KATE KELLNER THROWS A FILTHY DROP CURVE

Kate Kellner Throws a Filthy Drop Curve

MINDY KILLGROVE

Contents

Chapter 1

Thud...whomp...

The white and black soccer ball soared high in the air after bouncing off Grady's forehead, then he took off running, giddily chasing after it. He was surrounded on both sides by defenders, but he streaked by them, running gracefully. He dribbled the ball easily, using a touch of finesse to keep the ball just within his own reach, but expertly out of theirs.

With the graduation ceremony just concluding, it would've seemed logical and appropriate even for Grady to be standing with the people who'd been his classmates for the last six months, taking photographs to treasure as keepsakes later, but that wasn't what my boyfriend was doing. He was tearing down the practice field outside of the Farrington Falcon's High School gymnasium, heading straight for the goal box, where there was already a goal tender standing fixed to his spot, waiting to block the shot.

I walked to the edge of the field, not wanting to interrupt the impromptu game, but also feeling slightly fascinated. Grady's long legs carried him quickly downfield. His nylon, black graduation robe had been unzipped and it flapped at his sides, making him look a little like a crow that was ready to take flight. He juked to the left, then feinted to the right, shaking off the defender who was racing alongside him and when he was only a few feet from the goal, he punted the ball one last time, kicking it hard directly toward the corner of the net.

"Goal!" Grady threw his long arms over his head and shouted victoriously. Call me crazy, but I'd never been more attracted to my smoking hot boyfriend than at that moment when he was schooling a bunch of other guys, using his athletic prowess to dominate them.

The two players who'd been trying to prevent him from having this triumphant moment rejoiced too by clapping him on the shoulders and ruffling his silky strands of sandy brownish blonde hair.

"Hughes! Hughes! Hughes!" The others chanted and Grady beamed brightly, his smile radiant. I lifted my hand to shield my eyes from the glaring early evening sun and watched as Grady did a little victory dance, bee-bopping from one foot to the other, celebrating his own fancy ball handling skills.

I laughed then said quietly aloud, "I didn't even know Grady could play soccer."

"He never told you?"

I hadn't meant for my comment to be overheard, so I really tried not to be startled when Mrs. Greta Hughes, Grady's mom, came up beside me and spoke in a soft, but firm voice. I turned to look at her squarely. She and her son only shared a few features in common. Whereas Grady was tall and broad shouldered, Mrs. Hughes was a petite woman, compactly put together. Her body shape always reminded me of a hungry Jack Russell because she was strong and sturdy, but also wiry and lean. The olive-green sleeveless blouse she wore today put all the rope-like muscles in her arms on display. Her hair was a bit darker than Grady's too. His was the color of dry sand, but her hue could've been better described as like that of the rocks which line a beach shore. It was dark brown, with threads of gray and silver streaking through. She wore her wispy locks short so that the tendrils curled around her ears and her bangs were swept off to the side. Her most striking feature, and the one she had in common with Grady, was her grayish blue eyes. They were beautiful and hypnotic and while looking at Mrs. Hughes, I felt relaxed and at ease because of those steely blue orbs.

"I knew he'd played lots of different sports these past few years," I answered after thinking it over for a beat. "But I thought he liked wrestling the best."

Mrs. Hughes laughed wryly. "Wrestling certainly is a favorite amongst my children, but Grady was rather good at playing soccer. He was a first-team all-conference player right before we left San Antonio."

My eyes flicked back toward the playing field. After he scored that first goal, the ball had been given to one of the others, but now, it was back in Grady's possession, and he was heading toward the goalie, trying to score a second time. "I wish he would've said something," I murmured, watching him coast right by the defenders who seemed to be no match for his superior ball handling skills. "But that's not who he is, is it?"

"Not my youngest." Mrs. Hughes' eyes crinkled at the corners as she smiled affectionately at her son. "He might've considered it bragging to tell you about playing soccer and that's just not his style."

A shout erupted from the pitch again and my eyes darted toward the sound. There was Grady, arms held high, cheering because he had managed to fake out the goalie, and kick the ball by him rather easily. The two defenders were laughing hysterically, almost as if they were amused by the lackluster job their goalkeeper was doing.

"What're we talking about?" Mr. Hughes joined us then. His smile was warm and gregarious, much like Grady's. He was a used car salesman and while some people in that profession got a bad rap for being overeager, pushy, or phony, Mr. Hughes never struck me as being anything other than genuine. He was a tall man, maybe even an inch taller than Grady, and his upper body was expansive and robust. He wore a light-weight suit jacket, that was a soft gray shade, but it was stretched slightly across his broad shoulders to accommodate the bulk there. He also had on a pale pink tie that added something to the over-all look. It seemed to scream that even though he was a large man, he was also gentle and kind.

"The boys," Mrs. Hughes answered matter-of-factly, nod-ding fondly at the soccer players.

"Wait...do you mean...?" Because the sun had been in my eyes, I hadn't been able to fully identify the other people who were playing against Grady, but it dawned on me then that the others weren't wearing graduation robes, and I didn't exactly recognize them. "Are those Grady's brothers?"

"One in the same," Mrs. Hughes replied. Then, her eyes met mine. "Would you like to meet them?"

"Oh...uh..." I glanced down at my dress. Just before the graduation ceremony had begun, I'd taken the opportunity to throw a few pitches in the multipurpose room. At that time, it'd been raining outside, so I'd sought shelter in one of my favorite throwing places. But after Grady found me and re-minded me that the ceremony would be starting soon, I'd run to the locker room, taken a quick shower, and slipped into a fluttery, white sundress that had tiny black polka dots all over it. The whole process of getting ready had taken a little less than ten minutes and that included coming outside and stow-ing my workout gear and ball mitt in Grady's truck.

My fingers coasted over the soft fabric of the skirt self-consciously, but then I remembered how my hair was still slightly damp. Even though the graduation ceremony had lasted more than two hours, the long blond tresses had yet to dry fully, and they hung lankly around my shoulders. Hastily, I tugged the elastic band I always kept on my wrist off and pulled my hair into a low bun. I tucked a few errant locks that managed to escape my haphazard hairstyle behind my ear. "I...I think I'm ready now."

Mrs. Hughes shared a soft smile with her husband then said, "There's no reason to be nervous, Kate. Grady's already told the boys all about you. And...you look wonderful."

"Thanks, Mrs. Hughes," I said, smiling sheepishly.

Gently clearing her throat, Mrs. Hughes glanced out at the field once more. "Troops," she called in a voice that registered just four notes below her normal speaking tone. I knew that Mrs. Hughes served in the Air Force, because her relocation to Wright Patterson Air Force Base had been the catalyst for bringing Grady into my life this winter, but I'd never seen her behave like the staff sergeant I knew she was. The effect was magnificent. It was as if a referee had blown a whistle and halted the game. The four boys on the playing field stopped exactly where they were standing and turned to look in her direction. When she added, "Fall in," they got motivated. Grady scooped the soccer ball up and into his arms and using the same easy strides that I had come to recognize as his signature way of moving through the world, he and his brothers loped along the field, jogging slowly before realizing they could race each other. Grady surged forward into the lead, but his brothers were right behind him. He might've won the race had he not been wearing his graduation robe. It wasn't that the satiny material held him back, but that two of his brothers were able to get their hands on it and yank him so that he fell behind them a few paces.

"Cheaters!" Grady shouted, but the smile never left his face. He put on a burst of speed and sprinted, catching up to one of his brothers who was the shortest of the four and had fallen a step behind the others who had the longest legs.

"You rang?" the tallest one said, sidling in front of his brother, elbowing him in the ribs so he could be the one to stand right in front of their mother. She arched her eyebrow high at them and that was all it took for the boys to stop horsing around. He ran a hand through his curly brown locks, sweeping the longest bits out of his eyes so he could stare intently at his mother. "Did you need us, Mom?"

She nodded stiffly. "Kate wanted to meet you."

"This is Kate?" The brothers said in unison. And that was when Grady and his other brother finally joined us. Grady moved forward, flipping the soccer ball to his dad, then flapping his graduation robe wide as he encircled me with his arm. He wrapped his long fingers around my shoulder and pulled me to his hip.

"Guys, this is Kate," he said, making the introduction official.

"*The Kate*?" the tallest one, with the curly brown hair asked, giving me a smile in which he displayed dazzling white teeth.

"*The Kate* who throws a sixty-five mile an hour fastball?" the brother with dark brown hair, sort of like Mrs. Hughes', asked.

"*The Kate* who got to see Triple B destroy JBT?" the third brother, one who looked a great deal like Grady, questioned, while simultaneously swiping a big bear paw through the air.

"*The Kate* who drives Grady crazy?" The siblings chorused, then erupted into peals of laughter.

I glanced at Grady to see him smirking all over himself. "Do I drive you crazy?"

"Come on," the tallest one cajoled, pantomiming whipping out his cell phone and typing a text furiously. "Not a day goes by when Grady doesn't send a group text, telling us how you've got him tied up in knots."

"You've gotta know that, right?" the one with the dark hair asked, giving me a playful smile.

I grinned at Grady. "Is this all true?"

"Yep," he said, squeezing my shoulder and pulling me in even closer. "But I don't mind being a little crazy over you."

"A little?" the three brothers scoffed, which made me laugh. It was as if they'd rehearsed this bit and that's why they kept speaking in unison. I liked them all immediately.

"Maybe you ought to properly introduce your brothers," Mrs. Hughes suggested, nodding at Grady, indicating that her words were more than a recommendation.

"Okey dokey." He jutted his chin toward the brother standing on the far left. This was the tallest of the group. His smile was a touch wider and maybe even a little brighter than the others. All four boys had their father's grin and their mother's eyes, but this brother's wide eyes were bluer than the rest. They were the shade of the sky on a cloudy day. "This is Graham. He's the eldest."

"And the most handsome," Graham supplied before reaching out to shake my hand.

I giggled. "Are you sure about that?"

The other three boys hooted with laughter, but Graham was undaunted. He just tossed his head, flicking his long, curly locks out of his eyes, then held my gaze. "All right. I might not be the most handsome, but I'm definitely the smartest." I didn't make any quips about that, and the boys didn't guffaw either, so I figured the statement must be true.

While spinning the soccer ball on his finger the way a basketball player might do, Mr. Hughes said proudly, "Graham just earned his bachelor's degree in chemistry from the University of San Antonio. He's joining us today as a college graduate."

"Congratulations." I beamed at him. "Chemistry...what do you plan to do with that? Do you have a job waiting for you back in San Antonio?"

"Not yet," Graham replied. "But I'm working on getting something together."

Mrs. Hughes' face fell. "I thought you were thinking about getting a job around here."

Graham gritted his teeth. "We'll talk about it later, Mom."

"These are the twins," Grady said, taking the spotlight off what might turn into a small family squabble. He gestured with his free hand toward his fraternal twin brothers. The one on the left shared Grady's features almost exactly. He had heavy brownish blonde eyebrows and even the way his hair fell across his forehead, every so often floating into his eyes, was precisely the same. The only discernible difference was that this brother had decided to grow out a goatee. "That's Giles." I shook hands with Giles and his cheeks turned bright pink, which I thought was sort of cute.

So, there is a shy and reserved Hughes brother.

Then, Grady jerked the thumb of his free hand toward his last sibling. Even though he was one of the twins, he looked the least like his brothers. He was short, so much so that he and I were nearly eye to eye. His hair was dark brown, and he wore it heavily gelled and in a spiky, messy fashion. He resembled his mother a great deal because, like her, he had cord-like muscles that looked so tightly wound, they might snap if they weren't flexed regularly. His biceps strained against the sleeves of his buttercup yellow dress shirt and, if Grady hadn't just said so himself, I'd have thought this brother was the youngest, while Grady was part of the twin grouping.

"Meet Gregory," Grady said, smiling smugly.

That earned him a low growl from his brother. "Rory," he grumbled, reaching forward to take my hand.

"Rory," all the boys mimicked, some of them making the sound more animalistic.

Mrs. Hughes laughed. "You'll have to forgive my boys, Kate. When Gregory was a baby, he'd cry so loudly sometimes that we said he sounded like our little lion. That's how he grew into the name Rory. But ever since we told the others how he got his nickname..."

"Rory," the three brothers roared mockingly.

"Can it," Rory muttered, letting go of my hand, and falling back into line with the others.

Grady snickered, then tickled my elbow playfully. He was in such a good mood, and I loved seeing him interact with his siblings. I'd almost gotten used to thinking of him as being an only child, like me. But now, watching him interact with his brothers and seeing how much they all looked alike, I felt like I was getting to know him much better. "Don't pout, big bro," he said, reaching forward with his free hand to ruffle Rory's already disheveled-looking hair. "We're only messing with ya."

"Yeah, yeah," Rory said, jerking away from Grady quickly.

"So, what do we want to do now?" Mr. Hughes asked, driving away the tension easily by clapping his hands against the side of the soccer ball lightly and calling attention to himself. He tossed the ball up in the air to himself and caught it neatly. "Anybody hungry?"

"Starving," Graham said, rubbing his stomach.

"I could eat," Rory added while Giles nodded in agreement.

"What do you say?" Grady questioned, smiling down at me. "Do you want to...?"

"Oh...no..." I answered hurriedly. "It's graduation day. Time for you to be with your family. And your brothers had to have just gotten to town not long ago, so I shouldn't..."

"But we're going out to celebrate," Grady persisted. "You've gotta come with us."

"Yeah."

"Come on, Kate."

The other brothers joined in the wheedling.

"Special K," Grady added, leaning forward, and nuzzling his lips against my ear, "come out to dinner with us."

The affectionate urging didn't go unnoticed by his older brothers, and they all started making kissing noises, smacking their lips, and puckering up big time.

"You're welcome to join us, Kate," Mr. Hughes said, giving his older boys a look that evidently meant to knock it off because they hushed immediately.

"Please," Mrs. Hughes added, stepping forward and reaching for my free hand. "I'm always outnumbered. I need another woman around."

"All right," I agreed slowly. "Let's go get something to eat."

The whoops of delight that erupted from the Hughes boys were comical. Sure, they were here to celebrate Grady's graduation, but they made me feel part of the gang too by making such a fuss.

Mr. and Mrs. Hughes nodded and turned to walk toward their van, but then the three brothers chorused, "Shotgun!" and took off running.

"Are they..." I said slowly, "*all* racing toward your truck?"

Grady shrugged nonchalantly, keeping one arm draped lazily around my shoulders. "Looks that way."

I cast a glance over my shoulder. "Do you want me to ride with your parents then?"

"Not a chance," he said, pulling me nearer and dropping a kiss on my forehead. "You're with me, Special K."

"But your brothers..." I insisted, nodding at the three siblings who were elbowing each other out of the way and pawing at the door handle of the shiny, black truck.

"One of them will ride with us, but the others will take a hike and ride with Mom and Dad. We'll just hang back a minute and let them figure it out."

Grady was right. As we approached and he used the remote key fob to unlock the door, Rory boxed out his brothers and climbed into the front seat. Graham shrugged good-naturedly and Giles mumbled something unintelligible under his breath, but they eventually walked away and headed toward the family's SUV which sat on the other side of the parking lot that was nearly empty now.

"You be careful," Grady cautioned as Rory slid into the passenger seat, and he helped me climb into the cab. "I don't want you or any of the others to put a scratch on Adrienne."

Rory's eyebrows shot up. "You named your truck *Adrienne*?"

"Yeah." Grady relaxed in the driver's seat and started the ignition. "I thought you knew that." He was being his normal, easy-going self, but my eyes were fixed on Rory who was still staring at him in disbelief. "What?" Grady demanded, before backing out of the parking space.

"Nothing," Rory muttered. "I just can't believe you named your truck after your ex-girlfriend."

"Adrienne was your girlfriend?" I asked, looking from Grady to Rory, but neither of them answered right away, and so my cheeks flamed with embarrassment.

Chapter 2

Grady

"He didn't tell you?" Rory returned and Kate shook her head vehemently.

"You know," she whispered tersely, fidgeting in her seat, and fiddling with the hemline of her dress, "that's the second time in the last five minutes that somebody's said exactly that same thing to me." I could feel her eyes on the back of my head. "It seems that I'm discovering a whole new side to you today, Grady."

I sighed, while trying to figure out what to say. I had no idea what else she'd just learned about me, but I thought she might be making too much out of something that meant very little. Kate and I had only met in February and technically, we didn't start officially dating until a few weeks ago. I knew there were tons of things I hadn't had the chance to tell her about myself yet, and I imagined there had to be millions of stories from her past that I hadn't heard, either. But I wasn't upset by any of that. It was only natural to take our time while getting to know each other better.

"It's not a big deal," I said, steering the truck carefully out of the parking lot. We weren't headed far, just to A Slice of Pie, a local pizzeria that sat nearly adjacent to the high school.

"Right," Rory drew the word out long. "You only dated her for four, almost five years, so..."

"Four years?" Kate squeaked.

I snuck a glance at her in the rearview mirror. It was odd not to have her sitting right there beside me because, at this moment, I desperately wanted to give her hand a reassuring squeeze. "It wasn't that long," I said placidly, trying to make it clear this was not an issue worth discussing.

"Yeah, it was," Rory retorted. "I remember the day the two of you got together...vividly. And then I remember how..."

"What do you think we should order?" I interrupted, hoping to successfully change the subject, steering it toward safer waters. "You want garlic knots, Special K?"

Kate's face was bright red, and I got the feeling from the way she was breathing slowly in and out through her nostrils that she was schooling herself, trying to keep her emotions in check. I'd seen her do this dozens of times on the mound. When other pitchers might get rattled because an ump wasn't calling the game fairly or when the other team was batting around, it'd be awfully easy to lose her cool. But Kate was practically a professional at mastering her emotions. She knew how to calm herself down and mask what she was feeling. That made it tricky to be her boyfriend because I was never quite sure exactly what she was thinking.

"Order whatever you want," she said, scooting forward in her seat and smoothing down her dress. "You know me. I'll eat anything."

I laughed, still hoping to lighten up the atmosphere. "We both know that's not true."

"Are you a picky eater?" Rory asked, swiveling in his seat so he could look back at Kate.

"I guess I am," she said slowly, "but Grady's never said anything about it before."

There was something slightly off in her tone, and I detected it at once, but I figured it was better to ignore it and keep forging ahead. "We usually split garlic knots, a large pepperoni, sausage, and mushroom pizza, and a slice of chocolate silk pie for dessert. Sound good to you, Kate?"

I waited for her to nod approvingly, but that never happened because Rory said, "How do the two of you put away that much food?"

Sneaking another peek in the rearview, I saw that Kate was looking down at her dress, fiddling with the seams near the midsection.

What is she thinking?

"We do our best," I said at last, but thankfully, the awkward ride ended right then and there because I turned the corner, pulling us into the A Slice of Pie parking lot. Rory was out of the truck the second I'd put it in park and as I helped Kate out of the backseat I whispered, "Sorry if that was...uncomfortable." Slowly, I took off my graduation robe and flung it in the backseat, watching it fill up the space right next to where my girlfriend had just been sitting.

She frowned. "It's just that I've been wondering for a long time why you named your truck Adrienne. I'm pretty sure I even asked you about it, but you said it was only..."

"Are you talking about Adrienne Gladwell?"

That came from Graham who was already out of Mom and Dad's SUV and standing at my elbow for reasons I simply could not explain. He must've sprinted over here. "No," I said insistently, hoping to end the conversation right there.

Kate sucked in a sharp breath. "You had more than one girl-friend named Adrienne?"

"No," I said, forcing myself to stop before I could begin grinding my back teeth in frustration. "I only ever dated Adrienne Gladwell and..."

"You know I saw her the other day," Graham continued, completely oblivious to the signals I was trying to send him. It wasn't that I minded talking about Adrienne so much, but I could see and feel Kate's discomfort, so I wanted to end the conversation abruptly. And I wished he'd just let me finish up my thought so I could get out of this potentially complex situation.

"Okay," I said, offering Kate my hand, then, once she was fully out of the truck, wrapping an arm around her shoulder.

"Don't you wanna know what she was doing?" Graham drawled, giving me a smug smirk.

"Not especially," I replied, using my free hand to close the truck door, and nodding toward the entrance of the restaurant.

Graham snorted. "That can't be possible. The two of you were practically inseparable all through high school. You've got to wanna know…"

"I said I don't care," I snapped, then instantly regretted it. I'd meant to alleviate tensions, not make them run higher, but with those few little words, I'd caused Kate's shoulders to stiffen underneath my touch.

"*Sheesh*," Graham grunted. "Can't imagine what's gotten into you. I'd have thought you'd be glad to hear what your old friend was up to."

I held the door open with my free hand, ushering both Graham and Kate inside the restaurant. The place was fairly crowded, and I recognized a few others who had come straight from the graduation ceremony. Most of them were still wearing their graduation gowns and I was glad I'd had the idea to chuck mine. I nodded at Danny Williams, who sat with his family in a booth over toward the corner and waved to Micah Caldwell who was at a two-top with his girlfriend, Autumn. My folks were being led to a big, round table right in the middle of the restaurant and as we approached, I paused to hold out the chair for Kate. She nodded gratefully before sliding into the seat.

"What's with you guys?" Giles asked, using a discreet tone that was barely above a whisper as I slumped into the last vacant chair next to him.

"Rory wouldn't shut up about Adrienne on the way over here and when we got out of the truck, Graham wanted to talk about her, too," I hissed leaning close to him, whilst shooting an annoyed glance at my other brothers.

"Adrienne?" Mom perked up. I should've known that she'd be listening. She always was and we often liked to joke that she had super sensitive hearing, making it possible for her to eavesdrop on even our most private conversations. "How is Miss Gladwell?"

I shrugged, then cast a quick glance at Kate. "I haven't got a clue."

Mom tipped her head to the side thoughtfully and tapped her short fingernails idly on the laminated menu. I knew she wanted to say something, perhaps to reprimand me for so callously brushing off the idea of communicating with my ex-girlfriend, but then her eyes fixed on Kate too and I knew she could pick up on the palpable tension.

"She's great," Graham supplied, either because he was ignorant of Kate's feelings, or simply because he wanted to say what was already on his mind. "We ran into each other last week. She was taking a tour of the university, but I have to admit that I was surprised to see her there."

"Why were you surprised? Isn't she a senior, like Grady?" Kate asked, which shocked me. Based on her reactions in the truck, I was certain she wouldn't want to prolong this discussion, but she was the one asking the questions now.

"She just graduated," Graham said, picking up his menu and using the pad of his thumb to smear away a spot of grease. "But I was surprised to see her at U of SA. She wanted to go to Felding and..."

"She *what*?" Kate interjected, leaning so far forward in her seat that she was squashing her chest against the edge of the table. She blinked rapidly at Graham, then turned her gaze on me. I shrugged.

Attempting to keep this explanation as simple and concise as possible, I said, "Adrienne wanted to go to Felding because they have an amazing fashion design program. She was the one who got me interested in going there too."

Kate's eyes narrowed, and she sat up impossibly straight in her chair. "Uh-huh," she mumbled, then, without looking at me, or anyone else for that matter, she picked up her menu and held it right in front of her face. I was seized by the urge to reach over and lower the menu, so I could look her directly in the eyes and tell her there was nothing to worry about. Adrienne and I had ended things a long time ago, but I didn't want to make a scene in front of my parents or the other people in the restaurant.

A baby boy, dressed in a royal blue pair of overalls and a delicate white onesie sat in a highchair behind me with his family. The kid was waving around a garlic breadstick, and it came dangerously close to hitting Graham upside the head. He must've felt the grazing of the breadstick on the back of his neck because he made a disgruntled face, ruffled his hand through his hair, then scooted forward in his chair.

Ha. Serves him right for bringing up Adrienne.

I was just applauding the universe for intervening so spectacularly when Rory said, "Kate, did Grady *never* tell you about Adrienne?"

"Not really," she muttered, still hiding her face behind the menu.

"That's a shame," Mom said softly, giving me a mildly disapproving look. "She was such an important part of your life back in San Antonio."

At that, Kate lowered the menu and stared squarely at me. Her blue eyes were wide and curious. "Was she?" Then, she barked a quick laugh. "I guess she must've been for you to name your truck after her."

"Oh no," Mom groaned, allowing a small burble of laughter to sneak out. "You didn't."

I felt like dropping my head into my hands and hiding my face. Everyone was staring at me, and I knew if I didn't go ahead and tell the story, my brothers would beat me to the punch. And, if I left it to them, it was likely that they'd manage to blow just about everything out of proportion. Unfortunately, Graham was only too eager to jump into my nightmare and splash around for a while. "Grady never talks about anything or anybody," Graham began, "but you've got to know the story behind this, Kate."

She shook her head. "I'm clueless."

"Let me tell it," Rory chimed in. He sat forward in his seat and was on the verge of spilling everything when a waitress appeared. I recognized her as Lucinda, a lady who had served me and Kate on several occasions through the last half of the year. She was in her mid-fifties, with coal black hair that was threaded with white streaks, and she always had a cheerful grin for us.

Dad waved Lucinda over to his side of the round table and after rattling off an enormous order—two baskets of garlic knots, three large pizzas, one with pepperoni and extra cheese, and the others with sausage, and a whole chocolate silk pie for dessert—she sauntered away, after gifting Kate with an encouraging smile.

"Where was I?" Rory said, tapping his chin, feigning forgetfulness.

"This really isn't necessary," I interceded. "Kate doesn't want to know about Adrienne."

"Sure, I do," she piped up, nodding at Rory and Graham. "And you're right. Grady never tells me anything about anybody, including himself. So, let's hear it."

I groaned and slumped a little in my seat, allowing my long legs to stretch out underneath the table. I was on the verge of sending a couple of sharp kicks toward my brothers, but refrained because I couldn't be sure which set of legs belonged to which person and I definitely didn't want to kick Mom, Dad, or Kate.

"I think Grady and Adrienne first started going out..." Rory said, pausing to waggle his eyebrows significantly, "...when Grady stole Graham's car."

"You stole a car?" Kate asked, staring at me.

"I borrowed it," I clarified.

"Yeah," Graham snorted. "You stole it. You were only thirteen years old, and I'd just finished giving you something like your third driving lesson." He leaned forward, placing both elbows on the table. "Dad told me to go out and start up the car, so I could run a few errands for him, but it was gone."

"How did you find Grady...and Adrienne?" Kate questioned, peering at Graham.

"They were sitting in front of Adrienne's house, and they had their..."

"That's enough!" I shouted, maybe a little too loudly, but not wanting to give Graham the chance to finish his story. I recalled the event perfectly. Not only had it been the first time I'd ever driven a car without supervision, but this had also been the moment when I'd had my first real kiss. I didn't so much mind telling Kate about these things, but I didn't like the way the story was shaping up, being told, as it was, by my brothers.

All eyes at the table turned toward me and even the little guy behind us stopped waving around his breadstick.

"Boys," Mom said, coming to my rescue, "I think Grady's been embarrassed enough for one day. Why don't we give him a break?"

"But he's the one who named his truck after her," Rory argued. "If he didn't want to talk about her, why'd he do something like that?"

Graham rolled his eyes. "Adrienne Gladwell...Grady's first passenger and the girl who broke his heart. How could he not pay tribute?"

I cringed, sure that this tidbit would set off another round of horrific storytelling, but when I looked at Kate, her expression had softened. Her thin lips were no longer drawn into a straight line and even her posture had relaxed infinitesimally. When her eyes met mine, I saw something there that made me want to take her in my arms and tell her everything, but I knew I couldn't do that right here or now.

Later...we'll talk about all that came before.

To make the best of things, I reached out and took hold of Kate's hand, raising it to my lips, and kissing her knuckles gently. A small smile tugged at the corners of her lips and while I could see all her qualms rapidly melting, my simple gesture also drew a wealth of comments from my brothers.

"Grady and Katie...sitting in a tree..." Rory said in a sing-song voice.

Graham had just taken a slurp of his iced water and nearly spit it out, but he recovered quickly and joined Rory, "K-I-S-S-..."

"You two are so immature," I pointed out, but that didn't stop either of them from taunting me a little more.

It wasn't until Kate looked directly at Graham and said, "I know Grady's working at the auto mall with Mr. Hughes this summer. But what are you all doing? Are you staying in town or heading back to San Antonio?"

I was so grateful to her for coming up with a way to shift the focus off us that I nearly applauded. But I settled for just continuing to hold her hand instead.

Graham sobered up rather quickly. "I've gotta get my ducks in a row," he said, nodding stiffly at our parents. Lucinda reappeared then, carrying one large pizza in each hand. She was followed by two other waiters who were also laden with food.

The piping hot pepperoni pizza was placed right in front of me, and the basket of garlic knots was put directly in front of Kate. She let go of my hand so she could start loading her plate and I did the same, piling two knots and one slice onto the yellow ceramic plate.

"What does that mean exactly?" Kate asked, taking a small nibble of a garlic knot, then rolling her eyes heavenward, clearly appreciating the taste of the food.

"I'll be sending out resumes all summer and hoping to find a job where I can use my chemistry degree." Graham took another sip of water and sloshed it around in his mouth before proceeding. "Until I get the job I want, I'll be working at a place called Granny Renee's Diner. Have you ever heard of it?"

"Sure," Kate said, smiling broadly. "Everybody knows Granny Renee's. She serves the best homemade French fries in town."

"Good," Graham said, reaching for a slice of sausage pizza, then stuffing almost half of it in his mouth. He chewed quickly, then said, "If you know where it is, you ought to stop by sometime."

"I will." Kate finished off her garlic knot, then swiveled in her seat to look at Rory. "What about you? Any plans for the summer?"

"We're all sticking around." He nodded at Giles. "He's working at the gas station on base. And I've got a job at the car wash that's right outside the gates."

"Wax and Shine?" Kate asked as her smile grew even wider.

"That's the one," Rory said, tearing his garlic knot into pieces before dunking one half in the ramekin of marinara sauce. "You ever go there?"

"I don't drive much," Kate replied, bending forward to take a drink from her water. "But my best friend, Ty, works at the car wash."

"Ty?" Rory turned his eyes on me and blinked twice, silently asking me if this was the same Ty I'd already mentioned on several occasions. I tried to give him a discreet nod in return, but Kate didn't miss a trick.

"You told your brothers about Ty?" She turned her brilliant smile on me, as if she were impressed by this sort of action.

What she didn't know was how often I'd complained about her pal, Ty Masterson. The guy was like an angry wasp guarding its mud dauber. It seemed that no matter what I did, Ty was always around, constantly trying to win Kate over, and that often left me feeling stymied. He had been her best friend forever, but I also knew that he was in love with her. So, what could I do other than talk to my brothers and lament the fact that Kate always had another guy hanging around, waiting for me to make a big mistake?

"I did," I said softly, quickly casting a look around the table, silently begging the guys not to say anything inappropriate.

You had your fun talking about Adrienne. Please, just let this thing with Ty go.

For once, my big brothers didn't let me down. Almost as if on cue, they dove into their slices of pizza, stuffing their mouths, and making it so they couldn't say a word, unless they wanted to dare Mom to rebuke them for talking with their mouths full.

I sighed relievedly, then picked up my own slice of pepperoni. I had it halfway to my mouth when the little baby behind me started making an awful, retching sound.

"He's choking," the woman at the table with him, presumably his mother, yelled. "My baby's choking!"

"Somebody help!" the man with her said as his face turned ghastly pale. The baby continued spluttering, waving his breadstick frantically.

Kate was out of her seat in a flash, scooting around me, and flying to their rescue.

Chapter 3

Kate

I couldn't sit there and do nothing, especially when I knew just what to do. Quickly, I placed one hand on the child's small shoulder, then curled my index finger into a hook. Using a swift sweeping motion, I found the source of all his problems and towed it right out of his mouth. The poor babe continued hacking and coughing as I deposited a moist, limp chunk of breadstick on his plate. The baby's face had gone beet red, but with his airway clear, his color soon returned to normal. Subtly, his puppy-like cough turned into soft whimpering sounds and that was when his mother unfroze from her horrified pose. Her hands had been covering her mouth and her eyes were wide with terror, but then, when her baby reached for her, she hopped from her seat, unbuckled him from the highchair and took the young boy into her arms.

"How...how...?" the woman whispered, gazing up at me, still slightly awestruck. She clutched her child to her chest, patting the baby's head and cheek, continuing to soothe him.

"How did you know what to do?" the father finally asked, articulating evidently what his wife had been unable to say. He wasn't as pale as he'd been a moment before, but I could tell he was still rattled too because his voice was slightly tremulous.

I shook my head slowly. "My best friend has six younger siblings. So, his mom's a champ at performing the finger sweep. I can't tell you the number of times I've seen her rescue one of her children from a choking situation."

"You...you saved our baby," the man said, scooting closer to his wife and child, reaching out to put his hands on them.

"It was nothing, really," I said, shifting a few steps backward, wanting to give them a little space.

"Do you think you could show me how to do that?" the mother whispered. "Just...just in case it ever happens again."

I smiled sympathetically at her. "Sure," I said, dropping into a crouch so I could be on eye level with her, then remembering that I was wearing a dress. Hastily, I shifted so I was kneeling instead and that's when all the patrons at A Slice of Pie started clapping spontaneously. It was just a smattering of applause at first, but then, once the Hughes brothers got in on it, the cheers became louder and more robust. I laughed and shook my head. "Here, ma'am," I said, holding a hand up and creating a hook with my index finger. "Let me show you what to do."

The tutorial was over in about a minute and luckily, by the time I turned away from the little family and slid back into my seat, the restaurant had quieted down considerably.

"That was really amazing," Grady said, taking my hand and beaming at me.

"I didn't do anything special," I insisted.

"Yes, you did," Graham argued. "I had no idea what to do, but you...you got right up and went to work."

"Yeah, well..." I demurred.

"I'd have thought you'd done that a hundred times, rather than just watched someone else do it," Rory said, openly nodding his approval in my direction.

"What can I say?" I shrugged. "I guess I'm a quick learner."

"She's just being modest," Grady said, squeezing my hand tight. "Kate's going to be a doctor someday, so..."

"Is that so?" Mr. Hughes interrupted. "You didn't tell us you wanted to study medicine, Kate."

"I didn't..." I began, but my own words were swallowed by the swell of enthusiasm that arose from my dinner companions. They hadn't been half so excited to discuss their own summer jobs or future plans, but now that we were talking about my potential career, they were firing one question in my direction after the other.

"Where do you think you'll go to school?"

"Are you heading to Felding with Grady? Do they have a pre-med program there?"

"What specialty area do you want to study? Will you work in pediatrics so you can help kids just like that little one behind you?"

The questions swirled around me, but I didn't know how to answer a single one of them. Grady and I had only just decided to be a couple, so we certainly hadn't talked about going to school together next year, after I graduated. And as for becoming a doctor...my mind wasn't made up on that score yet, either.

"I...I like to make plans," I said, when the others finally took a collective breath and waited for me to answer. "But I haven't thought anything out much beyond next school year. I've got to make it through this summer first and hopefully some other things will just fall into place as we go along."

"What other things?" Mr. Hughes asked politely before taking a sip of his iced tea. The ice cubes clinked when he returned his glass to the tabletop.

"I didn't get recruited this year," I said, managing to shoot a weak smile at Grady, "but I'm trying not to let that get me down. I still wanna play softball in college, so I guess I'm kind of holding out hope that something'll turn up and I'll get an offer to play somewhere soon."

"I'm sure you will, dear," Mrs. Hughes said, smiling congenially at both me and Grady. "My son says you can outpitch pretty much anyone, so..."

"Is that true?" Rory asked, interjecting, and speaking over top of his mother. "Grady told us you throw fast, and you've got quite a few junk pitches, but do you think you can strike me out?"

I laughed. "Is that a challenge?"

Rory's eyebrows shot up, then his smile turned mischievous. "You bet it is."

"All right then," I said, letting go of Grady's hand, "let's do this right now."

Rory laughed loudly. "We can't. Unless you know someplace that'll let us onto the ball field after dark." He nodded toward the windows which were behind me. I swung around to have a look at what he meant. Night had crept in, while we were having our meal, and I was helping the baby. The parking lot was illuminated by a series of lamp posts, but other than that, twilight had descended, wrapping everything in inky blackness and deep indigo.

"We'll come up with something," Grady said, taking one last bite of his pizza, then pushing his plate away. "Whenever Kate's got the time and Rory doesn't have to work, we'll find a way to have this little showdown."

I loved that he said all that with a straight face. Even if Grady secretly thought his brother and I were being kind of ridiculous, he'd never say as much. He supported me fully and judging from the smile on his face, I was guessing he thought that I'd probably be able to strike out his big brother, which would truly be something to see.

Grady stared at me for a long moment, and we locked eyes. My heart started pumping madly in my chest. I liked gazing at him this way, trying to read his thoughts, as he so often did mine. I assumed he was relishing the idea of watching his brother be defeated by his girlfriend and I was feeling psyched up too at the prospect of proving my skills.

"Who wants pie?" Mrs. Hughes asked, leaning forward, and reaching for the serving utensil.

I considered refraining, because I wanted nothing more than to skirt out of there quickly and spend a few minutes alone with Grady but figured that was an impossibility. It took a whole lot of restraint not to lean over and kiss him quickly, just so I could taste his lips and satisfy my cravings, but again, I exercised an unbelievable amount of self-control and continued sitting primly in my chair.

Mrs. Hughes didn't wait for any of us to answer, but instead, divided the pie as equally as she could, considering there were seven of us. She carefully placed thick slices of heavenly chocolate pie on small plates, then passed them one by one to her husband so he could handle the distribution. I put one bite of pie in my mouth, savoring the silky texture by licking my lips when I felt Grady's hand on my knee, and I nearly dropped my fork.

"What're you doing?" I hissed, trying to keep my voice low enough that none of his family members would hear us.

"Let's get out of here," he whispered, brushing his thumb over the hemline of my dress which had slipped slightly upward to reveal my kneecaps.

"Okay." He didn't have to tell me twice. I took two more quick bites of my pie, enough to make it seem like I'd eaten my share, then when he stood, I did, too.

"I'm gonna give Kate a ride home," he explained, placing his hand on the small of my back, making my heart rate accelerate once more.

"Cool," Rory said, hopping from his seat after stuffing another bite in his mouth, leaving only the crust on his plate. "I guess I'm ready to go now too." He stepped around us, then called over his shoulder, "See ya at the house."

Grady and I shared a quick look.

He's coming with us?

I wasn't sure if Grady understood what I was trying to communicate, but he shrugged halfheartedly, then tipped his head to the side, indicating we should follow Rory out the door.

"Thanks for dinner," I said, turning back toward Mr. and Mrs. Hughes fast, lucky that I hadn't entirely forgotten my manners in my frenzy to get out of there and be alone with my boyfriend. "It was…" I glanced around. The little family behind us had already left, but my interaction with them had left a strong impression on my mind. Then, my eyes flitted toward Graham, who would've likely kept talking about Grady's ex-girlfriend all night if Grady hadn't stopped him. "…Interesting," I concluded.

"Yes," Mrs. Hughes murmured as a soft, secretive smile played on her lips. "You'll have to come over to the house soon and have dinner with us again."

"Sure thing."

"See you later, Kate," Graham called as Grady and I turned and started heading for the exit. "Don't keep our boys out too late."

"Bye, Kate," Giles whispered, continuing to eat his pie, then reaching over, and grabbing the crust off Rory's plate that had been left behind.

Grady pulled me to his side, then draped his arm around my shoulders. "I think you were a big hit with my family."

"Really?" I asked as he pushed the door open with his free hand and held it just long enough for the two of us to shimmy through. The air outside was warm, not stifling, but a tad humid. A light breeze ruffled the fringe of my skirt, and I remembered the way Grady's thumb had done almost the same thing a few minutes ago. A shiver started at the base of my spine and darted all the way up, making me feel both tinged with warmth and quaking with cold at the same time. Goosebumps appeared on my forearms.

Grady nodded at his truck. "Check it out," he said. "Rory hopped in the backseat. That must mean he's taken a shine to you. He doesn't just give up shotgun for anybody."

"Well, I appreciate it." I swung open the passenger door, then hopped into the empty seat. Grady only just started up the engine when I slid my hand across the console and reached for his fingertips, wanting, and needing to feel that electricity spark between us. Sure enough, when my fingers met his, a jolt flashed through my whole body, making everything zing.

Grady's eyes opened wide, so I knew that he must've had a similar experience and I was just about to lean forward, end the suspense, and kiss him passionately when Rory cleared his throat. "So, what's everybody doing tomorrow? You think you've got time to throw me a few pitches, Kate?"

I sat back in my seat and Grady fidgeted on the driver's side. Then, he put the truck in reverse and began steering us out of the parking lot. "I'm busy tomorrow," I said, once we were on the road, heading toward my house.

"Practice?" Grady asked and I nodded before remembering that he needed to keep his eyes on the road.

"Yeah," I said a split second later. Shifting in my seat so I could look at Rory, I explained, "I'm playing ball for a summer team this year called the Weatherfield Trailblazers. They're kind of a unique group because they play in a twenty-one and under league which means..."

"There'll be college girls on the team?" Rory guessed.

"Bingo."

"If I didn't have anything better to do, could I come watch you and your girls take batting practice?" Rory asked, smiling roguishly.

"You can come to any of the games you like, but I don't think you ought to show up to the first practice," I answered, twisting back in my seat slightly, so I could include Grady in the statement. "That goes for you too, ya know. As soon as I get my game schedule, I'll give it to you and..."

"I'll be there," he said softly. "Wild horses couldn't drag me away from watching you play."

Rory snorted. "Are you really that good, Kate? Or is my brother just making you sound so talented because he's madly in love with you?"

"I don't know," I said, smiling at Grady openly, then turning and winking at Rory. "You'll have to ask him how he feels about me. But as for my pitching abilities, once we both clear our schedules, you can decide that for yourself."

He flexed his muscles, making his biceps as big as a couple of softballs. "I'm not scared of you, Special K."

"You oughta be," Grady said, being perfectly serious while pulling into my driveway. "You'll never be able to get a handle on her fastball and you'll have to swing twice if you even want half a chance at catching her changeup." He put the truck into park, then turned in his seat to look at his big brother. "I can't wait to see how fast she strikes you out."

I giggled and Grady hopped out of the driver's side. He hustled around the front of the truck, then in a very gentlemanly gesture, swung my door open and offered me his hand. When our fingertips brushed against one another again I felt like my whole body had been set aflame. He used both hands to close the door behind me, and I leaned back against the cool metal. He kept his hands right where they were, framing them around my elbows, then sliding forward and pressing our bodies together. I tipped my head up and he ducked down. And just as our lips were about to meet, Rory coughed loudly. "Uh..." I murmured, tasting the sweet chocolaty goodness that lingered between us because of our last bites of pie. "Should we be doing this in front of your brother?"

"It's no big thing," Grady whispered, brushing his lips softly over top of mine, making my knees feel weak. "He's seen me kiss other girls before."

There were about a million reassuring or romantic things Grady could've said at that moment, but that exact phrase was not one of them. My spine stiffened and my eyelids fluttered open so I could look him fully in the face. "Like Adrienne?"

Grady groaned and I could tell by his pained expression that he wanted to kick himself for not thinking far enough ahead to know this was exactly where my mind was going to jump. "Do we need to talk about her right now?"

"No," I said quietly, "but we probably should've discussed her before, so..."

"She's not important to me," he muttered and when I backed slightly away from him, shrinking as far as I could against the passenger side door of the truck, he quickly amended his statement. "I mean she *was* important, a long time ago, but now...we haven't spoken in months. Nothing. No texts. No calls. No emails. I don't know what she's doing, and I don't...I don't..."

I felt an enormous amount of guilt, watching Grady stumble over his words in this manner. He was usually so relaxed, and he made me be a more mellow sort of person just because he was hanging around. It seemed almost cruel to torment him by forcing him to talk about a subject that was clearly distressing.

Graham and Rory's words from earlier in the evening came back to me.

She was the one who broke his heart.

I wasn't sure exactly what that meant, but I didn't want to torture him further by pressing the issue any more tonight.

Slowly, I draped my arms around Grady's neck, towing him closer to me. And abruptly, he stopped faltering over his words. "Kate," he said quietly, "I don't want you to think that..."

"Shh..." I hushed him. "You don't have to explain anything. Everybody's got someone in their past they'd rather not talk about and it's okay with me if you don't want to go there tonight."

"Really?" He perked up and it was then that dimples appeared in his cheeks. I moved my hands forward and cupped his face, rubbing my thumbs over those sweet, cherubic little specks.

"We can do whatever you want," I whispered. "Just for now..." His lips were so close to mine then that there was barely any air separating us, but then, someone coughed loudly. I knew it wasn't Rory because the sound came from somewhere behind Grady's back and immediately his shoulders became rigid and he straightened up, pulling away from me.

"Ty," Grady said, and I let go of my hold on him. Reluctantly, he pushed off the side of the truck with both hands and spun around, languidly draping an arm over my shoulder, but also making it clear that he no longer meant to kiss me. "Should've figured you'd be out and about tonight."

My best friend stood there in the patch of grass that separated my family's gravel driveway from his family's paved one. His thick red hair was freshly washed, and he smelled faintly of the orange citrus soap I knew his mom kept in the guest bathroom right next to the front door of their house. He had both arms crossed over his chest and was giving both Grady and me a critical stare. I wondered at Grady's words because I hadn't expected Ty to be anywhere in sight. He didn't usually go running this late at night, so I couldn't fathom what he was doing hanging out in his driveway at this hour.

"Congratulations," Ty said, jutting his chin at the backseat, where Grady had draped his graduation robe before heading into the pizza parlor. "You graduated. That means you can finally get out of Farrington."

Grady barked a quick laugh, and the sound made every muscle in my body relax. Even if Ty was being weird and slightly rude, Grady had reverted to his usual self—confident, calm, and totally unaffected by my neighbor's hostility. "I'm not leaving yet," he said, tightening his grip on my shoulder. "Special K and I've still got all summer to spend together." He peered down at me and winked. "And we're looking forward to every minute of it. Right?"

"Indubitably," I whispered as I stared up into his dreamy eyes. I'd never have said as much, but I wished fervently that both Rory and Ty would disappear. Grady and I rarely spent any time alone together and because of the two interlopers, I hadn't even gotten to give my man a proper kiss goodnight.

As if he could read my mind, the same way he had done so many times in the past, Grady bent forward and kissed me. It was not quite a quick peck, but it wasn't really swoon-worthy either. Just a nice, soft kiss, one that reminded me of how, in the future, when we didn't have an audience, there would be more to come.

"I guess I'd better get going," Grady said, backing a step away and swinging his hand off my shoulder. He looped around the front of the truck and opened the door, then paused before ducking inside. "Get ahold of me tomorrow when you're done with practice?"

"Absolutely," I agreed. I knew it was a silly thing to do, but I loved him so much at that moment that I lifted my hand to my lips and blew him a kiss. His smile broadened as he pantomimed catching it, then slapped it on both cheeks.

A few seconds later, Grady and Rory were backing out of the driveway, and as I stood there watching them go, Ty mumbled, "I don't know what you see in that guy. He's so corny. And he makes you act cheesy, too."

I jabbed Ty in the ribs with my elbow. "There's nothing wrong with being a little corny. Matter of fact, I happen to like it."

"Yeah," Ty muttered thickly, "I can see that."

I elbowed him again, this time more soundly and he winced, but then his expression broke, and he stopped scowling. "That's better," I chirped. He uncrossed his arms and when a smile finally touched his lips, I grinned back. "Now, did you come over for some special reason or…?"

"Just wanted to see if you were up for watching a movie," he said.

"Come on." I nodded toward the house. "We can watch whatever you like."

"Really?"

"Sure." I led the way toward the house and right before we mounted the first of the porch steps, Mom snapped on the exterior lights. That interaction between Ty and Grady hadn't gone as swimmingly as I would've liked, but I wasn't giving up hope on making friends out of the two of them yet.

Grady seemed obliging enough to, at the very least, tolerate my best friend. So, I figured that if I schmoozed Ty a little, let him pick the movie and all, I might eventually work up the nerve to talk about some of Grady's finer qualities. I knew it was a long shot, trying to create a friendship between these two people. But both were such a big part of my life, and I wasn't willing to give up either of them, so that meant I had to find a way to bring them together. My task loomed large in front of me because I knew that the only thing Ty and Grady had in common was their shared interest in me, so that made our whole situation awkward. I might be able to do a lot of things, but I wasn't sure if I'd be able to fix the uncomfortable edge that lingered around all our conversations.

I've just got to come up with a plan. Somehow…some way, I've got to make them both see that they have more in common than they think.

Chapter 4

Grady

"Who was that?" Rory asked the second we pulled out of Kate's driveway.

"Meet Ty Masterson," I mumbled, taking one hand off the steering wheel and twirling it in the air. "He's a regular barrel of laughs."

"Yeah," Rory snorted. "He seemed like it." I glanced at my big bro in the rearview mirror to see him crossing both arms over his chest, lowering his chin, and scowling at the back of my head. "If I hadn't got a close enough look at the guy, I would've sworn that was Kate's dad, coming outside to pull you off his little girl."

"Naw," I drawled. "Mr. Kellner's cool. He never gives me a hard time the way Ty does."

"Is that because Ty's in love with the girl next door?"

"Probably," I said, pulling slowly to the stop sign at the corner of Parkland Street. Kate's house sat right in the corner lot, so by flicking a quick glance over my shoulder, I was able to see the way she and Ty were walking toward her front door, elbowing each other like they were a couple of kids or maybe even siblings.

Rory laughed, then said, "Do you think when he walks her to the front door, she'll take the opportunity to kiss *him* good-night?"

I jammed my foot against the brake, then turned so I could punch Rory's arm.

"Ow," he groaned. "You know I was only joking, right?"

"Were you?" I countered, shifting back in my seat, and easing my foot off the brake before pressing the accelerator.

"You know what I don't understand?" Rory asked, scooting forward in his seat, poking his head forward so it was right by my shoulder.

"What?"

"Why you're pretending like it doesn't burn you up inside that your girl just walked into her house with some other guy," he said, continuing to rub his arm.

I snorted. "Who's pretending? I just slugged you pretty good for talking about Kate kissing someone else..."

"I really was only joking about that," Rory interrupted. "But now, I'm being serious. Does it tick you off that she's so close with some other guy?"

"There's not much I can do about it," I answered, directing the truck out onto the highway, and heading toward the base.

"That's not what I asked," Rory retorted. "You know, you're allowed to be annoyed. Maybe even hate the guy a little."

"I don't like him," I muttered.

"Have you told Kate that?"

"Of course not," I scoffed.

"Why not?" He leaned even farther forward. "If you told her how much it bugs you to see her hanging out with him, don't you think she'd pull back a little?"

"Maybe she would, but I'm not trying to be that kind of guy."

"What kinda guy?" Rory was sitting with his head poking so near to my shoulder that I wished he'd just crawl over the console and sit in the front seat. But that'd be dangerous to even suggest because he'd probably give it a go, so I refrained from saying anything.

"The kind who tells his girlfriend what to do. Who to be friends with. When she can talk to the people she cares about the most. You know..." I paused and clicked on my right turn signal as I eased into the far lane to take the exit. "The kind of guy that nobody likes."

"You're afraid Kate's gonna stop going out with you if you tell her how you feel?" I could hear the incredulity in my brother's voice.

"I always tell Kate how I feel," I countered. "But I don't try to control her, either. She likes Ty. They've been best friends their whole lives. What am I gonna do? Tell her to stop hanging out with him, even though he lives right next door, and then what? A few months later, I take off for college and leave her without her boyfriend *and* her best friend?"

The truck was oddly silent, so much so that I could hear the soft strains of rock music emanating from the radio. I always left it on in the background, but rarely listened, especially when someone else was in the car and I could have a conversation with them instead. But Rory was eerily quiet. I pulled up to our driveway and cut the engine. But Rory still didn't budge or say anything.

Is it possible he fell asleep?

I didn't think Rory could've been that exhausted, but now that we were at home, it was safe for me to turn around and check on him. But he was perfectly fine. He was sitting there, with his arms still crossed, gazing out of the passenger side set of windows.

"What?" I demanded, unsure of what to make of his posture.

"I just don't get it." Rory shook his head slowly. "You...you're trying to do that whole selfless thing again, but..."

"No, I'm not," I insisted. "Kate's allowed to have friends of her own and..."

"But you don't like him," Rory countered. "And with good reason."

I blew out an exasperated sigh. "If Kate wanted to be with Ty, she would be. It's that simple."

"Nothing's ever that simple," my big brother scoffed. "And I'm not buying your whole nonchalant routine, either." He lifted both hands and tapped his index fingers just below both eyes. "I saw the way that guy was looking at you. Daggers, man. If looks could kill, you'd be lying face down on the Kellner's driveway right now."

"So?" I said, adding a touch of sarcasm. "He's allowed to glare at me."

"But you can bet that's not all he's doing."
I turned around and stared at my brother furiously. "Did I not hit you hard enough a few minutes ago? You need me to do it again?" I lifted my fist and held it poised, ready to let fly.

Both of Rory's hands popped up in a mixture of self-defense and surrender. "Don't kill the messenger, Bro. But you've gotta see how what just happened back there wasn't right. Kate might've invited *you* in tonight. She might've even been a real peach and asked me to come along, rather than leaving me out in the truck. But then her *best friend*..." He paused, rolled his eyes, and made air quotes with his fingers, adding special emphasis to that phrase, "...showed up and suddenly, she had to dash inside with him."

"What're you saying?" I had no trouble following the recap he was giving of tonight's events, but I wasn't sure where he was going with this whole lecture, so I decided to speed him along with this gentle prompting.

"Do you think Ty just followed Kate into the house like some little puppy or do ya think he's whispering in her ear right now...telling her she ought to breakup with you? If he really likes her the way he seems to, is he honestly willing to just sit back and watch her make out with you in the driveway or is he trying to sneak in a kiss or two as well?"

"That's it," I said, cocking my fist back and preparing to hammer him.

"Wait!" Rory shouted, continuing to hold both hands up in protest. "Just hear me out. How do you know that Kate's fully committed to you? Didn't the two of you just start dating? Could she be..."

I breathed a heavy sigh. "You don't know Kate, so maybe I ought to let this one slide."

"You're right," he agreed. "I don't know Kate."

"If you did, you'd never even think anything like that, let alone allow the words to come out of your mouth." I lowered my fist, then stared at my palms, thinking of how her long fingers interlaced so neatly within my own any time we held hands. "She's all the good things any person could hope to be in this world. She's hardworking, determined, and loyal. I'm not worried at all about what Kate's doing with Ty right now."

"So, you love Kate?"

"Yeah."

"And you think that because you love her so much, you can't tell her to drop her best friend?"

I wound my fingers together. "I'm leaving Farrington in a few months, so I can't ask her to let go of someone who'll probably be there to provide her comfort later."

Rory nodded then said softly, "Don't hit me for saying this, but are you planning on breaking up with Kate?"

"No," I said quickly, glancing up at him. "What would make you say something like that?"

He shrugged. "You're worried about her having a companion once you're at school. If you were thinking of taking your relationship long-distance, you probably wouldn't care so much that she had a shoulder to cry on later."

"I'm not breaking up with Kate," I said emphatically. "If I had my way, I'd marry her tomorrow."

Rory guffawed loudly and the sound split the tension that had built inside my little truck's cab. "You can't be serious."

"Why not?" I countered. "I'm devoted to her. She cares about me. What's to stop us from getting married?"

"You're a couple of kids, for one thing," Rory commented in a sardonic way.

"But I've already told her I love her," I insisted.

"Yeah? So?"

I shook my head and laughed a little at my brother's obtuseness. "I didn't just tell Kate I loved her because that was the first thing that popped to mind. I actually meant it."

"Of course, you did," Rory said, inching back in his seat.

"I did," I persisted. "I do."

"Well, good for you," Rory sighed. "But I still think if you really loved Kate, enough that you thought someday you might wanna marry her, that you'd tell her outright how you felt about her spending time with Ty. It doesn't seem right that you're the one making all the sacrifices for your love and Kate's..."

"I'm not worried about Kate," I interrupted.

"Yeah," he grunted. "You already said that."

Rory opened the door then and a cool rush of night air blew across my face, helping clear my thoughts. I didn't like thinking about the future or what might happen next. Until I'd met Kate, I hadn't given much thought to what I might do or how I might behave three days from now, let alone three months in advance. But there was something so steady and stalwart about her. She might not have everything figured out down to the letter, but I could trust that before long, she'd have a plan in place, and fight tooth and nail to see her dreams come to fruition. She was the sort of person I wanted to tie myself to and plan out how our collective future would unfold.

But would I really marry Kate tomorrow?

The thought was appealing, but I knew I'd also said it glibly, so it bore further scrutiny.

Would Kate want to marry me? And where would Ty stand at our wedding? Right in between us?

Disgruntled by that unsettling image, I hopped from my truck and slammed the door shut behind me. I reached into the backseat to grab my graduation garb and it was then when I re-lived that last glimpse I'd had of Kate tonight, heading toward her house, laughing, and joking with Ty.

Maybe Rory's right. Maybe I ought to talk to Kate about Ty. It couldn't hurt to tell her how I feel...right?

Chapter 5

Sunday, June 4th

Kate

"What kind of a team is this?" I asked, stretching far to my left so I could whisper my question right in Abs' face. It was the first day of Trailblazers practice and the entire team was congregated in right field, doing some warmups. Our coach, Linda Davis, had urged two of the eldest girls to be captains and they were in the center of the ring. And there they remained, counting aloud, prompting everyone through the static stretching routine while Coach walked slowly around the infield, picking up pebbles with one hand and holding onto them with the other. Since I knew the coach wasn't looking in our direction, I seized the moment to talk with Abs.

Abigail DeWalt had been my catcher and good friend since I'd started pitching in the farm league. We'd both been nine years old when I got it into my head that I wanted to be a pitcher and she'd gamely volunteered to catch for me. Back then, she'd spent a lot of time hopping up and out of her catcher's squat, trying to snag the wild pitches that flew everywhere, but these last few years had been entirely different. As my control improved and Abs and I became closer friends, we developed a shorthand with each other, often communicating without using our words. But from the way Abs' face scrunched and she scratched at her curly black hair that had been swept into an untidy low ponytail, I could tell that my question had confused her.

"What's that now?" She leaned closer to me, almost like she hadn't heard my question, but I didn't bother repeating myself.

"You didn't tell me this team already had a stacked pitching staff."

"Yes, I did," she retorted, bending far forward, and touching the tips of her fingers to the edge of her cleats, demonstrating her superior sense of flexibility. "When we talked about playing summer ball, I told you expressly that we already had a full roster, but I was sure Coach would let you come aboard."

I bent low, reaching for my toes, smiling when the tips of my calloused fingers brushed over the worn edges of my cleats. "But I never would've even considered joining the team if I knew all *these* pitchers were going to be here."

Abs straightened up and smiled widely. "Geeking out, huh Lady K?"

"You can say that again." I turned so that I was only facing Abs and was hopefully shielding the others in the circle from overhearing our conversation. "I'm pretty sure that's Hope Sprang over there. And that's Lacy Rider. And...the girl in the middle...with the long brown braid...that's..."

"Becky Gardner," Abs finished. "Pretty neat to meet all your heroes in one go, eh?"

"Not pretty neat," I squeaked, but then, fearing that I'd permitted my voice to get too loud, I turned even further, putting my back to the rest of the group. "These pitchers were my idols just a few years ago. I used to follow Lacy's progress in the newspapers and Becky...*geez*. She's practically a legend."

"Yeah," Abs snorted. "I was pretty stoked when they showed up to the tryouts."

"You knew they were on this team?" I groaned, shooting her a desperate look. "Why didn't you tell me?"

"It's summer ball, Lady K. And we're on a twenty-one and under team. You had to have known some of the other players were going to be all-stars from the days of yore."

I groaned. "You make it sound like they're all ancient and we're just a couple of kids, lining up to get their autographs."

"No," Abs countered. "You're the one who's having a fangirl experience over here. Lacy, Becky, and Hope are your teammates now, Lady K. But you can't even look at them without going a little bonkers. How are you gonna make it through the whole season like this?"

"I'm not sure," I murmured.

Abs snickered. "That was a rhetorical question. I wasn't really expecting you to come up with an answer."

"All right, Trailblazers," Coach Davis called. "That's enough stretching. Run three laps along the outfield fence, then break into pairs and get to throwing."

I might be too intimidated to look my supposed teammates directly in the eyes, but I could certainly follow Coach's directions. I took off at a dead sprint, hoping to be in the center of the pack, rather than fall woefully behind. I wasn't a fast runner, not by any means. And it would've been easy to coast alongside Abs, who didn't seem to care one lick if she ran the laps quickly or not. But I wanted to be impressive, like my teammates, and so I streaked toward the right field foul pole, bounding through the dirt, kicking up plenty of it in my wake.

"Slow down, Kate," Syd said, jogging to my side. Sydney Shaffer played shortstop for the Farrington Falcons High School team and she, like Abs, had talked me into joining the Trailblazers at the last second. I meant to pummel her with questions too and ask why she'd held out on me about having a loaded pitching staff, but I couldn't talk while panting so hard. In typical Syd-fashion, she chugged along at my side easily, not getting winded at all. While I jogged regularly with Ty to build my endurance, Syd never had to do cardio workouts.

She was just naturally gifted. She moved with a lithe, graceful stride, and pumped her legs slowly, allowing her sinewy muscles to stretch. Her curtain of blonde hair, which was normally cut into a sleek bob, was growing a little long this summer and it made a tiny swishing noise as it flicked from one side of her shoulders to the other.

"Can't slow down," I said as we reached the left field foul pole and turned to head back across the outfield. "Gotta prove I'm worthy of being here."

"Of course, you belong here," Syd said, eyeing me closely. "Coach Davis wouldn't have asked you to be on the team at the last minute if she didn't think we needed you."

"The Trailblazers don't need me," I groaned, powering through when I felt a stitch attack the left side of my abdomen. Instinctively, my hand went to the spot and massaged it, then I slowed my pace a tad. "Hope and Becky are NAIA pitchers and Lacy plays for Felding. They've got years of experience on me and..."

"Knock it off," Syd ordered sharply. "You belong here. End of story."

"I don't know," I mumbled, trying to lengthen my stride to make up for the fact that we had slowed down marginally. Syd and I were still leading the pack, but I wanted to maintain our lead, and if possible, put a tad more distance between us and all the others. "I still think you should've..."

"You're just as good as they are," Syd said.

That made me laugh, which only caused the stitch in my side to flare painfully. "Stop," I said, wheezing a little. "I can't joke around right now. And we both know I'm nowhere near as good as any of them."

"You work harder than anyone I know," Syd countered, leaning into the turn, and holding out her right hand as if she were going to take hold of me and steer me right along with her. "Case in point, you're trying to break records here today in the four-hundred-meter dash."

"I can't be going that fast if you're keeping up with me," I said, setting my sights on the far foul pole, then ducking my head, and working through the pain.

"You don't have to try so hard," Syd chided. "It's only the first day of practice."

I shook my head. "I just wish I'd known who else was going to be on the team." I sucked in a deep gulp of air. "I know my fastball doesn't zip the way Lacy's does and my rise ball is nothing like Becky's. If I would've known they were on the team, I would've practiced harder these last few weeks. I would've..."

"Seriously, Kate?" Syd interjected. "How much harder can you practice? Weren't you in the multipurpose room throwing at the wall on graduation day?"

I snorted. "I thought only Grady knew I was doing that."

"Nope," Syd replied. "When I got there, I saw you going through the motions, but I steered far clear of the gym because I didn't want you to drag me in there so I could catch for you."

"I wouldn't have done that," I protested.

"You might've," she argued, tossing her hair over the opposite shoulder intentionally. "But I didn't have time for softball then." We pulled slowly to a stop and while we waited for the others to reach us, I panted, but she continued talking. "You know the big difference between the two of us, Kate?"

"I'm a pitcher and you're a shortstop?"

She rolled her eyes heavenward. "Nope. The difference is that I know there's more to life than this silly game."

"Silly game?" I echoed disbelievingly, glancing at the other players, hoping none of them heard her utter such blasphemy.

Syd tipped her head back and laughed haughtily. "I like softball. Sometimes I even love the thrill of playing the game. But there's a time for getting down in the dirt and tossing around a ball and a time for doing all sorts of other things."

"Like what?" I asked, honestly wanting to hear her answer.

She patted my shoulder. "Just don't overdo it this summer, Kate. The Falcons need you to be in top physical condition for fall ball and we don't want you throwing out your arm this summer trying to impress a bunch of girls who really couldn't care less." She nodded at Becky, Hope, and Lacy who were all loping along at the back of the pack, chatting with Abs. "They're here to have fun," Syd pressed. "Why are you here this summer?"

"I...I'm here to have fun, too," I said, but even to my own ears, my voice sounded unconvincing. "I *want* to have fun," I tried again, with more resolve. "But I also wanna do a good job for this team too." I gazed at the trio of pitchers. Seeing them in real life struck me the way seeing a group of celebrity actors might hit someone else. These weren't just my idols and heroes—they were softball legends. "And, if it's not too much to ask, I'd like to get some playing time."

Syd snickered. "You'll play, Kate. Coach Davis didn't bring you aboard so you could ride the pine all summer long."

"Maybe not," I agreed halfheartedly, "but she's going to expect me to be at the top of my game so when I throw, I don't embarrass our team."

Syd gave an annoyed snort, then waved her hand frantically in front of my face. "Yo. Earth to Kate. Are you even listening to anything I'm saying? It's summertime. Time to chill. Time to relax a little and just enjoy playing this game you claim to love."

"Yeah," I muttered, stepping away from Syd. "I'll relax...eventually. But for now, I think I need to work harder than ever before."

Chapter 6

Grady

"Kate, are you all right?"

After finishing up with my first shift at the auto mall, I'd checked my phone only to find that I'd missed several text messages from Kate. Apparently, softball practice hadn't gone very well, so she was heading out for a bike ride. By the time I got home and changed out of my work attire—a pair of gray dress slacks, a white button-down shirt, and a lime green and pink paisley tie—I sent Kate a message only to receive a response stating that she was going for a run. I begged her to wait for me, and when I got to her house, I suggested we take my pair of butterfly nets out to the reservoir and chase the moths, dragonflies, and damselflies around the rim of the water. That'd be a good way for her to get in more cardio. She'd agreed, but now that we were standing in the tall grasses, she wasn't even pretending to use the net or track down the insects.

"Kate," I called her name once more, this time more softly because I was approaching her side. "Is everything okay?"

She shook her head, as if she looked up and saw me standing right next to her and been startled. "Hey," she said softly with a dreamy quality blending into her tone. "Sorry. I think I spaced out there for a second."

"Yeah," I murmured.

That's so unlike her.

"Have you caught enough bugs yet?" she asked, looking down at the net in my hands.

"Have you caught any?" I shot a quick look at her net, which she was holding loosely by the wooden handle.

She giggled feebly. "Not a one, I'm afraid. I guess I'm just screwing up everything today."

"You're not screwing up anything, Kate," I said softly, wanting to soothe whatever it was that was really bothering her. Because I knew there was something lurking underneath the surface. She hadn't said much over the last hour, not when I picked her up nor while we'd been chasing moths, and I was starting to get a tad worried because Kate tended to say what was on her mind. "You're maybe just having an off day."

"I'm not sure that's it," she said, flopping down abruptly in the grass, tossing her net out to the side.

I sunk to my knees and placed my net right next to hers. "Then, what is it?" I prompted.

She sighed warily. "I'm tired of...Can't we just focus on something else?"

"Tired of what?" I asked, not at all following her train of thought.

"Tell me about work," she said, reclining a little and using her elbows to prop herself up a bit. "How was your first day working for your dad?"

"I barely saw my dad," I answered. "His boss, Mr. Barker, had me make so many cups of coffee...and it was my job to deliver bottles of water to potential customers, so..."

"So, you already did your fair share of running today?" she asked.

"You could say that," I murmured.

"You didn't like working at the auto mall?" she questioned.

I tipped my head back and forth in a noncommittal gesture. "It went kind of the way I thought it might. There was a lot of hustling back and forth, running from one spot to the next, but there was plenty of standing around too, talking to people about the cars that are still available in the lot."

"Which part didn't you like?" she asked, narrowing her eyes, looking for all the world like she was trying to read my thoughts. "I can tell something got under your skin, but I'm not sure which part perturbed you the most."

"It's the people," I said, ending the suspense at once. "I guess I don't mind talking to people when I've got something to say but going on and on endlessly about the deals Mr. Barker's running or the interior of a car...that's just not my thing."

"What is your thing?" Kate asked.

I smiled, then waved my hand at our pair of nets. "I prefer Anisoptera to people."

She wrinkled her nose in a cute way. "Are Anisoptera by chance some of your buggy friends?"

"They're not as cool as arthropods," I conceded, "but..."

She cringed. "Not the arthropods again." She shivered and I scooted closer to her. "Any time you just say that name, I'm sure I've got a centipede crawling up my shoulder."

"Like this," I said, tickling my fingers over her bare forearm, then wiggling my fingertips up and underneath the thin fabric of the t-shirt that was covering her shoulder.

"Yes," she giggled. "Exactly like that." I scooted my way closer to her and used my fingers to swipe her low ponytail away, then I buried my face in the crook of her neck and nibbled, which only made her wriggle and buck. "Grady," she whispered, "what're you doing?"

"I'm tickling you," I breathed before rubbing my lips over her earlobe.

"What if someone sees us?" she hissed, tipping her head back and allowing me further access.

"Who's gonna see us? We're lying in the grass at the far side of the reservoir and the sun has almost disappeared."

"Oh," she moaned a little, "normally, I'd push back, but tonight, I don't even care if someone sees us."

"You don't?" That comment caught me off guard. I didn't particularly want to stop kissing Kate, but I'd known something was wrong before and this statement only confirmed that fact.

She turned her head slowly and looked at me. "We've both had a rotten day. Can't we just kiss away all the worries and make it better?"

"That sounds nice, but I think I'm missing something here," I said, edging back a bit further so I wouldn't be tempted to lose all my self-control and kiss her fine, thin lips. "I told you my day was kind of lame... a little on the boring side. But you're still holding out on me. Did something happen at softball practice? Or did Ty say something last night that bothered you?"

She waved her hand dismissively through the air. "Ty and I just watched a movie last night. But at practice, things couldn't have gone worse."

"Really?" I tried not to sound too skeptical, but I was certain Kate was exaggerating the situation.

She took a deep breath, then proceeded to tell me a tall tale, centered around three pitchers named Becky, Lacy, and Hope who were all apparently gifted with talent which rivaled that of the Greek gods. Becky practically hurled thunderbolts across the plate. Lacy's arm was made of steel, enabling her to throw all day without ever tiring. And Hope? Well, she was simply a machine, able to place every pitch with perfect precision, so much so that she'd struck out each of her teammates twice before deciding to retire for the day.

"Kate," I said softly when she paused to take a breath. "Is that really what happened today?"

She buried her head in my chest and groaned softly, "No, but that's how I felt. They're just so good and I'm just so...mediocre."

"You are not mediocre," I said forcefully.

"Yes, I am," she replied, nestling so far into me that I had to lie down on the ground and cradle her so that we would both avoid toppling over. "You should've seen them, Grady. They're all so strong and powerful and they've got skills that I haven't even considered trying to develop yet."

"They're older," I said, wrapping one arm around her shoulder, trying to make her more comfortable, while also using my free hand to stroke the long strands of her ponytail. "They've had more time to add some junk pitches to their repertoires. That's all."

"That's not *all*," she sniffed, sitting up straight, and leaning slightly to my left side so that she was hovering over top of me. "When I'm comparing myself to them, I feel so...so inadequate."

"Then don't try to compare yourself to your teammates," I urged.

"How can I not?" she countered. "They're going to be right there. All the time." She hung her head, letting her chin fall to her chest and the long ends of her ponytail dragged across my cheek. "It's one thing to play against another team and lose because I know the opposing pitcher throws harder or is much better than me. But it's another ball of wax altogether to be stacked up against my teammates and realize that I'm the weakest link in the rotation." I didn't see any tears, but she used the back of her hand to wipe her eyes, maybe forcing herself not to cry or attempting to keep the tears at bay. "How am I gonna hold up this summer when I know that I'm just not as good as them?"

"Is that why you came home from practice and went right back to work?" I asked quietly and she nodded solemnly.

"I know that I can't make massive improvements over the course of one summer, but maybe, if I really buckle down, I can teach myself to throw a new pitch."

I wanted to ask about things we had just discussed yesterday. She'd promised that we'd spend our free time with each other this summer. And Kate had sworn that she'd only joined the summer league squad because she knew I'd already be busy with work, so we couldn't devote all our waking hours to one another. I really did want to question her on all those matters, but I knew how she'd reply.

She's changed her mind.

Somehow, in less than twenty-four hours, she'd determined that softball, once again, was the only thing that really and truly mattered in her life, and she was going to devote all her energies to being the best player she could be.

Well, I've got two options. I can either argue with her about this and get the both of us nowhere, or I can jump onboard the band wagon and give her the support she needs.

"Kate," I whispered, reaching up and touching her cheek. "I've got mine and Rory's ball gloves in the bed of my truck. Before the sun goes down completely, do you wanna toss me a few pitches?"

Her response wasn't at all what I was expecting. She closed the distance between us in a split second, pressing her lips to mine, kissing me fiercely. Her lips floated over mine, then skated across my cheekbones, heading for my neck. My heart skipped happily in my chest and just as I was about to reciprocate and wrap my arms around her, she stopped and sat bolt upright.

"You're just full of good ideas," she said, rolling away from me, and practically leaping to her feet. "Come on," she urged, offering me a hand up. "Let's go get those mitts."

I tried not to feel too dejected. For a second there, it looked like things were about to heat up between me and Kate. As much as I would've liked that, I also knew that she needed me to comfort her right now. And for Kate Kellner, kisses were nice and maybe a little soothing, but what she really liked to do, more than anything else, was to throw a few pitches.

If I wanted a nice, easy, and semi-normal relationship, I wouldn't have gone ahead and fallen in love with Kate.

I had to remind myself of that as she dragged me toward the truck. But when I tossed her Rory's glove and she smiled brightly back at me, I knew that my choices had been perfectly and totally the correct ones. Even if she was devoted to soft-ball, she loved me too, and having someone like Kate as my girlfriend was worth all the hard work.

Chapter 7

Wednesday, June 7th

Kate

"You're doing fine, Kate. Just hold steady."

I've never been so terrified in all my life.

The sun was beating down on my back, which I suppose was a blessing. I could've been the one facing the garish sun, having to squint into it, while performing this complicated task, but Becky had taken mercy on me and let me pick which side I wanted. I hadn't even factored in the blazing sunshine when I'd chosen to have the fence as a backstop, but now I was grateful to have one less thing working against me.

I put up my glove and tried my very best to keep my eyes open.

Zzzip...thwack.

Becky was just easing through her warmup routine, making slow circular windmill motions, but when she snapped her wrist and practiced her follow through, the ball zinged straight in my direction and I had two choices: keep my eyes open, hold up my glove, and catch that highlighter yellow orb or close my eyes, pray the ball didn't pop me on the conk, and hope that the fates aligned to let me at least knock it down. It took all the courage I could muster to keep my feet planted and mitt raised. But I caught that ball, then breathed a sigh of relief.

"Do you think I can move on now?"

She was being so patient with me, and I sort of felt sorry for her. It was near the end of our Trailblazer's practice. We'd all started in the outfield, catching routine fly balls. Then, Coach Davis had gotten creative and sent us running in zig zag patterns, only to hit more fly balls over our heads and make us track those down too. After fatiguing everybody with those drills, we moved to the infield and fought off an onslaught of grounders. But now, while the rest of the team was going through the mechanics of laying down the perfect bunt, the pitchers and catchers were standing in the outfield, throwing a few. While there were four pitchers on this team, there were only two catchers, so that made our numbers uneven. Since Lacy was going to be the starting pitcher most of the time, and she held seniority over everybody else, she'd snagged Abs as her catcher right away. That left Hope grabbing hold of her friend, Bianca, and claiming her as her designated catcher. So, Becky and I had been stuck together.

It was a whole new experience being on this end of the interchange. I wasn't afraid of the ball, per se. No one could be a pitcher for as long as I had and not taken their fair share of screamers that were belted right back up the middle. But this was certainly the first time I'd ever been asked to play catcher for someone else who threw the ball using the windmill pitching style. Moreover, Becky Gardner wasn't just anybody. She was six feet tall and had legs for days. When she strode off the pitching rubber, she made it almost halfway to home plate. And her fastball was notoriously speedy. She had often been clocked at throwing more than seventy miles per hour and if batters couldn't catch up to that heater, no one blamed them because once the ball left her hand the only way anyone knew where it went was to follow the bright yellow vapor trail that lingered. And here I was, holding my glove in front of my face, praying not to be beaned by one of Becky's patented fastballs.

"Uh...how about just a few more warmups?" I suggested. I tried not to sound weak or intimidated, but I was both of those things at present, and it was probably better to own my fears than pretend otherwise and get clobbered upside the head by a demonic rise ball.

"If you can't do this, we can switch," Becky offered, pausing for a second to wipe the dirt and sweat from her forehead using the tail end of her neon pink t-shirt. "I can catch for you for a while and then we can call it a day."

I frowned but gave her idea some serious consideration. It'd certainly make my life easier if I could just play my normal role rather than having to try something new against one of the very best in the game. "But you haven't even had the chance to work on your rise yet."

"My rise is fine," she said, shaking off my words by waving the tip of her glove dismissively. "It's my screw that needs help."

I cringed.

I can barely handle catching these warmup pitches. How am I ever gonna get a glove on her swerving and dipping screwball?

"Uh..." I summoned my bravery, then dropped into my best impression of a catcher's squat. "If you need to work on your screw, let's give it a go."

"You sure?"

A pit opened in my stomach, and I had to suck in a deep breath before I could answer. The scent of the baked dirt infield and the fresh cut grass of the outfield revitalized me, just as I'd hoped it would, so when I answered, I was able to ignore the ever-widening cavern of despair that was currently replacing my core. "Let's do it," I said, balling my fist and hammering it into the heart of my ball glove.

The first pitch Becky threw had a little pop on it and when I caught it my mitt made a cracking sound. "Looking good," I encouraged, tossing the ball back to Becky and she snickered.

"I'm still just warming up, Kate," she replied.

My knees knocked together then and I had to suck in another deep inhalation to steady myself. "No problem," I called. "Keep 'em coming."

A trickle of sweat started to weave its way down the side of my face, and I had to resist the urge to wipe my brow. Maybe because I was focused on that rivulet of perspiration or perhaps because I was scared to death of what it'd look like when Becky finally finished with her warmup routine and began hurling real firecracker-style pitches, when the next toss came at me, I missed it completely. Like, I didn't even get my glove on the ball. Instead, it grazed my left elbow and went flying, pinging off the metal fence at my back.

"No worries," I shouted, leaping to my feet, and dashing to retrieve the ball. After whipping it to Becky and before dropping into a squat once more I wiped the sweat away, then we got back to work. I clenched my jaw tight and willed myself to keep my eyes open the whole time, but it wasn't easy. Becky was still easing into her warmups, moving away from just working her arms to adding her legs into the mix. When she started striding toward me, my pulse quickened and that trickle of sweat that bothered me before was no longer a problem. I was perspiring profusely, and it was all I could do to stop myself from taking off my glove after every pitch and wiping my sweaty hand on the side of my mesh shorts.

"You ready for the screw?" Becky asked a few minutes later and I managed to nod weakly.

I'm definitely not ready, but if I admit that, everybody will think I'm a wimp.

That might not be precisely true, but I wasn't willing to take the risk.

Becky situated herself on the makeshift pitching rubber that was laid near the foul line and just as she was starting her windup, Coach Davis saved the day. "That'll do, Trailblazers."

I kept my eyes on Becky because it was my experience that even when Coach called practice for the day, I tried to sneak in a few final pitches and I wasn't about to put it beyond her to do the same, especially since she'd only done a little more than warmup today. But she paused and it almost looked as though she breathed a sigh of relief.

"Come on now!" Coach Davis hollered, waving her hand to beckon her players. "We only had the field booked until noon. And if we don't get out of here soon, the Little Leaguers are going to file a complaint."

My eyes darted down the left field line where a group of young girls were already depositing their equipment in the dugout. They were laughing and talking loudly. One girl was scurrying down the line, holding a gigantic plastic tub of bubble gum, offering pieces to her teammates. I sighed wistfully, thinking of how much easier things were when I was playing with the Falcons, practicing only in a position that was my own, rather than trying something new for the first time.

I jogged, along with the other pitchers, to the mound where Coach Davis was standing and waiting, rather impatiently, for us. Once we were huddled around her, she said, "Good practice today. I like what I saw in the outfield earlier. In this league, I don't expect any of our pitchers to be able to strike out the side, so we're going to need players who can stay on their toes and come up with those superstar catches." Her chocolate brown eyes roved over everyone, and they stopped when they reached Becky. "On Saturday, we've got our first game, and I expect that some of you will want to put in a little more practice time before then, but I couldn't get us another day back on this field. If any of you want to get together and maybe throw a few, use the group chat." She nodded stiffly at Becky and when Becky returned the gesture, my heart sank.

I really was a terrible partner today.

It hadn't occurred to me while we were in motion, but I was doing such a horrible job that I didn't even get the chance to take my turn throwing. Becky had only made it through her warmup, and I'd gone the whole practice without even tossing a few pitches. It was entirely and utterly a losing situation for everyone. Because now, not only did Becky need to find time to get in a few more practice sessions, but I did too. And I was already exhausted. Catching had taken something entirely different out of my body. It made all my muscles twinge and even my head throbbed and ached abominably.

I'd stopped paying attention to Coach's speech, but when she called for all hands in, I obliged. I hadn't heard what we were going to chant, so I just went through the motions, lifting my glove with the others, and yelling a nonsense word at the last minute. Maybe Becky could tell I was feeling dejected because as the group broke up and we turned to walk away, she stayed by my side.

"Don't sweat it, Kellner," she said, tucking her mitt underneath her arm, pinching it to her side. "You're not a catcher and nobody expects you to be."

"Yeah, but..." I started to argue, and she shook her head, silencing me almost immediately.

"It's not easy to try something new and I know how fast I throw." She snickered dryly. "I'd never have thrown full speed without making sure you had on the proper equipment first. And I'm pretty sure you don't even own catcher's gear, right?"

"That...that's what you think I was worried about?" I stammered. "You throwing full speed?"

"Sure." She shrugged.

I hung my head. "I just didn't want to take one of your warmup pitches to the face," I admitted.

I expected her to giggle, but instead she bobbed her head in acknowledgement. "That makes sense, too. Didn't your catcher get clobbered in the eye last season?" She cocked her head to the side indicating Abs.

"Yeah," I murmured. "The ball dinged her up pretty badly." That was, of course, an understatement. The ball had blasted Abs' eye, causing blood to spill everywhere. The impact had been dreadful, and the aftermath was painful, too. Her doctor had forced her to sit out for the remainder of the season and even now she was required to wear this squishy, foamy half mask thing any time she stepped onto the softball diamond.

"So, I get it," Becky said as we reached our dugout bench, and she dropped her glove into her bat bag. "You didn't want to get hurt."

Maybe that was part of it, but the other part was that I had been intimidated. Becky twirled her arm so quickly and her stride was so massive that I just didn't think I'd be able to catch what she was throwing. This practice hadn't exactly buoyed my confidence, but then, Becky said something that made me spiral even worse.

"We'll do better next time."

"Yeah," I snorted, "because next time we'll make sure you're paired with someone who can actually catch the ball."

"Right," she agreed. She was smiling and not looking at all perturbed, but I got the feeling that she was also speaking in earnest. She had to have been disappointed when she got stuck with me and now, because I was such a weakling and had put in such an abysmal performance, she was going to have to find time to throw a few on her own later.

Becky packed up her bag quickly and I tried to follow suit, but then I decided to linger a little, not wanting to prolong our conversation by trailing her out of the dugout. After she was done and gone, I swung my bat bag over my shoulder and sulked out of the dugout, heading toward Syd's car. I'd caught a ride with Syd and Abs this morning, but I wasn't ready to go home yet. Sloughing my athletic slides through the gravel of the parking lot and kicking at small pebbles brought me an enormous amount of satisfaction. And if the park where we'd practiced had been any closer to my house, I might've gone on this way, wandering all the way home, staring at my feet, and thinking about how I hadn't just let down my teammate today, but myself, too.

"What's with the face?" Syd asked when I reached her little, sky-blue car that she had affectionately nicknamed Dream Boat right after purchasing it.

"What face?" I retorted, doing my best to summon a smile that could replace the frown I knew was plastered in place.

Syd popped open the trunk of her car and dropped her bag inside. Then, Abs did the same and they waited for me to follow suit. "That face," Abs snickered. "You look like somebody just kicked you while you were already down." She laughed again, this time more loudly. "Did one of those Little Leaguers give you a hard time, Lady K?"

"Or did something happen with Grady?" Syd added. Her comment took me by surprise and that emotion must've registered on my face because Syd continued. "What's wrong? What did he do?"

"Nothing," I scoffed. "Grady's perfect."

Syd rolled her eyes dramatically. "Nobody's perfect."

"Grady is," I assured her. "I don't know how he manages it, but the guy always knows exactly the right things to say and do."

"I'll bet he does," Abs said, winking lasciviously at me.

I heaved my bat bag into the trunk, then slammed it closed. "Get your head out of the gutter, DeWalt."

She shrugged. "Maybe you oughta stick your head in the gutter more often, Kellner," she replied, using her merry sing-song voice. "It's a lot more fun there than stomping around the real world, feeling sorry for yourself."

"What's Kate got to feel bad about?" Syd asked as she climbed into the driver's seat and waited for us to take up our respective spots. Abs snagged the passenger's seat, leaving me on my own in the back. "Didn't she just tell us she had the perfect boyfriend?"

"Practice didn't go so well," Abs said quietly.

"You saw?" I slumped low in my seat. "You...?"

"Yeah," Abs cut me off. "I saw what was happening with you and Becky and I've gotta say, you really shouldn't beat yourself up over this one."

"What happened?" Syd was all ears. She backed the car out of the lot, and angled it toward home, but I could tell her attention was divided. She wanted to know what she'd missed while doing batting drills with the rest of the team.

"It was no big deal," Abs said, rolling down the window. "Lady K got teamed up with Becky because we were short on catchers and Kate's not built for being behind the plate." Warm air wafted in through the open window and I sat forward a little, letting it brush across the planes of my face.

"That's true," Syd snorted, then her eyes met mine in the rearview. "Have you ever caught for another pitcher before?"

I shrugged my shoulders helplessly. "This was a first."

"Well then, you shouldn't be upset about it," Syd lectured. "I'm sure Becky didn't expect you to do very well."

Reflexively, my nose snurled. "Then I guess I didn't disappoint her."

Abs pulled her hairband out, letting her wild locks whip around in the summer breeze, and then she swiveled in her seat so she could almost face me, rather than just peer over her shoulder into the backseat. "You're making way more of a thing out of this than you should."

"Am I?"

She nodded and Syd mimicked the motion. "You're never going to be catching Becky, or any of the other pitchers for that matter, during a game. So, it doesn't matter how you did in practice today."

"Practice matters," I argued.

"Yeah, yeah." Syd took one of her hands off the steering wheel and waved it flippantly. "We already know you subscribe to the theory that we all practice how we play."

"Doesn't everybody?" I countered.

Abs snorted. "Maybe," she conceded. "But nobody takes their practices as seriously as you do."

"I'm gonna have to agree with Abs on this one, Kate," Syd said slowly, making a wide turn as we pulled out of the park. "You've got to just let this thing today with Becky go. So what if neither of you got in a very good practice session. We all know you're going to be right back at it again tomorrow and..."

"Tomorrow?" I interrupted. "I can't wait that long. I've got to..."

"Woah," Abs said, drawing the word out long. "Slow your roll there, Lady K. You've already spent two and a half hours on the softball diamond this morning. There's no need to pick up your ball again the rest of the day."

"But I need to practice."

"No, you don't," Abs said firmly. She and Syd shared a quick glance, then she turned in her seat once more so she could meet my eyes. "What you need to do right now is give yourself a break."

"I can't take a break," I whispered fervently, wanting my friends not just to hear what I was saying, but also try to understand my situation. "I'm worried that if I don't stay on top of my game, I'll spend the whole summer on the bench, or even worse, I'll be forced to learn how to play a new position."

Abs scoffed. "What? You think Coach Davis is gonna want you to take over my spot as catcher? Sorry to burst your bubble, pal, but I'm not even the starter on our team. My injury last season set me back and I'm betting Bianca will get the nod. So, we don't have any room for other catchers, especially not newbies like you."

"And the infield is in good shape too," Syd added. "I may not even have a starting spot on the roster."

"See?" I said, lifting my empty hands and holding them out. "What am *I* gonna do? Just sit on the bench?"

"It's not so bad," Abs said, eyeing me keenly, almost as if she were daring me to argue. "I had to do it for the entire second half of last season."

"And you were a wonderful cheerleader," Syd said without a hint of sarcasm coloring her tone.

"Thank you," Abs chirped, but then she smiled brightly at me. "You've got nothing to worry about here, Lady K. You'll play or you won't. It really doesn't make any difference."
"It makes a difference to me," I said quietly.

"Yeah," Abs sighed. "I was sure you'd say something like that." She brushed back some strands of her dark hair that were whipping around and clinging to her cheekbones. "It's so hot out here today."

I knew that was her attempt at changing the subject and I didn't begrudge her that.

If I were Abs, I'd get tired of this conversation pretty quickly, too.

"It's too bad we don't know someone who owns a pool," Syd said snidely, then as she pulled into my driveway and put the car in park, she used one hand to slap herself upside the head. "Oh wait. We actually do know someone with a pool." She turned around in her seat to smile at me. "What do you say, Kate? Did Mama Kellner open the pool officially yet?"

"The day after graduation it was ready to go," I answered.

"What?" Abs feigned being shocked. "You've had pool access for almost a whole week, and you haven't invited us over yet?"

"I've been busy." I shrugged.

"Yeah," Syd snorted. "Hanging out with your perfect boy-friend." But then, her eyes lit up and I could tell she was culti-vating an idea. "Why don't you text that gorgeous boyfriend of yours? Tell him to gather up some of his smoke show friends and join us all for a little pool party?"

"Ehhh..." I pulled the sound out long, thinking over the possibilities. "I really need to..."

"Pitching can wait 'til later," Syd insisted. "Call Grady now. Tell him to get over here with his buddies and let's just have some fun."

I had to admit that the picture Syd was painting did sound awfully nice. My family had a rather small house, but the inground pool we had behind our little home was something special. It was a little more than nine feet deep, at the lowest point, so my parents had installed a small diving board that got plenty of use. In the shallow end, most people could stand easily and, if I really felt like it, I was sure I could coerce some of my friends to chuck a ball around with me while also splashing there. Plus, the pool had been open for a full week, and I had yet to get in or invite any of my friends, including Grady, to join me.

The thought of seeing him brought a smile to my face.

"Oh..." Abs said, pointing at me and laughing loudly. "I think you've struck pay dirt, Syd. If I know Lady K like I think I do, we're in for a pool party this afternoon."

"Come on," I said, reaching for the door handle. "If you don't have swimsuits of your own, you can borrow some of mine."

Cheers of delight filled the interior of the little compact car, and my smile stretched even wider.

Maybe they're right. Maybe I ought to try and just enjoy this summer.

Chapter 8

Ty

Great. Just great.

I was plugging my way through hour six of my eight-hour shift when Rory Hughes walked casually over to my designated post. I'd been put on towel dry duty today which meant every few minutes or seconds, depending upon how busy we were, as a car, truck, or van exited the express wash, I had to hustle forward and use a towel to hand dry away any residual water spots. He was carrying a stack of towels and moving at an almost glacial pace, which irritated me almost as much as the fact that he was smiling in that same goofy way his brother, Grady, always did.

"Can you hurry a little, please?" I asked tersely, eyeing the stack of fresh, black towels in his hands. "We've got customers waiting on us."

"Where?" Rory plopped the pile on the nearby rolling cart then gave a halfhearted glance around the parking lot. "I know we've been pretty busy all day so far, but I don't see anybody lined up right now."

His summation was accurate, but I wasn't about to agree with him. "I've just been needing those towels for the last ten minutes and..."

"If you needed more towels, you could've gone inside and picked up some more on your own," he reasoned, which irked me even further.

"I wasn't going to abandon my post," I said through gritted teeth while seizing a towel and wringing it between my hands, mostly to give myself something productive to do.

Rory shrugged. "If you really needed more supplies, you could've used the walkie-talkie to make a call." He nodded toward the walkie which was also perched on the rolling cart.

"I'm just glad you brought the towels," I muttered. "'Cause now I can get on with my work."

A shiny red compact car rolled out of the express wash and after Rory grabbed a towel of his own, he joined me in wiping down the automobile. Since we worked as a team, with him taking the back end and me attacking the hood and tires, we made easy work of the job, and the driver even rolled down his window and handed me a couple of bucks as a tip. "Thanks," I said, snatching the bills. I was tempted to pocket both dollars, but then thought better of it. Once the car rolled away, I held out Rory's share.

"There for a second, I thought you might keep the whole thing," he said, taking his dollar and shoving it deep into his back pocket. Then, in a leisurely manner, he snapped his towel and flung it over his shoulder.

"I don't work that way," I assured him, then corrected myself. "Well... I *might've* considered the idea of keeping all the cash, but I'd never have done it."

"Sure." Rory nodded. "You're a real standup guy."

There was something about the way he said it that made my insides rankle and I couldn't just let his comment slide. "What's that supposed to mean?"

Rory scoffed then fixed his lackadaisical grin firmly on his face. "You may wanna beat around the bush here, Ty, but that's not how I do things. We both know that you're gunning for my little brother's girl, so I'm not gonna pretend otherwise."

"What?" I barked. "I'm not trying to steal Kate from Grady. It was Grady who..."

"Did what?" He asked when I stopped talking in the middle of my sentence. "Had the misfortune to be uprooted in the middle of his senior year? Had the audacity to make friends with a girl who just happened to be your best friend, too?"

"You don't know anything about what went down between Kate and Grady," I grumbled.

"And you do?" Rory countered.

"I know enough," I retorted brusquely before turning away from him. But Rory Hughes was a tough guy to shake. Since another car wasn't coming out of the express wash any time soon, he followed me. And because I wasn't leaving my duties, I wasn't going very far anyway.

"I'm not sure what you think you know, Ty, but I can tell you one thing with certainty." Rory paused and I wondered if he was doing this for dramatic effect or just because he wanted to force me to participate in the conversation and come right out and ask the question. I obliged.

"What do *you* know?" I prompted.

"You're not being fair to my brother or Kate," Rory answered, which was slightly surprising.

"Fair?" I echoed. "You want to talk about *fair*? I've been in love with Kate forever and if Grady hadn't blown into town, I would've..."

"What?" Rory challenged. "You would've what?"

"Eh," I groaned. "Just forget it."

"You can't really be mad at Grady," Rory said, crossing his arms leisurely over his chest and leaning one hip against the rolling cart.

"Can't I?"

He arched an eyebrow, giving me a derisive look, but then chuckled lightly. "You're hard-headed, Ty. But I've got the feeling you're not entirely a bad dude."

"Uh, thanks," I muttered.

"No," Rory continued, "I mean it. And I admit that I don't know you well, but I'm pretty sure if you knew my brother better, you wouldn't hate him as much as you do."

"I wouldn't be so sure about that."

Rory snorted. "Yeah, Grady can be annoying. And I can totally understand why you've let him get under your skin, but..."

"But what?" I asked snidely. "Does Prince Charming have some horrible flaw he's been hiding up until now?"

Rory looked slightly taken aback. He stared at me for a long beat, then answered, "Grady's flaw isn't really such a bad thing." He uncrossed his arms and took the drying towel off his shoulder, then fiddled with the seams. "He's the youngest child in our family, but you already know that, right?"

"Yeah," I snorted. "So that means your parents have spoiled him, I assume."

"You assume wrong," Rory snapped, giving me a pointed stare. "Maybe that's true in some families, but that's not the way things have gone in the Hughes household. Ever since Grady was a baby, he always had this obliging attitude. Like he'd just be happy so long as everyone else around him was."

I rolled my eyes. "That must've been really awful."

"It was," he insisted. "Anytime it was Grady's turn to pick what everyone was having for dinner he'd turn to us and ask what we wanted instead. Then, when he told Mom he wanted spaghetti, which was obviously my favorite rather than his, Mom would come down on me and ask why I was telling my little brother what to do. I'd argue and say it was all Grady's fault, but even as a little kid, he'd just smile and say I could make the call. He didn't care what we had to eat, so long as everybody was in a good mood during dinner."

"So, what're you telling me?" I asked, bothered by this version of Grady that I'd never seen before. "Grady's a saint or something?"

"Far from it," Rory scoffed. "But he does lean toward being selfless." He flicked the towel over his shoulder again. "I'm just thinking about how things could've been very different for the two of you. If *you'd* have made friends with Grady when he first came to Farrington, and you'd told him you were harboring a crush on Kate, he might've..."

"What?" I demanded. "Stepped aside?"

Rory shrugged. "If you were his pal, he definitely wouldn't have made a move on your girl."

I grunted. "Do you think if I told him *now* that I wanted him to go away and leave Kay-Kay alone, he'd do it?"

Rory's grin returned. "Not a chance now, I'm afraid."

"Why not?" I challenged. "You just said that Grady had a self-sacrificing personality. If I..."

"Grady's different with Kate," he interrupted. "Maybe, if you'd been his buddy early on, he wouldn't have developed feelings for her, but now that he's in love with her..."

"Ugh," I said, interrupting because I really didn't want to hear any more. "Grady's not in love with Kay-Kay."

"Yeah, he is," Rory insisted. "And, from the looks of things, it'd take a natural disaster to make him give up on her."

I considered that notion. "Even when he leaves for Felding?"

Rory shrugged. "My little brother would take the shirt off his back and give it to somebody else, if he thought the person was in true need of it. But when it comes to Kate Kellner? He's not giving her up for anybody. Not now. Maybe not ever."

I scoffed, thinking how slightly ridiculous and melodramatic this whole thing sounded. "Why're you telling me this?"

"I thought it was only *fair*," he said, smirking as he recycled the word that he'd thrown out early on in our conversation. "You ought to know what you're up against, Ty Masterson. And...to be perfectly honest, I needed you to know the truth."

"Oh yeah? What's the truth?"

"Grady won't fight you for Kate, but he won't need to, either. She'll pick him every time because he's the one who loves her truly. So, you can interrupt them while they're kissing all you want or steal Kate away so the two of you can watch movies any old time, but that won't make a bit of difference."

"How do you know what Kay-Kay wants?"

Rory laughed brightly then nodded at the fresh from the express wash brown sedan that was gently easing toward us. He yanked the towel off his shoulder. "I don't know what Kate wants, but I know Grady. And he won't let her go now that he's got her."

"We'll see about that," I mumbled under my breath. As I skirted around the car, polishing the spots off the windows, I glanced at my own determined reflection in the mirrored surface. I was sure Rory had some of his facts straight because after all, he was Grady's brother, and probably knew him better than anyone else. But he didn't know me or Kay-Kay. She might be satisfied hanging with Grady right now, but she'd never make a go of it with him long-term. Once he left for Felding, their little relationship would be all over and things could go back to the way they were supposed to be. Me and Kay-Kay...spending all our time together.

***

Fantastic. They're doing that suction cup thing again.

I'd gotten Kay-Kay's text message about a pool party shortly after my conversation with Rory concluded, but since I had to finish up my shift at work, I didn't make it home or go over to the Kellner's until the party was in full swing. When I opened the gated fence and let myself into the backyard, Abs and Syd were already in the pool, laughing and singing along loudly with the song that was playing over the speakers. A guy I recognized from school named Will Hopkins was doing a cannonball in the deep end, some other guy I didn't know at all, but looked vaguely like Grady, was chatting with the girls, and Grady and Kate were sharing a lounge chair, practically glued together at the hip.

Perfect.

"Hey," I muttered, approaching Kate and Grady. He had on a pair of dark aviator sunglasses, so I couldn't see his eyes when he caught sight of me. Kay-Kay was wearing a red and navy-blue two-piece swimsuit. It wasn't revealing or anything because it was cut like the kit beach volleyball players normally wore, but Grady had one hand wrapped around her hip and his fingers were draped near her upper thigh, which didn't make me the least bit thrilled.

I've never liked that Grady Hughes...

Rory's words drifted back to me, and I recalled that if I had made the effort to like Grady in the beginning, I might've been able to save myself some of this heartache. But then, Grady opened his mouth to speak, and I remembered exactly why that was an impossibility.

"Hey, Ty," he said lazily. "Good to see you."

I couldn't tell if he was being facetious or not because those darned sunglasses continued shielding his eyes and the smile on his face was tranquil, so that gave away nothing, either.

"How was work?" Kay-Kay asked, yawning, and stretching, allowing herself to curl deeper into her boyfriend's side. I winced as his hand slipped over the curve of her hip.

"I had an interesting conversation with your brother," I said, nodding at Grady.

He lifted his sunglasses slowly, giving me a peek behind the mirrored lenses. "Did you?"

I nodded. "He seems to think that if I wasn't such a grump the two of us might just get along."

Kate laughed perkily. "That's what I've been trying to say."

"Cannonball!" Will yelled before jumping in the deep end, sending a spray of water in our direction. The water droplets touched the edges of my kiwi green flip-flops, so I kicked them off, tucking them underneath the lounge chair closest to the cozy couple.

"Maybe the two of you could have a nice, long conversation later," Kay-Kay suggested, positively bubbling with enthusiasm, and no longer looking all tuckered out. "You could sort through your differences and..."

"Whatever you want," Grady said, sliding his sunglasses back into position and snuggling further into the seat, pulling her closer to his chest.

"Yeah," I grunted. "So long as the two of you aren't suction cupped together during our little talk, I'm game."

"Suction cupped?" Kay-Kay echoed, as a bemused look slid onto her face. I hadn't realized that I'd just spoken my thoughts aloud and I sorely regretted saying exactly what I'd been thinking. "We're not..." she started to argue, but Syd must've been listening in because she burst out laughing hysterically.

"Did you hear that, Abs?" she cackled. "Ty just compared Kate and Grady to a pair of suction cups and..."

"But they're only attached at the hip," Abs said, popping up out of the water and draping her tanned arms over the edge of the pool. "Things could get a lot more suction cup like if they..."

Grady laughed, then pulled Kay-Kay nearer and before I knew it, I was granted a front row seat to him smashing his lips against hers and Kate kissing him back just as passionately.

Awful...and I'm to blame for this because if I hadn't opened my big mouth, they wouldn't be...

His hand slid around her backside and then he nibbled on her lower lip, which made Kate giggle, fortunately breaking the spell that had come over them.

"There," Grady said, smirking in a self-satisfied way at me. "Did we sufficiently mimic a set of suction cups, or do you need us to give it another go, Ty?"

Syd shrieked with laughter again and even though I wanted to turn and scowl at her, I knew I'd only make matters worse if I didn't pretend to be totally unaffected. "Great," I managed to mumble. The urge to flee suddenly overwhelmed me. I knew I could've beat a hasty retreat and headed back toward my house, but then I'd probably be forced to discuss this scene with Kay-Kay at some point later. So, the only option open to me was to bite the bullet, peel off my shirt, and plunge into the deep end of the pool.

As I whipped my shirt off and slung it at the lounge chair next to Kate and Grady, Abs let out a loud whoop. "Dang, Masterson! Where you been hiding those abs?"

Syd got in on the taunting too. When I walked by her, heading for the diving board, she let out a low whistle. "Looking good, Ty. Seems like all that running's been paying off."

I didn't care what either of them said because I was so steamed about the interaction I'd just had with Grady and Kay-Kay.

Selfless my left foot. That guy laid that kiss on Kay-Kay just to scorch my grits.

I leapt into the pool, making a small splash, but when I surfaced, I didn't even have time to catch my breath because Will had jumped right behind me. His cannonball made another massive splash, and the wave of water got me right in the face.

Syd and Abs giggled, then surged forward, and started pounding Will with sprays of crystal-clear water. The guy who looked like Grady lurked near the shallow end, but I ignored him too. Slowly, I swam to the side and as I reached the place closest to the filter, I pulled myself up so that my elbows were resting on the lip of the pool.

That's when Kate joined me. She sat so close to me that her hip nearly touched my elbow as she dangled her long legs in the water. "So..." she said slowly, "do you like Grady's brother, Rory?"

"Eh," I snorted. "He's pretty chatty, but I guess that's okay because at least he did his fair share of work today."

"You know, that's Giles over there," Kate said, nodding at the guy in the shallow end. "He's Rory's twin."

I twisted my neck slowly to look at her. She was smiling at Giles. "Exactly how many brothers does Grady have?"

She laughed. "Three."

"Terrific," I grunted. "The Hughes brothers are going to be everywhere this summer."

Right on cue, Grady jumped off the diving board, then, without needing to surface to take a gulp of air, he swam all the way to the shallow end and popped up right next to his brother. He clamped down on Giles' arm and towed him toward the action in the deep end. And that was when Kay-Kay hopped in the pool too. She took two quick strokes, stopped to tread water, and turned sideways to share an inviting look with me. "Aren't you coming, Ty?"

"Yeah," I said grumpily.

Even if I had to watch Kay-Kay kiss Grady a million times over *and* be surrounded by the Hughes brothers who irritated me immensely, I was doomed to follow Kate Kellner wherever she might go.

Chapter 9

"Watch, Kate. Just watch," Grady whispered right in my ear. It was difficult to focus on what he was saying when he was purring it in such a seductive manner and his warm breath was brushing against my cheek.

"What am I looking for exactly?" I asked, tipping my head back, leaning further into him and staring at the sky which showcased millions of twinkling stars overhead through the wooden beams of the pergola that encased my family's backyard pool area. "A shooting star?"

A few hours ago, my parents arrived home after spending all the livelong day at work. After Dad volunteered to grill hamburgers for me and my pals, and we all had supper together, the gang went home. Giles caught a ride with Will, Ty marched back to his house, and Abs and Syd hopped into the Dream Boat but not before making me promise we'd do this again sometime soon. So now, it was just me and Grady. We'd changed out of our wet swimsuits into some comfy t-shirts and mesh shorts and were cuddled together in the lounge chair that we'd mostly been sharing all afternoon once he joined the party after finishing his morning shift as errand boy at the auto mall.

"Not up there," he said, lightly grazing his fingers over my arm before reaching out and touching the tip of my chin, angling it downward. "Look at what's right in front of you."

A shiver raced up my spine in the same way it always did when I had the chance to be this close to my boyfriend. We didn't get to snuggle like this much, but after spending the day with him, practically locked in this position, I saw some merits in chasing this feeling and making it last for as long as possible.

I squinted across the pool, looking at the oak trees that covered the backside of our property. "I still don't see anything, Grady," I whispered.

"Really?" he murmured, and his voice was slightly disappointed. "You can't see all the Lampyridae?"

"Do you mean the lightning bugs?" I focused on the glowing hindquarters of one of the buzzing beetles that was drifting just a few inches above the surface of the still waters of the pool.

"Yeah," he chuckled lightly. "The lightning bugs...the fireflies...call 'em whatever you like."

"What was it you called them?" I asked, burrowing even further into his side, resting the side of my face against his chest so I could simultaneously listen to his heartbeat and the deep rumble he produced when he was talking in his quiet, melodic bass voice.

"Lampyridae," he whispered. "That's their scientific name."

"Tell me more about these Lampyridae," I urged.

"They don't get under your skin the way other insects do?" he asked, playfully tickling my forearm.

"Not so much." I grabbed hold of his hand to stop him from tickling me, but also so I could intertwine his fingers with my own. "I used to chase them around the yard when I was younger. I even kept them in glass jars until my mom said it was cruel to bottle them up like that."

Grady nodded. "She was probably right. According to most of the reading I've done on the species, fireflies only live for about two months." He shuddered. "Imagine what it would be like to spend even a single second of your already short life cooped up in a jar."

"What else do you know about lightning bugs?" I rubbed my thumb in a slow, circular motion around Grady's, enjoying listening to him talk about a subject that brought him such great joy.

"You see the way their tail end's light up?"

"Yeah," I snickered. "That's kind of their defining characteristic."

"Well, they do that because they want to attract mates." The hand he had wrapped around my waist squeezed my hip. "Some males flash their lights up to nine times, but others only do it once because they figure that's all they need to find the right female."

I giggled. "The laws of attraction, at least as far as they apply to animals, are fascinating."

"What?" he said, wriggling a little beside me. "You don't think human males behave in the same manner?"

At that, I laughed outright. "Yeah, Grady. I don't know about you, but I've never seen a guy spontaneously light up, just so he can get the attention of a girl."

When I turned to glance at his face, I saw that he wasn't laughing along with me. He was strangely serious. "Then I guess you missed the way Ty ripped off his shirt today before diving like an Olympian into the deep end of the pool."

"I...I saw Ty get in the pool, but I didn't think there was anything especially out of the ordinary about his behavior."

Grady laughed dryly, without any mirth. "So, he always showboats like that?" When I didn't say anything, he continued, "Come on, Kate. You had to have heard the way Syd and Abs made over him. They certainly weren't catcalling when anybody else joined them in the pool."

I fidgeted so I was better able to sit upright. It was difficult because our bodies were so closely pressed together, and

I had to put my left leg on the pavement so I could manage it. I swiveled so I could stare at Grady plainly. "What's wrong?" I questioned. "I was actually going to say something earlier...to let you know how happy I was to see you and Ty getting along so well today, but now that just seems..."

He scoffed. "You thought we were getting along?"

"You were," I insisted. "Today was the first time ever that the two of you have been in the same place for longer than a few minutes."

He shook his head. "Last spring, we went to your softball games all the time."

"But you never stayed next to one another for very long," I reminded him. "Even if you started out sitting by each other, one or the other of you got up, ceding your spot on the bleachers, and headed toward the fence line. Don't think I didn't notice."

"Yeah, okay," he agreed. "But just because we spent the better part of the late afternoon together today doesn't mean much."

"Yes, it does," I pressed. "You're my boyfriend and he's my best friend. I want the two of you to like each other." I leaned forward and smooched the side of his cheek. "Don't you think everything's better when we all can just hang out together?"

Grady shrugged, indicating his indifference on the subject. "I happen to think things are pretty great right now—just the two of us hanging out." He dragged me backward, pulling me to his chest, and hugging me close. I tittered.

"I like this too, but today was exactly what I needed, Grady. All the people I love, coming together at my house, spending time in the pool... Seeing everyone get along so well really helped me take my mind off softball for a minute."

"Well, I'm glad about that," he murmured, rubbing his chin over top of my head, snuggling me further into his chest. "But

I'd like to think I'd have been able to make you smile all on my own."

"I've always got a special smile, just for you," I said, turning my head and tipping my face upward so I could plant a quick kiss on the underside of his chin. "But with Ty..."

A low rumble resounded through Grady's chest, and I was surprised by this reaction. "Why do you have to..." he started, then stopped, and rephrased his question. "Are you attracted to Ty, Kate?"

I'd only been a tad taken aback by the low growl he'd just emitted, but this question caught me completely off-guard. "What...what do you mean?"

"It's an easy enough thing to answer," he persisted.

"No, it's not," I countered.

He adjusted his position behind me, scooting so that we were closer to being side by side. Then, he fixed an intense stare on me. "Why not?"

"Ty's not my type," I said, settling back into the chair, feeling bereft now that my head was resting against the cushions rather than Grady's warm and muscular chest.

"Right," he scoffed. "He has abs that look like they were chiseled from marble. I'm sure you wouldn't like anyone like that."

"I like your abs," I said, reaching out and running my fingers over his well-defined abdominal muscles which were discernible, even through the cotton of his t-shirt.

He snorted. "I'm not fishing for compliments here, Kate. And I certainly don't feel self-conscious. I'm cool with who I am and what I look like. All I want to know is how *you* feel about Ty."

I stared out at the lightning bugs, searching for divine inspiration, but nothing occurred to me. "The reason this is a tricky question to answer is because..."

"You won't hurt my feelings," he said hurriedly, talking over top of me. "I only want to hear what you honestly think."

"That's what I'm getting to," I assured him. "The thing is, I don't always think Ty's good-looking. Most of the time, he's just Ty—the guy I've known since we were both missing our two front teeth. But other times..."

"Yeah?" Grady urged.

I shrugged. "When he showed up to my house after the prom, wearing his tux, I thought he looked pretty handsome that night."

"Right," Grady agreed. "But don't most people look their best when they're all dressed up?"

"Maybe," I said halfheartedly. "So, that's why it's tough to say." I turned slowly to look at his face. Clearly my answer hadn't done much to assuage whatever misgivings he was having because Grady was chewing gently on his lowering lip, worrying the soft tissue between his teeth. "Why do you ask?"

Grady stopped fretting and turned his face toward mine. We were just a few inches apart, but I knew he wasn't going to kiss me. We were having a serious conversation and for the first time in what felt like a very long time, I felt like we were worlds apart. "I'm just wondering how long it's gonna take Ty to make a move on you once I'm out of the picture. And..." He paused and sighed deeply. "...I needed to know if you were attracted to him too so I could gauge just how long it'd take you to reciprocate his feelings."

I was gobsmacked. "What...? Why would you even think something like that?" Grady rarely lacked self-confidence and, unless I'd been missing something for the better part of the day, we'd just spent hours wrapped in each other's arms. "How did a thought like that even pop into your brain?"

"It's not such a far stretch of the imagination," he replied, still staring deeply into my eyes, piercing my soul a little with his words that felt almost like he was questioning my fidelity to him.

"You shouldn't be stretching your imagination at all," I said, leaning forward and resting my hand on his chest, glad to feel the warmth of his skin once more. "You've got nothing to worry about here."

"Nothing?" he asked, arching one eyebrow high on his forehead in an inquisitive style.

"Not. A. Single. Thing," I said, adding emphasis to each word. "I told you all about the dust up Ty and I had a few months ago, and I don't expect him to profess his love for me again any time soon. As a matter of fact, I was hoping he'd find someone new this summer and come fall, he'd have practically forgotten my name."

Grady covered my hand with his, pressing my palm deeper into his chest. "If only it was so easy to forget."

"But he *will* forget me soon enough," I promised. "He'll wake up one day very soon and I'll be totally gone from his mind and...wait..." I'd been about to say that I would've completely dropped off his radar and been out of the picture, but that phrase seemed all too familiar. Grady had just said something really similar a moment before and I had to search my short-term memory to recall exactly what he'd said. "Did you just say *you'd* be out of the picture? Where're you going?"

He tipped his head to the side and gave me a sympathetic look. "You know I've only got what's left of summer before I have to pack up and move to Felding," he said.

"Right," I said slowly, "but that shouldn't make any differ-ence. Should it?" I stared at him and the silence around us thickened. "Grady..." My throat constricted when I said his name and my pulse started thrumming wildly through my veins. I knew I had to ask this follow-up question, but I wasn't sure I wanted to hear his answer, so it pained me to eek out the next words. "When you go away to school in August, are you going to break up with me?"

Grady

"I wasn't planning on it," I answered and immediately Kate exhaled deeply. Her shoulders slumped and her evident relief was written all over her face. I decided to continue with my explanation. "Felding University's campus is only an hour and a half drive from here. So, I just figured we'd stay together."

"You did?" she asked, and I could see the shine of tears glistening in her bright blue eyes.

"Well, yeah," I said. "Didn't you?"

Kate nodded, then leaned back, resting her head against the cushions of the lounge chair, not saying anything, but glancing overhead at the night sky. Wanting to have her nearer to me, I draped my arm around her waist, and pulled her close, allowing our hips to bump then overlap so she wasn't quite lying in my lap, but we were definitely sharing our personal space.

"I know it's going to be tough, but I value what we have, Kate. It won't be a picnic driving back here during the weekends and I don't imagine you'll love giving up a couple of Saturdays here and there to drive and see me at Felding, but I guess I just thought we'd make it work. If...if that's what you wanted too?"

Kate wriggled against me and when she turned to gaze at me this time a completely different look was twisting her features. Gone was the pleasant, slightly relieved smile. It was replaced by a hardened stare, one in which her mouth was drawn into a grim line and her eyes were narrowed. "I'm not sure why you keep phrasing it like that," she said, and I could hear in her voice that she was miffed. "You make it seem like you're totally into me, but I'm just hanging out with you to pass the time. You...you're making me feel like you're questioning my devotion to you."

"I'm not," I said hurriedly, although admittedly, I could see how she'd spiraled in that direction. My questions about Ty had been rather blunt and I'd made it clear that I was sure they'd hook up just as soon as I packed my bags. Thoughts of Ty were muddying up everything and I groaned, trying to erase the vision of him ripping off his shirt, diving in the water, and then just a half second later Kate's graceful form slipping from our shared seat so she could go sit next to him when he surfaced. "It's just this whole thing with Ty."

"What about him?" Kate asked, allowing some of her hard veneer to crack.

I remembered how Rory had pushed me a few days ago to tell Kate exactly what I was thinking and feeling.

If I can't tell her I'm uncomfortable with the guy, how do I ever expect to see any changes around here?

"I can't explain it exactly," I murmured, "but he just rubs me the wrong way. It's like, when Ty's around, my skin starts crawling and it feels all prickly." I shook my head. "I think it's because you're a different person when Ty's around and..."

"Yeah, I am," Kate interrupted and that was a little shocking to hear her admit outright that she altered her behaviors when her best friend was nearby. "But that's only natural, isn't it?"

"Natural?"

She put a little distance between us by scooting back, but I didn't mind so much because this movement gave me a chance to watch her face. "You've heard of moral geography, right?"

"Sure." I shrugged. "I think Mrs. Townsend said something about it in ELA when we read *The Great Gatsby* at the end of the year."

"Exactly," Kate said, snapping her fingers. I should've figured she'd know exactly what I meant. Aside from being a star athlete, she was also a bookworm. She'd cruised through all the books on the senior class's reading list years before it was necessary. "Well, you know how in *Gatsby* the characters behave differently depending on where they are at the moment and who they're interacting with?"

"I guess," I said softly. "They all seemed a tad irresponsible to me, especially for a group of people who were supposed to be adults."

She waved her hand dismissively. "That's not the point, Grady." She shifted once more. "What I'm trying to say is that everybody acts differently, depending on the friend group they're hanging with or where they might be at any given moment. For instance, you wouldn't talk the same way you do to me while sitting out here as you would if you were having a discussion with a minister at the church on base."

I considered the idea. "Yeah, I would."

"No, you wouldn't," she insisted. "While we're out here, all by ourselves, sitting around my pool, you'll kiss me so deeply I can practically feel my insides being set ablaze. But if we were in church, you probably wouldn't even dare to hold my hand."

"Sure, I would," I told her honestly.

"Okay," she sighed. "Maybe you'd hold my hand, but you get my point."

"Yeah," I quipped. "When we kiss, I light up your insides like a Christmas tree."

She giggled. "That was what you took away from my explanation?"

I shrugged. "No. But I thought it bore repeating."

She tipped her head to the side and rested it on my shoulder. "You do get it. Right, Grady? I feel like there are many, many versions of me. There's the one I am when I'm playing softball..."

"Killa K," I guessed, and she nodded.

"Then, there's the girl I am when I'm with you."

"Special K?"

I gave her a sidelong glance so I could see the smile coast across her face, but it was only there a split second before she got back to the topic at hand. "And then there's the person I am when I'm with Ty. And Grady, I'm tired of being all these different people. I just wanna be one version of myself and..."

"I hear ya, Kate," I said soothingly, squeezing her arm, and tucking her close into my side. "And I think I get it." I breathed deeply, inhaling the sweet night air that smelled faintly of pool chemicals and the flowering lilac bushes that the Kellners had planted just outside the pool fence. "I just wish that Ty didn't pretend like he knew everything about you. Maybe if he didn't act like he was your best friend all the time...the only person who knew exactly who you were..."

"But Ty *does* know everything about me," Kate interceded. "Until just a few months ago...right up until the moment you walked into my pitching practice session...he *was* the most important person in my life. And he *did* know everything there was to know about me."

"I guess that's true," I whispered, grudgingly accepting this statement because I understood it was a fact. I had squeezed my way between Ty and Kate and now, even if he didn't know every single thing that passed between the two of us, the two of them still had this long, shared history, and he knew things about her that I hadn't even begun to question.

She snuggled into me then, finally relaxing back into the posture we'd been so comfortable adapting to earlier in the evening. "That's why I need you to do me this one big favor, Grady," she said, no longer looking at me, but staring straight ahead at the darkness and the fireflies. "I need you to try and be friends with Ty."

"All right," I agreed. "I'll do my best." Thoughts tumbled around in my head, and it was then that I realized Kate had neatly and effectively evaded my earlier questions about Ty. Oh, she'd said she wasn't interested in him, and she'd also gotten a little ticked that I'd had the nerve to put her feelings under a microscope, but she'd dodged away from the heart of my concerns and deftly steered the conversation toward her own purposes. "And Kate, if I'm going to do this one little thing for you, then I need you to do something big for me in return." "What?" she asked. "Name it. I'll do whatever you need."

I took a moment to carefully phrase my statement, because I didn't want to offend her again by implying that she was going to become Ty's girlfriend just as soon as I left for Felding. "If you decide, at any time, that you want to be with someone else—anyone else—all you've got to do is say so. I'd rather you break things off with me and avoid hurting our relationship than try to stay together and wind up making a bunch of bad decisions."

She tipped her chin upward and stared directly into my eyes. "I'm not going to hurt you, Grady. I love you."

"You say that now, but when I'm not here, sitting right beside you..."

She leaned even nearer and closed the distance between us. Her lips were soft against mine, but we weren't quite kissing, not yet. She stole away my breath when she started speaking. "Right now, spending time with you is the only really good thing about this summer and I'm not trying to ruin things between us. I just want these good moments to last and last and..."

Then, I kissed her because I felt like we'd already said enough.

Chapter 10

Saturday, June 10th

Kate

"Now, let's get out there and take it to those Cleveland Clowns!" Coach Davis shouted and all the ball players laughed.

"I think they're called the Cleveland Cougars," Lacy said, smiling from ear to ear and swishing her long platinum blond ponytail over her shoulder.

"Whatever," Coach Davis returned, shaking her head forcefully. "One way or another, the Trailblazers aren't letting them score this inning, are we?"

"No!" We all yelled at the top of our lungs.

Lacy, who was now the permanent team captain, called for all of us to put our hands in and as soon as we piled our mitts on top of each other's, she counted off. "One, two, three!" "Trailblazers!" The rest of us chorused and then, the first nine starters took off, sprinting toward their positions. Sullenly, I made my way back to the bench and sat right in the open spot that was available between Syd and Abs. Becky and Hope were already on the other end of the long wooden bench, twirling a couple of softballs in their fingertips, working on getting their grips quickly for different pitches.

"Well, this is a first," Syd said, reclining against the back of the bench, stretching her arms out and draping her right arm across my shoulder blades. "I don't think the three of us have ever been stuck riding the pine together since we...nope.

I'm almost totally positive that this phenomenon has never happened before."

Abs snickered. "I've gotta tell ya—it's nice to have company. It was hell sitting on the bench last season, making small talk with the sophomores. It's good to have my girls back where they belong."

"On the bench?" I wrinkled my nose distastefully.

"No," Abs replied. "By my side."

"I'd prefer it if we were on the field together," I said, leaning forward, placing both elbows on my knees and staring out at the pitcher's mound, trying to read which pitches Lacy was using on the first few batters in the lineup.

"We can't start every game," Syd said, showcasing an odd nonchalance that didn't normally mesh with her competitive attitude. She liked to be a starter just as much as the next person and as far as I knew, she'd spent just as much time sitting out as I had—which, before today, had been zero innings.

"We could," I muttered thickly, kicking the worn toe of my right cleat at a chewed up and spit out sunflower seed shell that was plastered to the cement just in front of me.

"We couldn't," Syd countered sarcastically, "and we shouldn't, either. Not in this case." She jabbed me in the ribs with her elbow. "We're the youngest players on this team. That means everyone else has earned the right to step on that field ahead of us."

"I beg to differ," I said, shifting backward in my seat so that my shoulder blades were resting against Syd's outstretched arms once more. "I don't think age has anything to do with it. Coach needs to put her best players on the field and..."

"She did," Syd interrupted and that brought me up short. Just then, Lacy struck out the first batter and Hope and Becky started applauding and stomping their feet raucously. Abs, who had apparently been paying closer attention to the game than either me or Syd joined in, hooting happily for our team-mate's accomplishment.

"What're you saying?" I asked, turning my eyes fully on Syd. She shrugged, which looked kind of silly because of the way her arms were all spread out.

"I don't mind riding the pine when I know I'm doing it for the good of the team," she said. "And Coach isn't just bench-ing us for giggles. She's got a strong set of players and she's utilizing everyone exactly the way she should be."

I heard what Syd was saying and while I recognized that Lacy was a superior athlete, it still stung to think that I was sitting the bench, while she got the start. "Sorry," I murmured, rolling my shoulders, trying to force myself to relax. "This is just all new territory for me. I've never sat out like this before and..."

Abs nudged me with her elbow. "I wouldn't worry too much about it. Your fan club is here to cheer you on, whether you spend a single second on the playing field or not."

Sure enough, when I followed her sightline, I spotted Grady. He was sitting on the bottom row of the bleachers, stretching his long legs out in front of him. When he caught me staring at him, he lifted his hand and waved and I nodded in reply, not wanting to draw attention to myself by returning the gesture.

"Who's that guy sitting next to Grady?" Syd asked, taking her arms off the bench, and leaning forward so she could get a better look. "Do you know him?"

I squinted in the distance. "That looks like his brother."

"That's not his brother," Syd retorted, flipping her hair. "You introduced us to Giles the other day at the pool party."

"It's not Giles. That's Gile's twin, Rory."

"What?" Syd's mouth dropped wide and hung agape for a split second. She snapped it closed quickly, then turned to look at me. "You mean Grady's got more than one brother?"

"Yeah," I snorted. "He's got a few."

"Shoot, Kate." Syd punched my left arm. "Why were you keeping Rory a secret?"

"I wasn't..." I said slowly, uncertain of how to interpret her reaction. Syd snuck another covert glance over her shoulder, but then held the pose, staring at Rory for what felt like much too long. I peeked around her, trying to see what she was seeing, but Rory just looked like himself to me. His dark hair was liberally gelled and spiked in his signature, messy, just rolled out of bed style. He was wearing a white sleeveless shirt though and not only did the color make his skin look very tanned, but it also showed off his taut, firm bicep muscles. He must've noticed her gazing at him because he lifted his hand and waved in a friendly gesture, mimicking the move Grady had made just a few minutes before.

Syd raised her hand slowly, then turned away from him and slumped against the bench. "Quick, Abs," she joked. "Get ready to catch me when I swoon."

Abs laughed. "I'm here for ya, girl."

I couldn't help but chuckle, too. "What's with you?" I asked. "I thought you and Danny were still going strong."

"Danny?" Syd blinked her eyes rapidly as if waking from sleep. "Danny who?"

"Danny Williams," I retorted, slapping her on the wrist playfully. "The guy who took you to prom just about a month ago."

"Right." Syd sat up straighter then and fussed with the ends of her hair, fluffing them. "We're ancient history. I've got my eyes on someone else now."

"Don't go getting too attached," I warned. "I'm pretty sure as soon as the summer's over, Rory and the rest of Grady's brothers are heading back to San Antonio."

Syd scoffed. "Who said anything about getting attached?" She shot a look at Abs. "You're the only person I know, Kate, who can't just seize the moment and have a little fun while it lasts. You've always gotta try to turn everything into some monumental thing."

"Hey," I said, feigning being wounded by her words, "if you're not nicer to me, I won't introduce you to Rory after the game."

"Sorry," she apologized at once. "Sorry, Kate. I didn't mean anything by it, I only..."

"Yeah, yeah," I said, taking a page right out of her book and dismissing her words quickly. "You just want to make sure the next time I have a pool party I remember to invite Rory to tag along with Grady."

"Yes," Syd groaned. "He's gotta be there."

"Agreed," Abs chimed in.

I swiveled to look at her curiously. "Things hit the skids with you and Layla again?"

"Yep," Abs confirmed. "And I think we're done for good this time. She's going to *the* Ohio State University in the fall, and she said she didn't want me tying her down back here at home." She snorted derisively. "So, I guess that's a wrap on me and Layla." She smiled sadly. "We had a good run. It was the most I could expect out of a high school relationship, I guess." She paused and sighed deeply. "Have you and Grady talked about what comes next? Is he ditching you too so he can hook up with a bunch of girls once he gets to Felding?"

I smarted at her descriptive use of words but answered the question just the same. "Actually, the other night, Grady made it pretty clear he wasn't interested in seeing anyone else. Instead, he was kind of worried that I might break his heart by going after Ty." After waiting a beat for my friends to laugh or, at the very least, chime in and say Grady was way off base, I glanced between them in disbelief. "Say something," I demanded. "You can't think he was right to have those kinds of worries."

"I feel kind of sorry for Grady," Abs said at length.

Syd snorted. "That's life, isn't it?"

"What's life?" I asked. "Why do you feel sorry for him?"

Once again, my pals exchanged a look that I didn't quite understand. Then, Abs said softly, "You and Ty have history together, Kate. And there's no denying that Grady will be leaving for school soon. I think it's smart of him to lay things out now and make sure the two of you understand each other."

"What's there to understand?"

"Grady's a smart guy," Syd said, defending him in a way I'd never heard her do before. "And I'm sure he doesn't really expect you to spend your whole senior year not dating a single person."

"I *will* be dating someone," I countered. "I'll be dating Grady."

Syd huffed. "That's not the same and you know it."

"Felding might not be super far from here," Abs pointed out, "but it's far enough away that Grady won't want to come home every weekend and you've got obligations, Kate. I know you. *We* know you. When fall ball starts, you aren't just going to ditch out on games so you can run over to Felding on a Saturday."

Syd leaned forward and lowered her voice to a whisper. "Kate, do you really plan to stay together with Grady—even if it gets to the point where you won't be able to see each other?"

Chapter 11

Grady

"Ugh," Rory groaned, stretching his short legs out in front of him, flexing his jacked quad muscles. "When's Kate going in?"

"I don't know," I said, glancing over at the Trailblazer's dugout. The first two innings had come and gone quite easily. The Trailblazer's pitcher, Lacy, had blown away the Cougars, sending them three up-three down while striking out four and allowing zero hits. I was only slightly astonished to learn that Kate had not been overexaggerating this girl's pitching abilities. She was the real deal and had made what she did look almost too effortless.

Then, at the top of the third inning, Coach Davis subbed in another pitcher. Her name was Hope and her windup was jerkier, less smooth and concentrated than Lacy's. I'd wondered if the batters for the Cougars might have been thrown off balance by Hope's uneven delivery, but they timed her up right from the jump. She had a wealth of junk pitches though and managed to get through the third and fourth, only allowing one run to score. But with the Trailblazer's offense providing blessed little assistance, they were just one out away from heading into the fifth and I was starting to feel almost as antsy as my big bro.

"You've been bragging about Kate's pitching abilities since February," Rory reminded me as he started to bounce his knees, clearly unable to stop fidgeting and getting rid of some of his own nervous energy. "Don't you think it's time she had her turn on the mound?"

"Yeah," I grunted. But there wasn't much more to say. I couldn't very well pick apart Coach Davis's style. This was only the Trailblazer's first game and based on what I had seen of it so far, she had been willing to give her pitchers equal playing time. At the end of the third inning, she'd sent Kate, Abs, and two other girls out to the corner of right field and had them start warming up. That led me to believe she meant give all her pitchers a workout today and I thought that was sensible. Kate had told me there were four pitchers on staff and while that seemed rather excessive, I appreciated that Coach Davis was cycling them through, letting them each hurl a couple of innings before putting them on the shelf.

The batter at the plate, a girl who wore the number forty-six, struck out swinging and Kate, as well as the rest of the Trailblazers and their fans, let out a collective breath we'd all been holding. It was tough when anyone struck out, but this game was especially close, with the Cougars only sitting on that one run lead, making it so the tide could swing back into the Trailblazer's favor if one of their batters just managed to get a single lucky hit. But they'd have to put off all that until the next half inning. I sat up straighter in my seat, which was a feat, considering it was just a bleacher which offered no back support, and craned my neck so I could watch as Kate picked up her well-worn ball mitt and pounded her fist against the webbing.

"See?" I said, swatting Rory on the knee. "She's going in right now."

Just as I'd hoped, Kate, Syd, and Abs hustled out of the dugout. It was the top of the fifth and since they'd been on the bench all game, it stood to reason that they were all taking the field together now. Abs hurried behind home plate, wearing two masks—the one that was part of her catching gear and the second that provided extra cushiony protection for her once-injured eye. Syd skipped out to the shortstop's position, straining, reaching for a grounder that the first baseman had lobbed in her direction. She scooped it cleanly then chucked it toward first, making what would've been an incredible play had this been the game and not just a bit of warmup. Then, my eyes locked on Kate. She was rushing toward the pitcher's circle, but there was a deep frown etched into her pretty features. She hopped right over the pitcher's mound, then took off running toward left field. I sat up even straighter and Rory did the same.

"Where's she going?" he asked, taking the words right out of my mouth. It was evident what she was doing, but I was shocked.

"I'm not sure she's ever played in the outfield before," I whispered, keeping my focus on her. The center fielder turned and tossed a lazy fly ball in the air. Kate caught it, then whipped the ball across the entire outfield, firing a blazing shot directly at the right fielder.

"Uh-oh," Rory murmured. "She's not happy about being out there."

"Yeah," I agreed. "I don't think she is." I knew it meant a lot to Kate that she had the opportunity to play ball this summer, but I was fairly certain her definition of getting playing time didn't include standing in the outfield rather than stalking around the pitcher's circle. I flicked my eyes toward Kate's parents who were not sitting in the bleachers, but just a little way down the line, in a couple of red and black camping chairs that had the Farrington Falcon's mascot embroidered on the seatbacks. Kate's dad was on his feet, striding toward the nearest fence line and Mrs. Hughes had a hand to her mouth, chewing on her fingernails.

They know Kate can't be happy about this situation, either.

"It seems extreme and unnecessary for the Trailblazers to have so many pitchers," Rory remarked, drawing my attention back to him, practically speaking aloud a thought I'd just had a moment before. "But look at this girl. She sure can whip that ball in there." I thought the third pitcher's name was Becky and watched closely as she hurled what looked like a fastball right down the pipe.

"Whew," I whistled. "Kate wasn't foolin'. She's got some speed." I remembered what Kate said about the Trailblazers last practice and how she'd cringed when she'd had to squat down and try to catch whatever Becky threw in her direction.

"That ball hits a batter and they're going down for the count," Rory muttered under his breath.

"Let's hope she doesn't bean anybody then."

Abs called for one final warmup pitch. The outfielders and infielders alike sent their practice softballs whizzing toward the dugout, then Abs fired a spectacular throw down to second base, right where Syd was waiting to catch it and put the pretend tag on a ghost runner.

As the infielders did a quick cheer and Becky knelt to wipe the dirt off the pitching rubber, my eyes drifted back to Kate's corner of the outfield. She looked tense. Her knees were bent softly, and her feet were shoulder width apart. Her glove and free hand hung limply and maybe, to the spectator who didn't know her so well, they would've thought she'd been in left field a thousand times and looked perfectly well-situated to catch anything that came her way. But even from this distance, I could discern the way her lips turned gently down at the corners. She was concentrating, surely enough, but she was also perturbed and that wasn't good.

Come on, Kate. You can do this. It's just for a half inning.

I sent as many happy thoughts her way as I could, praying that my good vibes would reach her and make her feel marginally better, but she didn't relax her posture one bit and I was sure she wasn't just dreading what might happen if and when the ball was hit in her direction, but she also must be worried wondering why her coach had chosen to let everybody else take a turn on the mound, while sticking her in left field.

It's all right, Special K. You've got this...

But I felt the fruitlessness of my endeavor. I'd wanted to see Kate take over the pitching duties just as much as Rory did and it broke my heart to think of the turmoil that was likely battering around inside her head.

"You think she's gonna be all right?" Rory asked, leaning close to me, and lowering his voice to a whisper.

"Playing left field or after the game?" I returned.

He made a confused face. "I don't know. Both."

"She'll be fine where she is and after the game...well, I guess I'll just have to think of some way to cheer her up then."

I searched my mind for all my greatest ideas—throwing a few pitches, getting an ice cream cone, but nothing seemed sufficient. It felt like Kate was fighting a losing battle and even though I wanted to tag in and help her, there was so very little I could do.

Chapter 12

Kate

"Good game, good game. Hey. Yeah. Good game to you, too..." I wandered down the line of Cleveland Cougars, respectfully slapping hands with my opponents, congratulating them on their narrow victory. We'd lost the game with a final score of one to zip and so I didn't look totally out of place, hanging my head, muttering my words, and scuffing my cleats through the dirt of the infield.

I felt terrible...just awful. I knew I should hold my head up and be proud that my team hadn't gotten totally annihilated, but I just couldn't muster the energy.

I ought to be grateful to Coach Davis for letting me in the game at all.

Coach called our team to meet her in right field and I jogged along with the others, for once, not concerned about being the first to the designated spot. I slumped onto the grass, taking a knee next to Abs, but while she leaned forward, evidently listening intently to every word Coach had to say, I was lost in my own thoughts.

I got zero action today. Zero.

Nothing was hit to left field during the last few innings and because our batters just couldn't manufacture any hits, I never even got the opportunity to step in the batter's box. I'd had my helmet on, but the player before me, Lila Bateman, our first basemen, had struck out, watching the third strike, so that ended my hopes of saving the day and the game by belting a line drive to center field.

Fortunately, Coach Davis was a woman of few words. She didn't labor over our defeat or point out the errors some of my teammates had made, both in the batter's box or around the field. She just said the Cougars were a tough team and she expected that when we saw them again during tournament play that we'd give them another run for their money.

Maybe she's right.

I stood when the others did, but my movements were jumpy. Instead of moving mechanically, almost sluggishly like my teammates were doing and as I'd been inclined to do just a few minutes before, I was suddenly wired and ready to burn off some of my excess energy. When Lacy called spiritlessly for all hands in, I was the first to the center and I cheered exuberantly when it was time to shout, "Trailblazers!"

"What now?" Abs said, coasting up beside me as we headed for the dugout. She was still strapped into her catching gear and her shin guards rattled as she walked. "You look like you're ready to take on the world, Lady K."

"I've gotta do something," I whispered feverishly. "My muscles are warm and I'm ready to throw." I cast a quick glance over my shoulder. "Do you think you'd want to hang around and catch a few for me?"

"Can't," Abs said, nodding toward the team wearing scarlet and gold uniforms that were standing just outside our dugout. "The field is already spoken for."

"Shoot," I muttered, kicking at a pebble, and watching it skitter toward the fence line.

"We could go swimming again," Abs suggested, wiping her wrist across her sweaty forehead. "I know I could go for a dip in your pool. And while I don't love the idea of inviting myself over, I'm not gonna pretend like I'd turn down an offer from you, either."

"Yeah," Syd added. "Let's go swimming. You promised to introduce me to Rory, and you could just sort of mention that we're all heading to your house for a pool party later and..."

"Nah," I said, cutting off the scheme before my two friends took it any further. "I *will* introduce you to Rory, but I'm not up for having everyone over. And I don't feel like swimming."

"What're you going to do then?" Abs asked, prying a tad more than I would've liked.

"I think I just want to be alone for a little while," I answered.

Abs snickered then made her eyebrows dance. "Alone with Grady."

"Maybe," I said sourly, "but also maybe not."

I found Grady and Rory talking with my folks, standing near the fence line. Dad was trying, unsuccessfully, to fold up the camping chairs and jam them back into their carrying sleeves, so Grady was assisting him, doing most of the work, while making the endeavor look effortless. Mom was talking animatedly to Rory, waving her arms, and gesturing toward the pitcher's mound.

"Hey, Katie," Mom said when Abs, Syd, and I trooped to her side. "I was just telling Rory about the game you girls played against the Lucasville Leopards last summer." She turned back to include Rory in the conversation. "You should've seen it. Kate struck out thirteen. Syd made two double plays at short, and Abs even threw out a runner who was trying to steal third. Our girls were on that game."

"Hey," Syd said, nodding at Rory, playing the whole scene coolly. "I'm Syd."

He jerked his chin at her, smiling devilishly. "That's what I hear. I'm Rory, Grady's older brother."

"Yeah," Syd breathed. "I met your other brother, Giles, last week." She tipped her head to the side, eyeing him shamelessly. "Kate says he's your twin."

"Kate's never wrong," Rory said, smirking at me like we were sharing some private joke. I blew out an exasperated sigh and shot a look at Grady. He was smiling all over himself, clearly not as irritated by Syd and Rory's coy flirtatious routine as I was.

"Hey, Special K," he said, reaching forward and rubbing my right shoulder. "You want me to carry your bag for you?"

"I've got it," I replied, shifting my weight, and bumping the bag just a little higher on my arm. "No tired arm today."

"You girls played a good game," Mom said, looking at me with wide eyes.

"Thanks, Mama K," Abs said, taking a water bottle out of her bag and squirting a couple of ounces into her wide-open maw. "Too bad we couldn't pull this one out."

"There's still a lot of ball yet to play this summer," my dad said, staring directly at me. "No reason to get downtrodden yet."

"You want to go get some ice cream?" Grady offered, reaching for my hand a second time, but including all the others in the invitation. "I'll spring for extra sprinkles." He winked at me, and I smiled in return, but I didn't feel like having ice cream and I said as much.

"I was actually thinking I'd go home with my parents," I said, nodding at Mom and Dad. Everyone, including my folks, gawped at me. Grady squeezed my hand.

"Really? You don't want ice cream?"

I shook my head and that's when the group started to go their separate ways. Mom and Dad excused themselves, saying they'd wait for me in the parking lot and Syd and Abs disappeared too, taking Rory with them, mostly because he was still busy grinning at and flirting with Syd. When Grady and I were left by ourselves I looked up and met his gaze. There was a look of confusion flitting through his eyes, and I wanted to smooth away the worried lines that were creasing near his eyebrows.

"It's not that I don't want to go get some ice cream with you," I tried to explain. "I think it's just that I need to be alone right now."

"You...you don't want to talk about the game then?"

I shook my head slowly. "What's to talk about? I barely got the chance to play."

"You were good in left field," Grady commented, stating the words as if they were irrefutable facts. "You looked like you were ready to..."

"I really can't do this," I said, letting go of his hand and taking a step back. The look of sorrow that stole over his features in an instant had me regretting my hasty actions. Guilt swarmed throughout my body, stinging every part of me, making me feel like the worst sort of girlfriend. "I know you gave up your afternoon to come sit at my ballgame, and I'm glad you were in the stands, but I need to sort through my feelings on my own." I peered up at him. "You can understand that, right?"

"Of course," he said, taking a step back, giving me some space and making the awkwardness less palpable. "You're disappointed and the last thing you want is to have to dissect the game with someone else. I get it."

"You *do* get it," I murmured, giving him an appreciative smile.

He nodded simply and his happy-go-lucky grin returned. "Take your time working through this, Special K. And, if you change your mind later, and want some company, shoot me a text."

"Will do." I watched as Grady walked away, wanting partially to run after him and simply spend some time soaking in his warm, cheerful presence. But the other part of me was glad to be all alone.

I need to work out my frustrations without other people around. I can't answer any questions and I know I wouldn't be able to stand it if everyone was dancing in circles, bending over backwards to try and make me feel better.

Adjusting the strap on my bat bag, I turned my feet and headed in the opposite direction Grady had just walked, stalking toward my parent's SUV.

I think I finally know what Coach Cobb meant last year when he said I spent too much time in my own head.

My thoughts were all bouncing around, careening into one another, making it hard to pull together even the simplest of cohesive statements.

I've just got to work through this and the only way to do that is to power through the pain and not even pretend to be happy right now.

Chapter 13

Ty

Left, left, left, right, left...

Sometimes, when I'm out on an extra-long run and the time spent alone starts to feel tedious, I chant marching orders in my head. I know I could listen to music or even cue up an audiobook or podcast on my iPhone but since we're not allowed to run with earbuds during meets or practices, I've never gotten into the habit of using those sorts of motivators when I'm just out by myself.

I miss Kate.

Even though Kay-Kay generally set a much slower pace, she had always been an excellent running partner, knowing just when to chatter away, but also when to back off and let me roam around in my own head.

I've had these same feelings about Kate a lot lately. Since February, our regular running routine had been stilted and instead of jogging together four or five times a week, I'd been lucky if I had her by my side fifty percent of the time.

Nothing to be done about that. She'd rather be with Grady than slogging along with me.

It was painful to admit this fact, even to myself, but I was nothing if not a realist.

All I can do is pray that this summer passes quickly and that Kay-Kay loses interest in Grady once he's out of sight.

That was an uncharitable thought to have about my best friend, because I knew she wasn't the type to just give up on someone or something so easily. But I had to hold out hope that this thing with Grady was just a minor blip and she'd be back to focusing on softball and all the other things she'd once treasured, like our friendship, soon enough.

As if I had been thinking so hard about Kay-Kay, I'd managed to manifest her image, I glanced up at the entrance way to the reservoir and saw her figure climbing the steep hill.

It can't be...

I sped up, because I'd really just been cruising around the rim of the reservoir, trekking along, looking to put in a few miles but not hoping to break any records tonight.

"Kay-Kay," I called when I got within shouting distance. "That you?"

She spun around but didn't stop moving. Instead, she started backpedaling, lowering her arms so they hung near her waist, righting her center of balance just as I'd taught her to do years ago.

"Who wants to know?" she yelled in response, but I could hear the levity in her words.

I put on a burst of speed and closed the distance between us, then turned and started jogging backwards too.

"One of us has got to face the right direction," she quipped. "Otherwise, we're likely to both go careening down the hillside and tumbling into the waters below."

I laughed. "You must've forgotten, but I've got a perfect sense of direction. We could run like this all day, and I wouldn't let either one of us fall."

"So confident," Kay-Kay said, shaking her head slightly. "You know what they say about hubris. Don't you, Ty?"

"Nope," I joked. "You tell me."

She huffed. "Forget it. My mind isn't working properly, so I can't even be bothered to come up with a proper punchline."

I frowned. She'd seemed to be in a playful mood just a moment ago, but as she hit the skids and abruptly turned so that she was once more running uphill, facing the right way, I could see that everything had shifted. I desperately wanted to ask what was wrong, but I knew Kate well. If she wanted to tell me what was going on, she would've done that the second I joined her.

We jogged on in silence for nearly a full ten minutes, making it to the far side of the reservoir while moving at a moderate pace. When we got to the farthest reaches of the rim, I said quietly, "You can tell me, ya know. Whatever it is...no matter what...I'm here to listen to you."

She stayed totally quiet for a minute longer and I was afraid she might never say another peep, but then, all at once, the words came tumbling out of her. "I'm worried about summer softball. Things with the Trailblazers...they're not going at all the way I thought they would." She proceeded to tell me everything she'd been keeping inside all summer so far. There was a horrible practice where she had to play catcher for one of the other pitchers and the game today...her coach had callously not even given her a shot to show what she could do on the mound. My indignation rose on behalf of my friend, but I didn't dare interrupt her. "It looks like I won't be getting much playing time," she continued explaining, "and I think I might've made a mistake by joining this team."

"A mistake?" I couldn't help but ask. "How so?"

When we rounded the bend and headed back toward the park entrance, Kay-Kay kept talking, not at all paying the least bit of attention to the path we were traversing. "I thought it'd be nice to spend this summer taking it easy. I told myself that it might be...relaxing... to ease up a bit and not be solely devoted to playing softball this summer. But, as it turns out, riding the bench isn't a whole lot of fun."

I grunted. "A new experience for you, was it?"

"The worst possible experience," she returned as she started to drag her feet a little. She might not admit as much at present because she had that determined look on her face, but this was her tell. I knew that her legs were getting tired. "And the worst of it is that I think Coach Davis was right to sit me out."

"Huh?" I questioned. "That can't be right."

"But it is," she argued, turning to glance at me. "You should see these other pitchers, Ty. Next to them, I look like one giant ball of incompetence."

"Now I know you've got things twisted, Kay-Kay," I said softly. "The other girls might be good, but you're the one who throws a filthy drop curve, and nobody can touch that pitch, even if they're reaching for it with a ten-foot pole."

She smiled, nodding a little, as I recited a quote from one of the newspaper articles that had been published following a thoroughly successful pitching outing last season. A local reporter had written those lines about Kate, and he'd been right. When she was on, nobody could hit what she was hurling.

"I do like throwing the drop curve," she said softly, "but I might not get the chance. If Coach never lets me step foot on the mound, then..."

"She won't keep you on the bench," I assured her. "And you probably only played left field today because she didn't want you to get too discouraged. I'm sure she'll rotate you through the pitching lineup, just like the others."

"Maybe," she breathed, then chugged along in silence.

"Is that it?" I asked, sure there was something else Kate was keeping to herself.

She shook her head. "How am I supposed to stay in shape and keep up with my normal regimen if I'm playing for a team which is already so stacked with pitchers that they don't need me? I'd considered taking a break but now..."

"I thought you were only going to take a break because that's what Grady wanted you to do," I interjected. "Wasn't he planning to monopolize your whole summer?"

"Of course not," Kay-Kay said, jerking to a halt. She stared at me as if I had caterpillars crawling out of my ears. "What made you think that?"

"You told me that you weren't playing summer ball because you wanted to spend time with Grady," I reminded her.

"I guess I did say that," she said slowly.

"Well, doesn't this make him happy?" I ventured. "Now that you're disgruntled and not getting much playing time, isn't he excited to spend more time with you?"

Her lips pressed together, forming a thin, almost invisible line and her eyebrows wrinkled in consternation. "It's not like I'm quitting the team, Ty. I'm just complaining to you because you're my friend and I thought you'd be willing to listen."

"Is Grady pushing you to quit the team?" I asked, stepping closer to her. "Is he telling you it's not worth your time and that if you gave up the Trailblazers the two of you could have the whole summer to..."

She shook her head so forcefully, I decided it'd be best to back up a pace and put a little space between us once more. "I'm not sure where you're getting any of this," she mumbled. "But you've got Grady all wrong. He's not even thinking about this summer anymore. He's already planning for next fall and..."

"Oh," I said softly, feeling a tad sorry for my best friend. "He's been talking about going away to college and that makes you feel..." I allowed my words to peter out so that I wouldn't be speaking on her behalf. I knew, after having an argument with her last spring, that she hated it when I tried to push her too much in one direction or the other, so I wasn't about to make that same mistake again here and now.

"I don't know how I feel," Kay-Kay blurted. "Grady said he wanted us to stay together, but then he said this thing about you and..."

"He mentioned me?" I was surprised. "What'd he say?"

"Oh, nothing," she grumbled. "He just thinks that as soon as he's gone, we'll start dating but I think he only said that because..."

"Because what?" I prompted.

"Because he's worried our relationship won't last," she finally admitted. "He said he didn't want to breakup, but I think that might not be entirely true. He's going away and he can't really want to stay tied to me, a girl he's only been dating for a short while. And..."

I felt like Kay-Kay was spinning out of control. Her sentences were starting to run together, and I was, frankly, having difficulties keeping up with her meandering thoughts.

"I said you were handsome, and Grady thinks you're trying to steal me away from him and then he said..."

"Woah, woah," I said, holding up my hands, trying to slow her speech. My mind had vaguely registered her last couple of statements and while it pleased me to no end to know that Kate thought I was good-looking, I knew I shouldn't dwell on that fact right now. "Let's get you home before you roll with these thoughts any further. Take a shower. Calm down. And get a good night's sleep."

"Whatever you say," Kay-Kay mumbled, rolling her eyes, but then, dutifully she started leading the way, jogging down the hill, and heading toward our houses.

We ran the next few miles in silence and just as we were rounding the corner, coming up on the intersection where Granny Renee's Diner sat on one side of the road and Mr. Fletchley's Chicken Shack occupied the other, I decided that I'd let her stew in her own thoughts long enough. "Kay-Kay, I know you're probably going to ignore this next bit of advice, but at least, let me say it."

"All right," she said, swirling her hand through the air, making a prompting gesture. "Go ahead."

"Don't worry about anything. Everything with the softball team will be all right. You've only played one game so far. So, you can't know how the rest of the summer is going to turn out based on just this one instance. And try not to worry about what's going to happen with Grady, either."

She huffed. "That's easy for you to say. You don't even like him."

"It doesn't matter if I like him or not. You do and you're the one we're talking about right now," I said, punctuating my thoughts by articulating each word clearly. We pulled to a stop right in front of Granny Renee's because there was a red light halting us at the intersection. I hurried to finish what I wanted to say, knowing that if I didn't get it all out now, she might start reasoning through everything again, and I'd probably lose my chance. "The two of you could possibly stay together forever. Or you might break up eventually. But if that happens, then that's just the way things are going to be." I tried not to sound too gleeful while saying that last bit, but I couldn't keep the smile from my face. Personally, I looked forward to the day when Kate came to her senses and dropped Grady Hughes.

"So, what you're saying is that once again, I've just got to roll with the punches and take whatever life decides to give me?" She snorted. "Is that really all you've got in your counseling repertoire, Ty?"

"Hey," I said, shrugging it off. "There's a reason those ideas are cliches and maybe even a little bit trite. Everybody has to learn to make the best of a bad situation and..."

"Are you saying my relationship with Grady is a bad situation or are you referring to my position on the softball team?"

I stared at her. "What do you think?"

She didn't say anything, but I could see the seed of doubt swirling behind her brilliant blue eyes. I didn't consider myself a conniving sort of person, and it really didn't bring me any sort of joy to stress out my best friend, but she needed to consider all the possibilities. This was all a gray area because I knew I hadn't sabotaged her relationship exactly. All I meant to do was force her to fully evaluate her feelings, to examine all the moving parts before proceeding further. And while it was slightly guilt-inducing to think that she was so torn over what to do next, I kind of relished the thought that this little prompting might lead to her imminent breakup with Grady.

Chapter 14

Grady

"Hey man, thanks for picking me up," Graham said as he climbed into my truck and slammed the passenger side door, indicating I was free to take off. He smelled of French fry grease and hamburgers, which might've bothered some people, but I kind of liked it, and the scent made my stomach growl loudly. He laughed. "Hungry?"

"Not especially," I replied. "But you smell good."

Graham lifted the collar of his white button-down shirt, part of the uniform he wore when he worked at Granny Renee's Diner and sniffed. "Fried foods mixed with body odor. I think I'll call it, Hunger Pangs, a new fragrance for men." He snickered at his own joke. "You think the chicks around here will dig it?"

I backed the truck out of the parking space I'd been occupying while waiting for him. "I don't know."

"Maybe we ought to ask Kate," he suggested playfully, but then he laughed loudly once more, and I snuck a quick sidelong glance at him.

"What's so funny?"

"Speak of the devil and she appears," he whispered in a semi-awed voice. My big brother jabbed his index finger at the windshield, pointing to a spot in the distance. "Isn't that Kate right there?"

The sun had practically vanished for the day, so even though my headlights were illuminating most of the road ahead, I couldn't quite make out much more than the shape of two people, idling at the corner, seemingly waiting for the crosswalk sign to light up and tell them it was their turn to move across the street. "Can't be," I said, dismissing the notion out of hand. "It may look like her but..."

"Grady, I know she's not my girl and all, but I'll swear that's Kate."

As I pulled the truck to the stoplight and the crosswalk machine did its thing, I watched as Kate, accompanied by Ty, dashed right in front of us. There was no mistaking the matter when she was darting right in front of my windshield, chattering away happily to her best friend. That was Kate, all right.

"What the..." I muttered.

"Who's that guy she's with?" Graham asked, leaning forward, nearly pressing his nose to the dashboard.

"Ty," I growled.

"Out for a late-night run, I see." Graham fussed with his seat belt as he sat back a little. "Do you wanna pull over and have me hop in the back? You could talk to her for a few minutes or even offer her a ride home?"

"I...She's supposed to be..." I couldn't quite get the words to materialize. I was dumbstruck, staring at Kate as she and Ty made it safely to the other side of the road, then started jogging leisurely once more.

"What's wrong with you?" He punched my arm. "The light just turned green."

I shook my head, forcing myself to focus and not gun the engine, but it was difficult to get the image of Kate and Ty together out of my mind because it was still so freshly imprinted there. My brother gifted me a few minutes of silence, but as we reached the highway, he reclined in his seat a tad and asked,

"So, do you wanna tell me what's going on or should I just keep making up my own version of your story?"

"When I saw Kate earlier today, she said she wanted to be alone."

Graham scoffed. "She's definitely not alone."

"Thanks, Sherlock," I grumbled. "I'd already made that astute deduction."

"So, what are you gonna do?" he prompted. "Call her when we get home and ask what gives or... do you want to turn around now and see if you can't talk to her face-to-face?"

A foul, bitter taste rose in the back of my throat and suddenly the fact that my brother smelled like cheeseburgers made me want to vomit. I turned away from him and rolled down my window so I could suck in a few deep breaths of fresh air. "I...I'm not going to confront her."

"Too bad," Graham mumbled. "I'd kind of liked to have seen you wrestle that guy to the ground."

"And I'm not getting into it with Ty either," I added.

"Why not? I can tell you're annoyed, so why don't you vent some of those frustrations and at least find out what she's doing with some other guy at this time of night?" I thought he was sort of egging me on, maybe even making the situation into a bigger deal than it ought to be, but I answered his questions just the same.

"First of all, it was obvious what they were doing—going for a run," I said in my most practical tone. "But also, it doesn't matter if I'm annoyed. Kate was busy and if I turned around right now and we pulled up to her side I'd look like I was a crazy person. Then, I'd probably say something to either Kate or Ty that'd make a mess of everything. And I'm not up for ruining things with her just because I don't like who she's hanging with."

"Yeah," Graham agreed, rolling down his window too and making it so there was a nice cross breeze drifting through the cab. "It's probably better not to get too worked up over something like this. Relationships like yours and Kate's are unstable. They don't have a very long shelf-life as is and throwing a temper tantrum every time you..."

"What'd you just say?" I interrupted.

"Huh?" I quickly glanced at him to see that he was leaning against the doorframe, perfectly at ease, using his big, bear paw-like hands to comb through his curly brown hair. "What's your problem?"

"I don't have a problem," I said through gritted teeth. "Well...at least I'm not sure that I do. But you seem to have lots of opinions about my relationship with Kate, so don't stop now on account of my feelings. Proceed," I said, layering that last word with a hefty dose of sarcasm.

Graham's forehead scrunched in confusion. "I'm not sure why you're taking out your anger on me, baby bro," he said, shifting his position and sitting up straighter. "I get that you like Kate, but I thought you knew the score. High school relationships tend to fade away once you get to college. I was sure you understood that. I mean, *you* were the one who broke up with Adrienne last fall and I just figured you did that because..."

"I broke up with Adrienne because I didn't want to be with her anymore," I interrupted. "It was really simple."

"Yeah," Graham snorted. "Sure. You were moving to Ohio, and it was going to be hell to keep a long-distance relationship going."

"It was more than that," I argued.

"Right," he said smoothly, pulling out the word longer than necessary, cutting off the explanation for our breakup that I had sitting on the tip of my tongue. "But things are suddenly somehow very, very different with Kate? She's the kind of girl who makes you want to carry this relationship with you to college?"

"And beyond," I breathed.

"What's that now?" He scooted closer to me.

"I wanna be with Kate...forever."

"Woah," Graham breathed. "Forever is an awfully long time."

My lips twitched as I turned slightly to smile at my brother. "Yeah. I'm aware of that."

"But--" he persisted, "are you sure you really understand what that means?" He leaned forward and drummed his fingers on the dashboard. "You said Kate told you she wanted to be alone, but right now, she's out with some other guy. Are you sure you can handle spending a lifetime with someone who's so...duplicitous?"

"Kate's not like that," I countered defensively. "I mean...she *was* with Ty when she said she wanted to be by herself, but I'm sure there's a good reason for the two of them hanging out right now. And she's not like Adr..."

"Hey," Graham said, tapping out a drumbeat even more vigorously, "you don't have to jump all over me, kid. I'm just asking questions here. And..." He stopped making extra noise abruptly and even softened his tone. "Maybe you ought to consider your answers more thoroughly before you just spit them out. You say you want to make this grand commitment, but are you sure you're ready for all that?"

I sighed in a beleaguered fashion. "Don't you ever get tired of guarding your feelings? Making sure never to give your heart to someone else because you're afraid they might trample all over it?"

Graham snickered. "That's life, bro. You can't control the way other people are going to act. All you can do is concern yourself with your own behavior."

"That seems like a very self-centered way to live," I pointed out.

"Does it?" he returned, pursing his lips thoughtfully. "Or is it just a fact that you don't want to accept?"

We went through the rigamarole of entering the base then. Our conversation had to pause so I could hand over my ID and let the guard know we were just headed home for the night. But once I pulled away from the check-in depot, we picked right back up where we'd left off.

"I tried not to get too attached to Kate. I told her, for months, that I only wanted to be her friend, but that didn't work for us. We needed to be something else."

"That's cool," Graham said simply. "And you ought to enjoy this time you have together while it lasts." I pulled into our family's driveway and cut the engine. It was a relief to be able to stop and look directly at my brother's face. He'd pushed all his joking aside and was looking at me with wide eyes, his concern apparent. "Just don't make Kate...or yourself...any promises."

"But..."

"You'll thank me for this bit of advice later," he insisted, not letting me protest one bit more. "Just don't decide anything right now. It'll hurt a lot less in the long run if you don't have to go back on your word."

"You know me," I argued once he permitted it. "I never make promises I don't intend to keep."

"Yeah." He sighed softly. "I know that, Grady. But you also aren't seeing things clearly. While you're over here, devoting yourself completely to Kate, what's she doing? Out running around with some other guy?" I knew his questions were rhetorical and didn't require an answer, so I sat silent. "If she's telling you these kinds of fibs now, while you're still in the same town with her, what's she gonna do two months from now when you're at college and she's hanging around here...supposedly all by herself?"

Had I not seen Kate and Ty before with my own two eyes, I would've argued vehemently. I would've defended Kate with every breath. But the proof was right there in front of me. My whole life, I'd been so cautious, never allowing anyone to take more than their fair share of my heart. But now, I'd let my guard down with Kate and what *was* she doing exactly?

The answer, an unsatisfactory one, materialized, and I hopped out of the truck, hoping to shake it off. But the image of Kate running along at Ty's side, talking to her best friend as if she didn't have a care in the world, haunted me.

Chapter 15

Sunday, June 11th

Kate

"Uhh..." Grady groaned, fidgeting in the lounge chair we were sharing.

"What's wrong?" I asked, scooting to the side to give him more room. "Can't you get comfortable today?"

It was blazing hot outside, but I didn't think it was the heat that was bothering him. My parents had gone out for the day to celebrate their twentieth wedding anniversary and I'd taken the opportunity to invite all my pals over for another pool party. Abs, Syd, Grace Smith, a.k.a. Smitty, and Jennica were all scattered across the deep end, playacting as judges, giving scores each time one of the guys—Ty, Giles, Graham, Will, and Rory—jumped in the pool. Grady and I had been pretty cozy at one point, but now he seemed restless.

When he didn't answer any of my questions, I stared at him, but his features were inscrutable. With his pair of aviators fixed in place, I couldn't read his eyes and for some reason, that worried me a little. "Grady," I said slowly, "is there something you want to..."

Huffing, he slid away from me completely and quickly got to his feet. He tossed his sunglasses on the nearest brown wicker end table, then in a series of swift movements, walked to the edge of the pool and dived neatly, surfacing right next to where Abs had been bobbing in the water. She giggled delightedly when he popped up right next to her and flashed her a coy smile.

Maybe I'm reading too much into this. He seems fine now.

I stretched out on the lounge chair, which suddenly felt oversized now that I wasn't sharing it with my boyfriend. But I didn't have much time to ponder Grady's absence because his older brother, Graham skipped over to my side just then. He was wearing a pair of bright orange swim trunks and dripping water all over the place. I snatched a beach towel off the nearby table and tossed it to him.

"Thanks," he grunted, dabbing at the water droplets that were trickling down his face, then rubbing the towel down his torso. "You mind if I sit next to you?"

I nodded toward the vacant row of lounge chairs. "Be my guest."

He slipped gracefully into the closest seat, then ran his hands through his hair, flicking a little pool water in my direction, but I didn't mind. It really was hot out here.

"So, what're your plans after high school, Kate?" he asked, settling back into his chair, and reaching for the pair of sunglasses Grady had discarded.

"What?" I quipped. "You don't make small talk?"

"I *am* making small talk," he said, perching the glasses on the bridge of his nose, then pushing them higher, covering up his very blue and inquisitive eyes. "Since Grady spends almost all his free time with you, I'd like to get to know you better, too."

"All right," I said, shifting in my chair so I could look more squarely at him. "What is it you wanna know? What I'm doing after high school?"

"Let's start there," he suggested. "I'm pretty sure after you saved that little boy at the pizza place, Grady said you were going to be a doctor but..."

"I'm not one hundred percent sure about that yet."

Even though the sunglasses were doing an effective job of covering his eyes, the way Graham's eyebrows shot up inquiringly was not to be missed. "If you don't want to study medicine, what do you want to do?"

I exhaled deeply and reclined my head onto the cushions of the chair. "Last year, I thought I had it all figured out, but then Grady moved to town and..."

"*Grady* changed your plans?" I could hear the skepticism in his brother's voice.

"Not exactly," I conceded. "But he did force me to reevaluate them."

"Huh," he grunted. "So, what exactly did you want to do before Grady made you start to think otherwise?"

"I was going to be a middle school teacher and I wanted to coach the varsity softball team. The plan was to go to college, then come right back here and work at Farrington Middle School."

Graham nodded slowly, then he folded up the towel he'd been using and leisurely placed it back on the tabletop. "When I first started at U of SA, I wanted to be a teacher, too. I was even majoring in education."

"Really?" I was slightly surprised by this news. When I'd told Grady my dream last year, he hadn't reacted very enthusiastically. Immediately, he'd come right out and said I ought to be doing more with my future and I'd listened to him, assuming that for reasons I didn't fully know or comprehend, he had some grudge against an old teacher. I shot a quick look toward the pool only to find that Grady had moved away from the others. He was draped lazily over the edge of the pool wall, with his chin resting on his hands, listening quietly to this conversation I was having with his brother. I waited for him to interject or maybe try to explain himself, but he stayed mute.

"Yeah," Graham proceeded. "I wanted to be a P.E. teacher, but once I got into it, I realized I didn't like being around little kids."

I laughed. "That's sort of a big part of the job description."
"I know." Graham chuckled too. "I was just glad I figured out early on that I wasn't cut out for that kind of job. Can you imagine how awful it would've been to train to become a teacher for four years, then to get out of college, take on my first job assignment, and discover that I couldn't stand being stuck in a classroom with a whole bunch of children?"

"Catastrophic," I murmured, picturing a few teachers I'd had over the years who probably had come to the same realization at some point, but stuck with it, because they weren't qualified to do anything else after the fact. Those few teachers had wound up making themselves, and most of their students, miserable.

"Incidentally," Graham asked, leaning forward, and lowering his sunglasses just slightly so that I could finally peer directly into his eyes, "how do *you* feel about kids?"

I snickered and in that split second in which I didn't answer immediately, Ty put in his two cents. I'd known that Grady was floating near the side of the pool, but I hadn't registered it when Ty got out and came to stand right next to Graham. "Kay-Kay *loves* kids," he said, crossing his arms over his chest, dripping water everywhere. "I've got six younger siblings and she's always been great with them. And they practically worship the ground she walks on, too."

"Thanks, Ty," I said, shooting him a sincere smile, before turning my focus back to Graham. "You see? I adore the Mastersons, and they feel the same way about me."

"Yeah, but they're your neighbors, right?" Graham gestured toward the eight-foot privacy fence that separated our pool from their backyard. "You sort of have to be nice to them, don't you?"

"I guess it wouldn't be very polite or neighborly if I was rude all the time," I agreed.

"So, you don't really know how you'd get along with a bunch of little kids, if you had to be their teacher?" Graham prompted.

"I...I guess you're right."

"Don't you think you ought to figure that out? It'd be better to know how you really feel about becoming a teacher before you firmly settle on that career path." He ruffled his fingertips through his hair again. "I'm no expert, Kate, but I think it's always better to have too much information than not enough. And the best way to understand what you like or don't like is to get a little experience on the subject."

"How am I supposed to do that?" I asked.

Graham shrugged. "Before I decided on studying chemistry as my new major, I worked in a chem lab part-time, cleaning out beakers. It wasn't glamorous, but when I watched what the other technicians were doing, I was intrigued by the processes. That's how I wound up studying the subject. I simply wanted to know more."

Ty scoffed and when I turned to look at him, he was frowning. "It's not like Kay-Kay can shadow a teacher over the summer or..."

"She shouldn't be shadowing anybody," Graham said waspishly, cutting Ty off right in the middle of his sentence. "Kate should be putting her own skills to use, and trying to understand if what she's already got will translate into something she'll find to be valuable later."

Grady perked up a little then. His head bounced off his hands and he suggested, "What if you host a pitching clinic, Kate? You could sort of combine the experiences of teaching and coaching and..."

"It's brilliant," I beamed at him. "*You're* brilliant."

Chapter 16

Grady

There were times when I worried about Kate because she got so wrapped up in her need to plan, calculate, and make everything just right. But now, was not one of those moments. With Graham's prompting, and my quick suggestion leading her onward, Kate was off and running. She sat bolt upright on the lounge seat and immediately started charting a course for success.

While Syd and Rory continued flirting with each other in the shallow end of the pool and Will and Giles tossed a ball back and forth, Kate called out to Abs and Smitty, asking them to join her so she could begin handing out assignments.

"First, we'll have to pick a date and time," Kate said, scooting to the edge of her chair and staring up at Smitty and Abs who were still soaking wet from just climbing out of the pool. "When's everybody free?"

"For what?" Abs asked, giving Smitty a strange look, which was met with a shrug of confusion.

"I'm going to host a pitching clinic," Kate explained quickly, motioning for her friends to pull their chairs closer. I continued listening from my position near the edge of the pool, taking pleasure in watching Kate do her planning thing. "But I need to decide when and where to have it." She tapped her chin thoughtfully. "It's gotta be toward the end of the summer, right?"

"Sure," Abs agreed. "Right before school starts ought to work for everyone."

Kate's eyes flicked toward mine. We both knew that Farrington High was going to be back in session just about a week or so before I left for Felding, but she was obviously making sure I'd be around long enough to help her run this thing. I nodded. "End of summer should be all right."

"And you'll probably want to use the softball field at the school, right?" Smitty questioned, leaning forward to snatch a beach towel off the stack. Hastily, she wrapped it around her swimsuit clad body.

"I don't know," Kate murmured pensively. "I like the idea of being on the Falcons home turf, but I might have better luck drawing in more people if I talked to someone at the Farrington Parks and Rec. Department and reserved one of the softball diamonds there."

"Yeah," Abs said, nodding amenably. "People don't like coming to the field at the school because the parking lot is so far away. You'd be better off reserving a diamond at Farrington Park."

"Speaking of the high school, I'd probably better call Coach Cobb, too."

"Good idea," Abs enthused. "He'll be able to help you get the word out to the middle schoolers. He can contact the softball coach over there or something."

"Right."

I could practically see Kate's brain whirling. She wasn't writing any of this down, but I was certain she wouldn't forget a thing.

"Do you want me to send out a text to the other pitchers and catchers?" Smitty questioned.

"Yes," Kate groaned. "I know we're going to need lots of help on hand and if the other girls agree to stop by..." Her eyes floated toward mine again and I gave her an encouraging nod, letting her know, once again, that I'd be there. She didn't even have to ask for my assistance.

"As soon as you pick a date, I'll get the others on board," Smitty promised.

All in all, things shaped up pretty quickly. It helped that Kate was an expert at planning and setting workout routines and that Abs and Smitty were immediately willing to co-operate. Graham seemed thrilled by the prospect too. "If I'm still hanging around Farrington by the time you get this thing cooking, count me in as a chaperone or catcher or something," he offered, which made Kate giggle.

"I thought you didn't like hanging out with little kids," she reminded him.

"I don't," Graham replied, "but I'd like to help you, if I can." Slowly, I flexed my arms and lifted myself out of the pool. I meant to go clap my brother on the back and congratulate him on helping motivate Kate, but then I caught sight of Ty. He was still standing rooted to the same spot where he'd been a moment before, but because Abs and Smitty had both crowded the area and Graham was now leaning forward, offering his opinions, Ty had just sorted faded into the background.

His eyebrows were furrowed, and he was staring at Kate almost like he was trying to read her thoughts but having a rough go of it.

I wanted to laugh, but because I didn't want to draw Kate's attention to her scowling best friend, I decided against it. Picking up a beach towel and patting my stomach, I turned and gave Ty my best winning smile. "What's the matter?" I asked, trying to keep the teasing note out of my voice. "I'd have thought you'd be downright ebullient right now."

"Huh?" Ty shook his head, then leveled his gaze at me.

I jutted my chin, gesturing toward Kate and the others. "She's moving in the direction of becoming a teacher and coach. She's doing something to actually promote her own future. I'd have thought you'd be jumping up and down with excitement be-cause she's doing exactly what you always wanted her to do."

Ty shook his head slowly. "*I* don't see it that way. Kate's testing out her teaching skills, sure, but that may mean..."

He stopped talking right in the middle of his sentence, but from the look on his face, I knew that he'd already said too much of what he was thinking. I could easily infer the part he was keeping to himself. "You don't think Kate will like teach-ing, do you?" I shucked the towel onto the nearest chair then turned to size up Ty. He refused to meet my gaze, but that didn't prompt me to back down one bit. "You've been pushing her to be a teacher and coach all these years, but you're pretty sure she's not cut out for it, aren't you?"

Slowly, Ty twisted his neck and when his eyes met mine finally, not only did I see uncertainty there, but his hostility toward me was on full display as well. "*I'm* not the one who's pushing Kay-Kay to do anything."

"Really?" I snorted, then leaned forward, and added in a faux whisper, "That's not the way Kate tells it."

I knew in that instance that I was maybe going too far with Ty. He struck me as someone who was wound up so tight that when he eventually snapped, there would be a whole wealth of repercussions. But oddly enough, I didn't much care. I still had the vision of Ty, running along at Kate's side yesterday, as a reminder that he wasn't all that concerned with *my* feelings, and that urged me to keep right on taunting him.

"You know, Ty..." I continued and at that, Kate stood.

"What's going on?" she asked, but I ignored her and so did Ty, because he continued glowering at me.

"You may think you know everything about Kate, but I've got the feeling there're some massive holes in your knowledge bank." I smirked at him, silently daring him to ask for more information. He didn't, so I kept right on. "But now, I can see the truth, Ty. Even the things you do know about Kate, you're unwilling to acknowledge, especially if they don't fall right in line with the person you want her to be." I snorted scornfully. "I'm sure it's purely coincidental that *your* dream of being a teacher and coach just happens to be *hers* as well. What did you think? If you followed her around forever one day she'd wake up and just decide that..."

I'd gone too far. I could feel Ty's hatred for me rolling off him in waves. So, I sort of expected his next move. He lifted his hands, as if he meant to push me, but I was too quick to let him lay a hand on me. Instead, I sidestepped, but that was a mistake. Because even though I was ready for Ty's reaction, Kate wasn't. She'd moved right in between us and because Ty was so greedy to get his hands on me and give me a good hard shove, he ended up pushing Kate into the pool instead.

Chapter 17

Kate

"What... what was that?" I emerged from the pool spluttering. "Why'd you push me?" I'd heard Grady and Ty going at each other and while I must've missed some of their conversation because only half of what Grady said made any sense at all, I'd been compelled to step between the two of them.

And look at the thanks I get for playing the pacifist.

I ran my hands through my hair, then swam toward the side of the pool. My eyes darted toward Abs and Smitty, but both were sitting there with their mouths hanging wide open, not saying a word. When I turned my gaze on Ty and Grady, I was surprised to see their expressions. Neither of them was stepping forward, either to apologize for pushing me or explain what had been evolving between them. And while Grady looked guilt-ridden, Ty still seemed steamed. He shot a withering stare at Grady, and I knew that whatever had really happened, he was on the verge of blaming Grady for everything.

"Go on," I said, waving my hand impatiently. "One of you'd better tell me what's going on here right now. Last I knew, we were all planning a pitching clinic, then the two of you were squabbling and..."

That's when Grady stepped forward to offer me his hand. "Sorry, Kate," he said. "We just got carried away. You know how Ty and I can get."

"Actually, I don't know," I retorted, annoyed by the way he was trying to brush things off and make this incident seem totally normal. I might've said more, but then Abs rose slowly out of her seat. She pressed her index finger to her lips, shushing me, and crept forward. I knew exactly what she meant to do, so I ignored Grady's proffered hand and swam backward, pushing away from the wall.

"Kate," Grady said and there was a pleading tone in his voice, but that's all he had time to say before Abs sprung on him and Ty. She was incredibly strong and especially since she caught them both with their guards down, it didn't take more than a gentle shove to send them both flying into the deep end of the pool. Abs cackled at her own high jinks. And Syd whooped loudly too. I laughed as well while I watched the wacky, surprised grimaces that registered on both of their faces just before they hit the water.

Ty reemerged first and he had a furious look on his face, but that was soon wiped away when Abs shouted, "Cannonball!" She took a flying leap and landed just a few inches away from where he was treading water.

Grady swam to the surface then, looking a whole lot less flustered than he had a moment before.

Maybe getting in the pool cooled him off a little.

It was disconcerting to see Grady and Ty getting into it for a number of reasons—the least of which being that Grady normally operated on an easy, even keel. Seeing him behave in any other way just didn't sit right with me.

As the others jumped into the pool and a water war proceeded to unfold, I swam forward and grabbed Grady's hand. His eyes lit up, almost as if he hadn't recognized me until my hand grasped his. Gently, I towed him toward the middle area of the pool, on the other side of the filter, just out of the splash zone.

"What's wrong?" I asked as he swam a little further, then turned and pressed his back against the wall of the pool. Grady shook his head slowly, but I insisted. "A minute ago, everything was fine. But now, I can see that both you and Ty are really upset with each other."

"We're cool," he said, letting go of my hand just long enough so he could wrap both his hands around my waist.

"No, you're not," I persevered. "If I hadn't stepped in the way, he'd have pushed you in the pool instead."

"You rescued me," he joked, pulling me forward so that our bodies were pressed together. "I guess that makes you my hero, Special K."

"Grady," I groaned, draping my arms gently around his neck, "just tell me what's going on. You know I won't be able to concentrate on anything if I think the two of you were fighting and..."

"Are you having trouble concentrating?" He interrupted, then, out of the blue, leaned forward and brushed his lips against mine. "How about now?" But he didn't give me a second to answer because before I could even catch my breath or formulate a response, his lips were coasting over mine again, but this time, much more insistently. I was so startled by the sudden public display of affection that I tried to back away, but Grady only pulled me closer, making sure there was nothing separating us other than our swimsuits.

He crushed his lips to mine, but when I opened my mouth, allowing him to slip his tongue inside, the kiss softened quite unexpectedly. He kissed me sweetly then and his hands drifted lower, cupping my backside. I stood on my tiptoes, which prompted him to glide his hands down the length of my legs and tuck them behind my knees, hitching them upward. Because it felt so good and totally like the right thing to do, I swung my legs and wrapped them around his torso, so that I was clinging to him baby-monkey style. We stayed locked in that position for what felt like ages and had he not nibbled on my lower lip, making me giggle, we probably could've remained that way even longer.

Grady didn't say anything when we broke apart and I was too dazed to conjure up much speech, so I just unlocked my legs from around his waist and floated there, still resting in his strong arms. I leaned my head against his chest, listening to the rapidity of his heart rate—which was racing.

"Better?" Grady said softly.

"The best," I whispered. I burrowed my face further into his chest, pressing my lips right over his heart, and he rested his chin on top of my head.

"I'm glad you think so," he breathed, and that would've seemed kind of sweet, if I hadn't felt his chin graze my wet-slicked hair, making me think he wasn't exactly speaking to me, but directing his words at someone else entirely. No one was paying us any mind, or at least I assumed they weren't because most everyone was still splashing around and laughing loudly. Plus, if Abs or Syd would've caught sight of that steamy kiss, I'm sure they both would've said something wildly inappropriate. But I couldn't shake the feeling that Grady wasn't fully with me, relishing this moment.

"What are you looking at?" I asked, slowly raising my head off his chest so I could meet his gaze.

"Nothing," he said, snapping back to attention so quickly that I knew I'd caught him in an obvious fib.

I twitched my head slightly to the left and that's when I saw Ty climbing out of the pool. He hadn't bothered to walk to the stairs or even use the ladder which was in the deep end. He'd just heaved himself out of the pool, over near the diving board, and was stalking toward the gate.

Without stopping to say goodbye to anyone or even grab his beach towel and shirt off the chair where he'd dropped them upon first arriving hours ago, he marched toward his home.

I blinked in confusion, then looked up at Grady. A small, nearly indiscernible smile was creeping onto his face. "Grady," I said softly, gazing up at him, scrutinizing his features, "what was that all about?"

"What was *what* all about?" he returned as his smile turned teasing and the surface of the pool water around us reflected in his cloudy bluish gray eyes, making them look like they were sparkling.

"That kiss," I whispered. "Did you just get swept away by a moment of passion or did you do that because you were trying to send Ty a message?"

His brows wrinkled and his smile twitched. "What kind of message would I have been trying to send?"

"I don't know." I continued gazing at him. "Maybe you were trying to tell him to back off?"

For a split second, Grady's features hardened. If I hadn't been looking at him so closely, keenly paying attention to every movement he was making, I might've missed the way his brows contracted, and his nostrils flared. But I didn't miss a thing. I knew that what I'd just said had struck a nerve. I wasn't precisely sure which nerve or what his reaction meant, but there was something about my words that had distressed or maybe perturbed my boyfriend.

Before I could point out what I'd just noticed, his face went completely back to normal. His eyes were alight with joviality and his smile was firmly sitting in its lop-sided cradle, making both dimples appear in his cheeks. "Come on, Kate," he whispered, draping his hands leisurely around my hips, towing me toward him once more. "I don't need to tell Ty to back off. I'm not even thinking about Ty right now." His next words were so softly spoken that if I hadn't been so close to him, I might've missed them. "I'm only thinking about you, Special K."

Once again, Grady had said precisely what I wanted to hear, but that didn't bring me much comfort. I hugged Grady, because I loved him and because it felt so good to stand this close to him, wrapped in his arms. But I couldn't shake the feeling that despite all my better intentions, I was, in fact, missing something.

Something did pass between Grady and Ty just now and it is possible that Grady was only kissing me like that to prove a point. But what point? What does he think he needs to prove? I was loath to think that the two of them had been arguing or maybe even fighting over me because I was pretty sure I'd settled this issue before it had even become a problem. I'd chosen Grady and Ty knew that. But, if everyone was on the same page, why had Ty pushed me into the pool?

Chapter 18

Tuesday, June 13th

Grady

I really don't like working at the auto mall.

It had been another long day of making one coffee after another and running bottled waters around to anyone who looked like they could use a thirsty sip, and I was feeling ragged. When I had the chance to watch my dad do his thing, that was kind of cool, because he was an excellent salesman. He never overcharged for a vehicle or hyped it too greatly, but he listened to his customers, heard their needs, then tried to show them the best they could afford for their buck. But I rarely got to stick close to Dad. Mr. Barker had too many things for me to do, including washing some of the cars that had been parked out back for the last two weeks, getting a layer of grime baked over their windshields. Normally, I wouldn't have minded washing and waxing the vehicles, but I'd been wearing my business casual work attire and after all that hard work, I'd sweat right through my dress shirt.

The only thing that made me put on real clothes, rather than pajamas, when I stepped out of the shower was the thought of pulling up to Kate's house and seeing her again. That notion had led me to hop into my truck and barrel over here as fast as I could, without breaking any speeding laws, just so I could wrap my arms around her and tell her all about my rotten day.

But when I rounded the corner of Parkland Street and my headlights flashed on the Kellner's driveway, I felt like someone had punched me right in the stomach.

He's here...

Kate's back was turned to me, but Ty stood right there, checking his watch, and mumbling something. I could see his face clearly and was suddenly overcome by the urge to pounce on him. Normally, I was a pretty even-tempered guy, but just thinking about the way he'd taken his aggression against me out on Kate the other day by shoving her into the pool made me want to bash him over the head.

If I could get my arms around him right now, I'd give him one of Triple B's patented bear hugs.

It was mildly satisfying to think of grabbing hold of Ty and squeezing him until he begged for mercy. He was well-built and a runner, but I was the youngest of the Hughes brothers. I'd pretty much crawled out of the womb ready to grapple, so I was sure no matter how scrappy Ty might be or what kind of fight he tried to put up, I could take him easily.

But then, just as the image of obliterating Ty was coalescing in my mind, Kate spun around and started waving. She was glowing. Her ponytail was pulled into a messy topknot, but it bobbed as she continued enthusiastically gesturing for me to pull the truck forward. She was wearing a white tank top that was drenched through with sweat and even her skin looked slick from the way she was perspiring.

No matter how much I want to destroy Ty, I won't tear him apart in front of her.

It irked me supremely that the jerk was constantly manipulating her and doing it all under the umbrella of being her best friend, but as I put the truck in park and climbed out of the cab, I refused to look at him. Instead, I focused all my energy on returning Kate's cheerful smile.

"Hey, Special K," I said, shutting the driver's side door softly behind myself. "What's happening?"

"We're just finishing up and yep..." She stopped and pretended to sniff her armpits. "One, or maybe the both of us, needs to head inside and shower."

"See ya," Ty muttered and thankfully, that was all. He stalked toward his house so fast that I wondered what could've possibly motivated him to slip away like that. If Kate had directed words at me like that, I might've winked at her and asked if she was inviting me to join her in the shower. But Ty practically ran away, darting across the divide between their houses and disappearing immediately.

Good riddance...

"Give me five minutes," she said, leading the way toward her house. "I'm disgusting and..."

"You look fine to me," I interrupted, reaching forward to grab ahold of her hand. Her palm was sweaty, but I didn't care.

"You say that, but that's because you haven't gotten close enough to smell me yet." She wrinkled her nose and made a repulsed face. "I'm grosser than ever." I started to open my mouth to protest and tell her I'd take her anyway I could get her, stinky or otherwise, but stopped because she kept talking. "Why don't you wait for me by the pool? I'll shower and meet you there in just a few minutes."

She pushed open the door to her house and I trailed after her. "Aren't your folks home?"

"They will be soon," she said, heading for the staircase. "At least, I think they're on their way."

I nodded, but then realized that Kate was already in the process of closing the bathroom door behind herself, so she couldn't see me. "I'll just take up some space out back," I drawled. Sauntering slowly through the dining room and kitchen area, I headed out the sliding back doors and onto the Kellner's patio. The only light was emanating from the house behind me, and it made the surface of the pool water look an oddly greenish-blue hue. Feeling the exhaustion that had nearly kept me home this evening overtake me, I slid a little less than gracefully into one of the lounge chairs, tipped my head back, and watched the lightning bugs do their thing.

It was possible that I dozed off for a second because when I scented Kate's shampoo and body wash, my eyelids fluttered open and I looked up to see her standing over top of me, smiling beatifically.

"Hey," I whispered.

"Hey," she said, sinking into the lounge seat beside me, burrowing right into the only space that was available. "You tired?" She reclined her head back, letting her wet locks rest against my chest and I inhaled deeply.

"How do you always manage to smell so good?" I asked.

She snickered. "I only smell nice like this when I first get out of the shower, but I guess I owe it all to my new bath products."

I lowered my face, burying my nose in her hair. "You smell like caramel and peanuts."

"Ha!" she laughed perkily. "That'd be my Take Me Out to the Ballgame conditioner. It's supposed to smell like peanuts and Cracker Jacks."

"It does," I whispered, angling my lips closer to her ear. "I like it very much."

"And I like that you're here," she said, twisting so that she could kiss me lightly on the lips. "I didn't know you were stopping over tonight."

I smooched her once more, then sighed contentedly. "I wasn't planning on it, but when I got off work, all I wanted to do was see you and talk for a little while."

"Rough day?" She snuggled into me, and I wrapped my arm around her hip, cuddling her as close as we could get.

"Working at the car dealership really isn't for me," I mumbled.

"Right," she agreed. "You'll take Arthropods over people any day."

"Yeah," I whispered, "but it's more than that. I knew that my summer job wasn't going to be anything out of this world, but I guess I didn't expect to find it so boring either."

She fidgeted and looked at my face. "You don't like getting to interact with all the customers?"

I shrugged. "They come and go. Sometimes, I don't say more than two words to any of them."

"It's funny, I guess," she said slowly. "When you told me you were working at the auto mall this summer, I just figured you'd like being a car salesman."

"Why's that?"

She reached up and traced the tip of her index finger along the curve of my mouth. It wasn't a seductive move, but rather something she was doing to try and make me smile, I think. So, I obliged her. "You're so personable," she whispered. "You always know the right things to say and when you smile...well...If you offered to sell me a car and smiled at me the way you do, I wouldn't be able to say no."

"Hmm..." I hummed, leaning forward, and nuzzling the tip of my nose against hers. "I wonder just how far my silly little smile could get me with you."

She giggled. "Where exactly do you want to go?"

"Wherever the mood takes us." I kissed her then, but it was a soft, playful kiss, one that I meant to last for a long time without really going much further at all. Slowly, I ran my hands through her damp wet locks, feeling them slip and slide through my fingertips. It was nice just to be with Kate, admiring everything about her, and not feeling pressure to do anything else.

"You're quite the salesman, Mr. Hughes," she said, wriggling against me, and pulling out of the kiss.

"I'm not trying to sell you anything, Kate."

She rubbed her fingers over my cheeks, then brought them up higher and massaged my temples. "Maybe not, but you probably could. Have you ever thought of asking Mr. Barker if you can be on the sales team, rather than running the errands for everyone else in the office?"

"I'm not old enough to make the sales yet...or at least that's what my dad told me when he got me the job." I leaned back against the lounge chair cushions, pulling Kate right along with me. "And besides, I really don't think I'd like it."

"But you're so gregarious and out-going," she insisted. "You make friends so easily."

I laughed. "I made friends with *you* easily."

"No," she persevered. "You charm practically everybody. Don't you remember when you first met Syd and she did little more than snarl at you? But now, she thinks you're adorable."

"I am pretty adorable," I joked, which made Kate smile. "But I think Syd thawing toward me has more to do with her interest in Rory than anything else."

"Nope," she countered. "Syd changed her mind about you months ago, all because you just relaxed and made her feel comfortable around you, too." She paused and sighed heavily. "That's why I can't understand why things still have to be so difficult between you and Ty. I'd have thought that the two of you would've been best friends by now."

Are we really talking about Ty again? Can't she just forget about her best buddy for a few seconds?

"What would make you think that?" I asked, instead of saying what I was really thinking.

She shifted once more so that we could lock eyes with one another. I could see the hopefulness lingering there and even hear it when she answered, "I already told you how important it is to me that the two of you at least try to be friends. It'd be easier for everybody if you just worked some of your magic and charmed him the way you do everyone else."

"Easier for everybody...or easier for you, Kate?" It was an audacious thing to say, mostly because I knew that pressing this issue would probably get me nowhere. I was exhausted beyond compare and suddenly, the nice and cozy night I'd planned to spend cuddling with my girlfriend was turning into another conversation about why I could be chummy with everyone else yet despise the boy next door.

"I just know that if you gave Ty a chance, you'd really like him." Her hand drifted to my chest, and she tapped her forefinger right over my heart. "I mean, he and I have been so close for years that we've practically become the same person." Her eyes searched mine. "And you love me, so I don't see how you can hate someone who is almost my twin."

"Kate," I said forcefully, cupping her chin and making it so she couldn't look away from me. "*You* are one of a kind. Don't you ever let anyone make you think otherwise. You may have things in common with people, like Ty, but you are truly unique. And that's why I love you...not him, not any of the other players on your softball team...just *you*."

She kissed me and I got a heavy whiff of her Take Me Out to the Ball Game conditioner. It wasn't enough to put my mind totally at ease, but for now, that simple kiss and the smell of caramel and peanuts was plenty.

Chapter 19

Wednesday, June 14th
Kate

Focus.

I kicked at a clod of dirt that was sitting much too close to the pitcher's mound.

I've gotta get this next out myself. Go after her. Don't let her even get the bat on the ball.

The sun was setting low in the western sky, but there was a canopy of trees on the other side of the fence, shielding the softball diamond from the brunt of the golden, pink, and bright orange rays. I glared at Abs' glove, trying to memorize the spot where she was positioned, hoping that when I whipped my arm and flung the ball, I'd be able to hit it precisely.

It was the bottom of the fifth inning and things weren't going so well for me or the Trailblazers. After sitting out the first four innings, Coach Davis called me to the side and told me to get ready to pitch. I was relieved, mostly because I shuddered at the thought of making the long jaunt out to left field again and missing another opportunity to show what I could do on the mound. But, instead of dazzling the spectators and my coach, I was struggling.

The batters in this league are just better—flat out—than any others I've had to face before.

It was then that it occurred to me exactly how out of place I was playing in this twenty-one and under league.

I could be pitching for an eighteen and under team right now, taking on local girls, competitors I've faced before and know exactly what pitches will make them whiff.

Thinking wistfully of my wicked sweet changeup and how gratifying it was when I took a batter down by throwing it, I kicked at the pitching rubber again, clearing away all the dirt that had accumulated there.

Get it together, Kate.

There were two outs, a runner was on second base, and the number nine batter was striding to the plate. That would normally be a good thing if I were still playing high school ball. The coach tended to pile the weakest hitters at the end of the lineup and that would mean all I had to do was cruise a couple of fastballs, maybe slip a drop curve by the girl, and the inning would be over with a pretty neat strikeout. But in this league, position on the lineup card didn't mean a thing. All these players could hit.

I snuck a surreptitious glance over my shoulder at the runner on second and spied Syd, stalking close to her, keeping her in check, and relatively close to the bag.

Good, good. Syd's ready for a throwdown, should it come to that.

But I prayed it wouldn't. If I could do my job, and weave enough junk pitches past this batter, we could close the books on the fifth inning and head into the dugout to prepare for the sixth.

Abs dropped into her catcher's squat and instantly flashed me the signal for a fastball. Her index finger pointed down and off to the left, indicating she wanted a shot on the outside corner. I nodded stiffly, then moved into my windup, rocking back gently, twirling my arm rapidly, and releasing while exhaling in a hearty grunt.

"St-rike!" the man in blue behind the plate yelled. The batter had just missed nipping the ball with the end of her bat, but she was so close to catching up to it, I knew I'd never be able to get away with firing a fastball a second time.

Abs called for a change, but I shook her off, fearing what might happen if this batter got ahold of it. She was a big girl, with thick arms and legs, and I was certain that if she turned on the ball and even hacked at it slightly, she'd be able to hammer one right back up the middle and send the runner at second base flying for home. Abs gave me the sign for the drop curve and immediately, I began performing the necessary sequence of movements.

My fingers gripped the two seams hard. I stretched my left foot as far to my right side as it would go, making it so when I brought my throwing arm around, I was going to have to sling with all my might to avoid hitting my hip. I whipped my arm, almost like I was tossing a frisbee, and when I let go of that bright yellow ball, it sizzled toward the plate, arching, then dipping just as I'd planned. But even my filthy drop curve wasn't enough to stump the girl in the batter's box. She dropped her back elbow and her hands, almost like she was teeing off on a golf ball rather than swinging at a softball, and she sent the ball soaring over our right fielder's head.

I didn't even need to turn and watch the trajectory of the hit. Our right fielder, who happened to be Becky, getting her playing time as I had last game by taking a few innings in the outfield, was on her horse, racing with all her might to track down the ball, but she could only move so fast. The ball crashed into the fence, rattling it loudly. Then, thankfully it started rolling right toward Becky. She scooped it up with her bare hand and turned to fire the ball to the cut-off, Syd. Cottoning on after just a second's delay, I raced toward home plate, circling around behind Abs, to provide backup support, should she need it. But Abs didn't need me standing there. The runner from second had already scored and it was best that

Syd held onto the ball instead of making the throw home so she could keep the number nine batter locked in at second.

Crud...

I stomped on home plate as I marched back toward the mound.

There's no one to blame for that run but me. I tried to put too much movement on the curve and wound up letting her take it for a ride.

Glaring at the girl who had just smashed one of my best pitches to the fence, I stalked to the mound.

"Take it easy, Kate," Syd called softly, tossing me the ball, because she was walking toward me, rather than her own position. "You don't have to strike out every batter. Just let them put the ball in play and allow us to do the rest."

I was furious. Apparently, Syd was choosing to ignore what had just happened. That girl had knocked the ball nearly out of the park and even though my teammates had worked hard to make the right play, it didn't make much difference because *I'd* allowed a run to score.

"Breathe," Syd coached. "We're back at the top of the lineup and you know it's only getting tougher from here."

She was right, at least in this instance. Since I'd had the first part of the game to watch all our opponents stride to the plate, I knew that the number one batter was tall and built like a bean pole, but boy-oh-boy could she run. In the first and third innings, she'd laid down bunts both times. And even though our third baseman had been expecting as much the second time around, the girl with wings on her feet had managed to beat out the throw and get called safe at first.

"Okay," I said, flexing my jaw, which I hadn't realized I'd been clenching. "I've got this under control."

I sucked in a deep, steadying breath and attempted to clear my mind, which was never easy. I knew that all good pitchers were able to transcend and get to a place where nothing mattered, nothing existed other than the tasks their bodies needed to accomplish. But it wasn't one of my gifts to let things go. One runner had dashed off second base only to be replaced by another and if I didn't get this batter out, who knew what might happen next...

I was so mired in my own thoughts that I missed the sign from Abs, so I decided to throw a rise, just to be on the safe side. I figured if the girl bunted, as she'd proven she was so adept at doing, she might possibly pop it up and that'd give Abs or me a chance to catch it and have her called out.

Thank you!

As if I had written the play out ahead of time myself, the girl at the plate chased the rise ball, dangling the thickest part of her bat in front of the plate, then following the ball upward as it drifted higher and higher. The ball kissed the top side of her bat and soared high, high up in the sky. "Got it!" I yelled, darting forward, and readying myself. It was an easy, loopy fly ball, and as soon as my glove closed around it, the inning was over.

"Not bad, Lady K," Abs said, taking off her mask and grinning at me. She didn't look like herself because of the foam mask that still stayed locked in place, but I returned the smile and added a compliment of my own.

"Not bad yourself."

We raced toward the dugout and that's when Syd came up behind me. She was holding my water bottle and helmet, offering me both. "Stay in the game, Kate," she advised, handing me the bottle first. "I saw your concentration slip out there, but you can't let that happen. These batters are better than we're used to and..."

"Don't remind me," I grumbled, taking the bottle, and squirting some of the tepid liquid into my mouth. Since the day was so hot, the icy cool water had long ago heated and become little more than a way to wet my lips rather than quench my thirst.

"You're in the hole," Syd continued talking, as if I hadn't interjected. She shoved my helmet at me. "But don't worry, the coach for the Sparks isn't changing pitchers like we keep doing. The same girl's been in all game and she's looking a little worse for wear."

I stared at the player on the mound and had to admit that she did look a tad rattled. She'd started the game strong, not allowing much action during the first two innings. But in the third, our hitters caught up with her fastball and when she was forced to throw her junk, it was clear that she didn't have much outside of that stealthy heater. During the fourth inning, we'd nearly batted around. And if I hadn't botched things in the last half inning, our team would be leading the game with a score of 4-3. But since I'd let that number nine batter send the ball soaring, we were all tied up. And soon enough, I'd have my chance at redemption because it'd be my turn to step to the plate.

I jerked my batting helmet onto my head and wiggled the face mask covering, trying to get the thing to sit right and quit squishing my topknot painfully against the side of my head. While pulling my bat from its cubbyhole, I darted a glance into the outfield, searching for my parents. I hadn't heard my dad during the last half inning, and I was sure he was just as keyed up over what happened as I was. When I spotted him, sure enough, he was moving along the fence line, pacing from one end of the baseline to the other, muttering to himself. My eyes then floated toward Dad's abandoned camp chair. But his seat wasn't empty. Grady was sitting in it, or at least he had been sitting in it. Because as I watched, he stood up, waved over his shoulder at my mom, then walked away from the ball field.

"Where's he going?"

"Where's *who* going?" Syd snapped. She was still standing nearby, but instead of turning and looking over her shoulder so she could figure out exactly who I meant, she just clapped her hands on both sides of my helmet and gave me a little shake. "Snap out of it, Kellner. We need you to bring your A-game right now."

For the second time in just a handful of minutes, I knew that Syd was the one who had her head on straight and I was the one acting like a space cadet. So, I nodded, silently promising to do better. But even as I did all that, I couldn't help but wonder where Grady was going and why he was leaving after only watching me pitch just the one inning.

Chapter 20

Grady

"Come get me," Rory said as soon as I dialed his number, and he picked up the phone.

"Yeah," I snorted. "I got your text. Is something wrong?"

"No," Rory drawled, "but I wanna see Kate and Syd play, and I just finished my shift at work, so I need you to drive over here and pick me up from the Wax and Shine."

"Ehh..." I said slowly, thinking of how if I went over there, I was likely to run into Ty.

"Get over here," Rory ordered, "or I'll put you in a headlock."

"You'll have to find me first," I taunted.

"I'm serious, Bro," Rory insisted. "I told Syd that I'd be there if I could and I know that if you don't come get me now, I'll miss the game altogether."

"You still might miss it," I said. "We're already in the fifth inning."

"Hurry," he demanded. "I want to be there for Syd...and Kate too."

It's Kate I'm worried about right now.

I didn't say that, because it felt like bad luck to give life to such thoughts, but they occupied my mind anyway as I started jogging to my truck, already plotting out the best way to get to Wax and Shine and be back at the ball field before Kate even had the chance to know that I'd slipped away for a few minutes.

"On my way," I whispered, then hung up the phone.

A few minutes later, I slowed the truck marginally, just enough so that Rory could swing the passenger side door open and hop inside. Some people might've been irked by this, but Rory seemed to think it was all part of a game, and he pounded on the roof of the cab, shouting, "Go! Go!" as I gunned it out of the parking lot, leaving the Wax and Shine without ever even having to see a streak of Ty's red hair.

As we headed back toward the ball field, Rory said, "Things must be pretty bad."

"It's not that," I muttered, "just that the game was tight. The Sparks had just tied things up when you called, and I think Kate was going to be up to bat soon."

He scoffed. "Then why'd you leave?"

"Because you told me to," I countered which made him snicker.

"If, when you'd called, you'd have said Kate needed you to stay, I wouldn't have pushed so hard."

"Yeah, you would've," I argued, edging the truck into the parking space I'd just vacated a few moments before. When I put the vehicle in park, I turned to look at my brother. He was smiling but also looking at me in the oddest way. "What?"

"Nothing," he said. "I just can't believe you left to come get me."

"You needed me." I opened the door and clambered out of the cab.

"*She* needed you," he corrected.

"Kate's fine," I murmured. "She's tough and besides, she was way too focused on the game. She'll never even know that I left."

Just to be on the safe side, I ran across the parking lot, past the bleachers, and headed straight for the baseline where Mr. and Mrs. Kellner had left their camping chairs. Now, not only was Kate's dad pacing near the foul line, but her mom was standing with both arms propped on the yellow tubing that capped the fence. She shouted, "Come on, Eight. You can do it, Katie!"

My heart started racing. I'd been gone long enough I knew it wasn't possible that Kate could still be up to bat but hearing that note of concern in her mother's voice put me on edge too.

Things can't be going well for Kate.

I propped my elbows on the fence and leaned close to Mrs. Kellner. "What did I miss?"

Rory pulled up beside me and poked his head around my shoulders so he could greet her. "Hey, Mrs. Kellner."

"Hello, dear," she said, giving him a warm, if feeble smile. Then, she answered my question. "Katie hit a grounder when she was up to bat, but it didn't go very far. The second baseman scooped it up--no problem. We were three up, three down."

"And now?" I nodded to where Kate stood on the mound. Her face was drawn into a series of impassive lines and her jaw was clenched determinedly. She twirled the ball in her right hand, evidently searching for the seams, then started into her windup. She fired a beautiful pitch toward home plate, but the girl in the batter's box bounced on her knees comfortably, acting almost as if she ate pitches like that for breakfast and had all the time in the world to get ready. At the last second, she snapped her hands forward and belted a line drive right up the middle. It flew past Kate, just missing her head, and even though Syd was ready and all over it, running to track it down, the ball streaked by her too.

"Go!" Mrs. Kellner shouted. "Get the ball!" She was frantic, flapping her arms, trying to direct the outfielders, but not calm or collected enough to be of much help. "Throw it home. Throw it home!"

That's when I saw what I had missed before. My eyes had gone directly to Kate as soon as I arrived back at the field, so

I hadn't noticed the runner on third who was tearing toward home plate, barreling straight for Abs.

But it didn't matter how fast that girl was moving or how loudly Mrs. Kellner was yelling instructions. The runner scored and by the time the outfielders got the ball back to the infield the batter had made it all the way around to third base.

A triple and an R.B.I...yikes.

Kate hung her head, and it was all I could do to stop myself from calling timeout and running right out onto the field so I could give her a pep talk. But there was nothing I could do. I literally had to stand there and do absolutely nothing.

"Come on, Special K," I cheered. "Go get this next batter."

I had half-expected Kate to look up and smile in my direction, but that didn't happen. She just caught the ball Syd tossed to her, then sidled right up to the mound, and prepared to throw her next pitch.

It was torment to watch her take on that next batter. I'd caught enough for her over these last few months that I knew when she was trying too hard. Kate twisted her body in jerky motions when she was trying to get her junk pitches to cooperate. And because she believed that her fastball wasn't as zippy as some of the other pitchers, she was trying to overcompensate for that by leaping and exploding off the mound. This might've worked a little, maybe allowing her to add one or two miles per hour to the pitches, but since she wasn't used to the motion, her hips got in the way, messing with her follow through and leaving her in a position where she wouldn't be capable of fielding the ball properly should it be knocked right back at her. Not that her fielding position seemed to matter any...

Oh, geez...

It was almost painful to watch when the next batter smacked the ball toward center field and went racing around the bases.

I could see the frustration clearly stamped on Kate's face and knew that if something didn't happen, if the tide didn't swing quickly, she'd sink into her sorrows and drown. I turned to look at Rory. "Have you seen Kate throw her changeup yet?"

"How would I know?"

I glanced at her mom, but she was nervously biting her nails, and I didn't want to bother her.

I searched my memory, trying to recall what the Farrington Falcon's varsity Coach, Mr. Cobb, would've said when he wanted Kate to slow down, take a deep breath, and throw her changeup. Try as I might, I couldn't recollect his exact words, but prompted to do something, I shouted, "Come on, Eight. Give her something she can hit!"

And that was when Kate turned and looked right at me. Her eyes were like a set of laser beams, boring into me, but outside of sharing that single glance, there wasn't much more to our interaction.

She popped the ball into her mitt, shuffled it around in her hand, and it was then that I knew she'd heard me and was following my lead. I was certain I hadn't gotten the phrasing right, but Kate understood what I thought she should do. And then, in one big sweeping beautiful motion, she sent a phenomenal changeup floating toward home plate. The batter whiffed so hard, she nearly spun in place, which made Syd laugh and shout, "Wicked!"

I saw a small smile gracing Kate's lips when she turned back toward the mound, but she didn't look in my direction again. Just firing that one pitch and having it land exactly the way she wanted was what she'd needed to do. She wasted no time before rocking back and firing a rise ball. It too was just out of the batter's reach, but the girl swung at it anyway.

"Strike two!" The ump called.

"Come on, Katie!" Mrs. Kellner yelled, pounding the palm of her hand against the yellow part of the fence. "One more pitch. One more!"

I closed my eyes and whispered a silent prayer that Kate would know what to do and finish the job right here and now, but when I opened my eyes, it was because Rory and Mrs. Kellner had let out a collective groan. I'd missed the windup and delivery, but I didn't fail to see what happened next. The girl at the plate, after spectacularly whiffing at those first two pitches, had hardened her resolve, and aimed for the fences. The ball flew over the heads of the infielders, soared beyond the outfielders, and didn't touch the ground until it was safely on the other side of the scoreboard.

"Home run!" the coach for the Sparks roared triumphantly, pumping her fists in the air. I wanted to plug my ears, so I couldn't hear any more of their celebratory chatter. But more than that, I wanted to pull Kate right off the mound, hug her close, and tell her that everything would be all right. I truly felt her pain.

Chapter 21

Kate

That was it. That was my first dinger.

Never in all the years I'd been pitching had anyone ever hit a homerun off me before. And the feeling was surreal.

My fingertips tingled and my legs ached to run, to chase down the ball, and collect it, but there was nothing I could do. There was no prayer to be uttered and no hope of one of my teammates making a phenomenal play by leaping into the air, snagging the ball, and towing it back over the fence line. That ball was just gone. And all I could do was watch...and, of course, try to keep myself from breaking down and crying hysterically.

With that home run, the Sparks surged into a commanding lead, making the score 7-4 and putting us at a very clear disadvantage.

Is Coach gonna bench me now?

Abs held up a new game ball, waving it a little to get my attention. I caught it easily, but then turned to look at Coach Davis, wondering what was coming next.

That'd be two firsts for the day.

Giving up the home run was awful enough, but I'd never been pulled out of a game before. Not that I would blame Coach Davis for doing as much, but it stung to think that the possibility was hanging out there.

We've got plenty of other pitchers. Becky hasn't even thrown at all today. She could take my place, be on the mound, and ready to strike out the next batter in no time.

But Coach Davis didn't move from her position near the dugout. She didn't even give me the nod or make eye contact. So, I pounded the ball into my glove and retreated to my pitcher's circle.

All right...what are we looking at here?

I'd lost track of which of the Sparks was up to bat next, but with the bases cleared, I figured it was sort of like starting all over again with a clean slate.

That's the correct way to look at the bright side of things, right?

Shaking off all my negativity, I stared at Abs.

Just let her call the shots. Whatever Abs dictates, do it.

And for once, it was that easy.

I never could completely turn off my inner monologue, but during the next few pitches and plays, I behaved like a machine, going through the motions, doing what I needed to do to succeed. Abs started by calling for a drop curve. So, I dug deep and fired mightily. The batter missed so completely that Abs went with the same call on the next two pitches. I didn't shake her off either time, which proved to be the best thing for everyone, except the batter, because number fourteen swung her bat like it was made of lead, but failed to make a connection, notching me my first strikeout in summer ball. The Trailblazer fans went wild, and Syd snickered before mouthing the word, "Filthy."

A tiny bit of relief poured into me, filling the empty cavities that had been ripped open and broadened by self-doubt, but I knew better than to get ahead of myself. This inning was far from over.

"One down!" I shouted, holding up my index finger and flexing it.

When the fourth batter in the lineup strode to the plate, I took a deep breath and once again relied on my drop curve to carry me. Thankfully, when the girl got the bat on the ball, she whacked a grounder right to Syd, which was dealt with quickly and efficiently.

"Thank you," I whispered, tipping my imaginary cap to my friend while she mock bowed in return.

With two batters down, number five in the lineup ground her heel into the backside of the batter's box, smearing the line of chalk. She was a skinny girl, with biceps so small I wondered if I could wrap my fingers around them. But I knew not to discount her abilities. I'd watched her smash a double earlier in the game off Lacy and I knew that even though she looked small, she was mighty.

I fired a four-seam fastball, because that's what Abs requested, but that didn't work out so well. The scrawny girl slammed her bat into the ball, sending it toward center field. It bounced right up to Lena, our center field, and she threw the ball in quickly to Syd, managing to hold the runner on first and just give up the single. I shot a look of despair at Syd, but she was too busy dancing on the balls of her feet, keeping one eye on this new runner, and the other on the player who was marching to the batter's box. I swerved my focus back to the task at hand and as soon as Abs called for a changeup to start things off, I gave it to her.

That old, faithful pitch worked like a charm, and it was then that I knew this was going to be my final out of the game. I followed Abs' orders to the letter, delivering a perfectly placed screwball right underneath the batter's hands, then dropping a curve across the outside part of the plate, painting it ever so delicately. And that was the third out. I'd struck out two, but that didn't matter in the grand scheme of things. As I hustled into the dugout with my teammates, Coach Davis tapped me on the shoulder and said, "Take a break now, Kellner. We'll let Becky go in for the seventh."

I was devastated and it took a tremendous amount of fortitude not to let my intense feelings of failure show on my face. "Sure thing, Coach," I chirped, but I was pretty sure the phony voice I'd just conjured wasn't fooling anybody. I slipped into my well-worn spot on the bench and stared at the softball diamond, wishing I was any place but here right now.

Chapter 22

Grady

It was difficult to know what to say to Kate. I rehearsed a few lines in my head throughout the seventh inning, but they didn't amount to much. I knew that she would need comforting, but part of me also wondered if she'd send me away, like she did before, and claim she needed to be alone.

Once the game had concluded and the Trailblazers packed up their gear, Abs and Syd joined us on the fence line. "That was a nice hit you had there in the top of the seventh," Rory complimented Abs and she beamed at him.

"I'm just glad I got the bat on the ball. I'm sure you probably couldn't pick up on it from over here, but that pitcher really had the ball moving tonight."

"Eh," Rory said, nodding at Syd. "You'll get 'em next time."

"I'm hoping there isn't a next time," Syd grumbled. "Unless we see the Sparks during the tourney, we probably won't have to face them again."

"Maybe that'd be best," Kate said, joining the group. Her face was stiff, her lips held in a rigid line. Even when I smiled at her, there was no change in her demeanor.

Mrs. Kellner surged forward then. "Not to worry, Katie. They were a tough team and..."

"Every team in this league is tough," she said quietly.

"How about we head home, and I fire up the grill?" Mr. Kellner offered. "Anybody hungry?"

I knew my brother was itching to accept the invitation and I figured Abs and Syd were probably starving too, but all eyes went to Kate because no one wanted to force their company on her, especially after the sort of game she'd just endured. "Actually," she said, taking a deep breath, "I was hoping I could go for a drive with Grady for a while." She blinked at her parents. "Is that okay?"

"Sure, Katie," her mom said, smiling gently at me. "Take your time. But let Dad and me know if the two of you go out to eat so we don't wait dinner on you all night."

"Okay." Kate leaned forward and hugged her mom quickly, but then she turned her wide eyes on me. "You ready to go?"

Rory shot a quick look in my direction, but before I could do much, he wrapped one arm around Abs' shoulder and the other around Syd's waist. "Let's get out of here, ladies," he suggested.

"Where are we going?" Abs asked.

"I don't know," Rory replied, smiling impishly. "Wherever Syd drives us, I guess."

With my brother and Kate's friends and family members dispatched, all that was left to do was for me to take Kate's right hand, squeeze her fingers, and lead her toward my truck.

I knew better than to ask a bunch of questions or try to whisper any of the soothing platitudes I'd been practicing, so I just stayed quiet, giving Kate the space that she needed. It was tough letting this kind of silence grow, but as soon as she climbed into the cab of my truck and I joined her, she let out a tremendous sigh. From the moment I'd first met Kate, I knew that she was an intense girl, maybe a little more serious than anyone our age had a right to be, but this new, brooding version of her was a little unsettling.

So, I was glad when I started the truck and she said, "Tell me something, Grady."

"Shoot," I prompted. "Whatcha wanna know?"

"No," she sighed. "Tell me something. *Anything*. Talk about your day. Recite a bunch of facts about creepy, crawly bugs. I don't care what you say, just talk to me."

"So..." I said slowly, "is this your way of saying you don't wanna talk about the game?"

She inhaled deeply in through her nose and out through her mouth. I wanted to accommodate her request and it was kind of nice to think that she wanted to discuss something other than softball, but I needed to make sure she was okay with sidestepping this subject altogether. "No softball. No game. Nothing that has to do with hitting a home run, either."

I pulled my truck out of the parking space slowly so I could look left and right carefully, then I steered us out of the park and headed toward the reservoir. "I'm not sure if you want to hear about what I did at work today."

"Yes," she pleaded. "I need to know all about the car lot."

I took my right hand off the wheel and patted her knee. "Okay, Kate. Let's talk about the auto mall." I was just about to replace my hand on the wheel when she clamped hers over top of it, holding it in place.

"Grady," she whispered, "I just want..."

"I know," I breathed. "I've got you, Special K."

From Kate's house, it didn't take very long to get to the Farrington reservoir, but the drive was a little further away coming from the park's softball diamond. I took the back roads, meandering slowly over the hilly curves, talking to Kate about the most mundane topics. But as we went along, her fingers relaxed on top of mine and her breathing synced into a much more normal rhythm.

By the time we got to the reservoir, the dairy stand hut was illuminated by bright, fluorescent lights and when I pulled into one of the empty parking spaces and shut off the engine, I saw that there was a whole gaggle of people lined up to get their tasty treats. "You want ice cream?" I offered. "With sprinkles?"

She'd shot me down the last time I'd made this suggestion, but today, Kate was nodding, letting go of my hand, and reaching for the door handle before I had the chance to ask her twice. I looped around the tail end of the truck and swung my arm around her shoulders, pulling her next to me. "So, what're you thinking, Special K? A scoop of vanilla with chocolate sprinkles?"

She shook her head. "I think I'll try something new."

"Really?"

We approached the ice cream stand, and she scanned the menu. "I'm thinking a hot fudge sundae with nuts sounds good. What about you?"

I was stunned that she'd changed her order, eschewing her beloved sprinkles altogether, but I tried not to let that show. "Whatever you want," I said. "I'll get the same thing you're having."

A few minutes later, after waiting in line and receiving our orders, I watched as Kate spooned ice cream into her mouth, then licked her lips. "That's delicious," she purred. Tempted, I leaned forward and kissed the side of her mouth, which made her laugh.

"What?" I asked, blinking at her innocently. "I wanted a taste, too."

"You have your own," she said, jabbing her spoon into the top of my sundae and scooping up a huge dollop of whipped cream.

"That's mine," I teased, leaning forward, and staring into her eyes. "I just might have to take it back from you."

"Oh, I'd love it if you tried," she whispered, and the inducement was just too much to ignore. I kissed Kate lovingly, or as much as I could while still holding onto my sundae cup. When we pulled apart, her eyes were shining, and there was a smudge of hot fudge on her lower lip. She beat me to it, by sucking that lip in and licking the smear. "Like I said," she whispered, "absolutely delicious."

It was hard to compare Kate's current behavior to the way she'd reacted after the Trailblazers last defeat. Before, she'd been a little surly and begged to be alone—only to go running around with Ty later. But tonight, when I'd been so sure that she'd push me away again, here she was, seemingly pulling me closer, allowing me to share these fun little moments with her. I wanted to make this last for an eternity, so I decided it was time to talk to her about something I'd been pondering for the last few days.

"You wanna sit over there?" I asked, pointing my spoon toward a picnic bench.

"Let's go back to your truck," she replied, lifting her free hand, and slapping at her knee cap. "The mosquitoes are eating me alive."

"They've got good taste, you know," I jested which made her laugh.

"Your jokes are still terrible, Grady," she said, smiling at me adoringly.

"Yeah, but you love that I try," I remarked.

"I really do," she whispered. We traipsed back to the truck and climbed inside, but because it was so hot outside, the windows fogged up immediately. "Uh-oh," she whispered. "We stay in here very long and all those people out there are going to think we're up to no good."

"We can get up to whatever you want later," I said, winking at her which caused a giggle to pop out of her thin, perfect lips. "But first, I've got something I want to ask."

"Okay," she said, swirling her spoon around her parfait cup, digging out another bite of hot fudge. "What's up?"

"Once a year, the Hughes family takes off during the summer to go on vacation. Depending on where we live, we try to head someplace we've never been before, but we're not much for hitting touristy spots. Mom likes to go hiking and Dad's all for taking a boat out and doing some fishing, so we usually end up holing up in a cabin somewhere for a week and just disconnecting from everything and everyone else."

"All right," Kate said slowly. "Is this your way of telling me that you and your family are about to disappear for a whole week?"

"I was hoping that you might wanna drop off the grid with us." I paused and waited for Kate to react, but she sat totally still and didn't say a word, so I continued. "My parents already rented our cabin this year. It's on Lake Erie, on the other side of the Pennsylvania and Ohio border. We leave the Saturday before the Fourth of July and if you want to come along, Mom and Dad already said you'd be more than welcome."

"I can't," Kate said, snapping out of her daze and answering immediately.

"Why not?" I countered, perturbed that she didn't give the notion much thought before turning negative on it.

"Plenty of reasons," she murmured, lowering her head, and rooting around in her sundae, scooting the vanilla ice cream to the side, and digging for fudge. "My parents probably won't love the idea of me shacking up with my boyfriend for a week."

"We won't be shacking up," I retorted. "You'll be going on vacation with me and my family. My folks will always be around and knowing my brothers, they'll make it their mission for the week to make sure we never get even a second alone with each other."

Kate frowned. "Well, even if we can get my parents on board, there's the issue with softball. I know the Trailblazers are in a big tournament over the Fourth. And because we'll have so many games, I'm likely to get some real playing time."

"I thought you didn't want to talk about softball for the rest of the night," I reminded her.

"I don't," she grumbled. "But I can't just make plans to go to the lake for a week with you without considering the commitment I've already made to the team."
"Why can't you take a break?" I jammed my ice cream sundae container into the cup holder between us, wanting to have my hands free so I could reach out and grab Kate's. I lowered my voice a little, making it softer, less pleading, and more soothing. "The team has got plenty of pitchers. Nobody will care if you take off a couple of days or even for a full week. They might even..."

But evidently, I'd just said entirely the wrong thing.

Kate tore her hands right out of my grasp and stared at me disbelievingly. "I don't care if the entire team is made up of pitchers and catchers. I want to be on the field. I wanna do a good job and be a true and contributing member of my team. Why can't you see that?"

It wasn't that I was shocked by her words or even by the strength of her argument, but it hurt that she was treating me this way—acting as if I couldn't possibly understand how much softball or being a good teammate meant to her. "I'm not asking you to quit the team, Kate," I said, scooting back in my seat, letting the space between us grow wider. "I only thought it might be nice if you took a couple of days off."

She snorted. "Even if I wanted to, my parents..."

"I'll talk to them," I promised, lightening up a little and trying not to be so defensive. "I'll explain the situation and tell them all about my family being there. We'll even set up something so my folks can meet yours. I swear, after all that, it really won't be a big deal..."

"But it *is* a big deal," Kate replied. "You're asking me to give up playing softball for a whole week. Do you know that I've never done that?"

I groaned. "Come on, Kate. That can't be true. There had to be a time in your life, before you started pitching, when you did something else other than fire a fastball at a catcher's mitt."

She shook her head, then whispered, "Take me home, Grady."

"But—"

"Take me home."

I could see that putting up an argument of any kind was futile. Kate had already made up her mind and nothing I could say was going to change a thing.

When we reached her house a few minutes later and I turned off the ignition, I swiveled in my seat to see that Kate was staring at me. She was caked with dirt and because of that, tear tracks were evident on her cheeks.

"Oh, Kate," I said, reaching for her. "I'm so sorry. I didn't mean to make you cry."

My fingertips had just brushed the sleeve of her jersey when she wriggled away from me. "I don't want you to hug me right now, Grady," she whimpered. "I know that if I do, you'll comfort me the same way you always do, then I'll give in and do whatever you want. But I can't let that happen this time. I can't just do whatever you want again."

I was stupefied. Dropping my hands, I gawped at her. "You never do whatever I want, Kate. You always make up your own mind and do what suits you best."

She shook her head. "This isn't working, Grady."

I scooted toward her once more, itching to reach for her hands, grab her shoulders...wanting to do something, but not sure if I ought to try and break through this invisible barrier that she was trying to construct between us. "If you won't let me comfort you, Kate, what do you want me to do?"

"I don't know," she whispered.

Chapter 23

Kate

It hurt to climb out of Grady's truck. Not because my muscles ached or were sore, but because the seriously dejected look on his face pierced me right to my very soul, making me feel like a horrible person. Plus, I knew that he wasn't done with our conversation yet. Unfortunately, my brain had stopped computing half of what he was saying, and I wasn't capable of continuing.

So, I closed the door gently, tossed a wave to him over my shoulder, then headed for the house.

"Katie!" Mom called when I pushed through the front door. "That you?"

"You ready for dinner, kid?" Dad added.

"I'm good," I replied, trying to keep my voice light and breezy. "Eat without me."

I heard some murmurs in response, but they were muffled because I swerved through the living room quickly, mounted the steps, and locked the bathroom door behind myself in a flash.

Phew...finally alone.

I luxuriated in the shower for much longer than I probably should have, but it felt good to let the warm water wash over my skin, clearing away not just the dust and muck, but also wiping away some of the cares that were bothering me.

After getting out of the bathroom and tiptoeing across the hall to my bedroom, I flopped on my bed, soaking in the stillness, satisfying my craving to be all by myself. But then, almost as suddenly as I'd needed to get out of Grady's truck and run inside so I could seek out just this sort of solitude, I was struck by a sickening bout of loneliness.

I shouldn't have left him like that.

The way he had just sat there, waiting for me to tell him what to do next, had only made things worse when we were trapped in the truck together. But now that I was alone, and missing him, I wished I could go back to that moment and just let him hold me. That would've made so many things better, rather than worse. And if I'd done as much, I wouldn't be alone right now.

Sometimes, I really am my own worst enemy.

I jettisoned my fluffy towel and fussed around in my pajama drawer for a few minutes before deciding against crawling in bed. I jerked open my t-shirt drawer and removed my favorite with the words *Softball is Life* stamped in enormous, black block letters, but for some reason, that didn't feel like the right shirt to wear tonight, so I tucked it back into place and grabbed a Farrington Falcons softball tee instead. After throwing on a pair of mesh shorts, I collected the latest novel I'd been reading and kept on the nightstand near my bed, then exited my room and headed for the lounge chair out back that I'd almost become accustomed to sharing with Grady. *Almost.*

I could call him. Or send a text. At the very least, I should be the one to reach out and tell him that I'm sorry.

But I hadn't brought my phone along with me and was feeling too lazy to lumber back inside after it. I slumped into the cushiony chair, propped myself up, and opened my book, but then recognized that it was much too dark to read out here.

Eh...I should've flipped on the exterior lights.

It felt like I just couldn't get anything right tonight. I dropped the book on the end table and stood, angling toward the sliding doors where the light switch was located and that's when the back doors creaked open, and Ty emerged.

"Hey," he said, nodding at me, before shutting the doors smoothly behind himself.

"Hey." I nodded, too. "What're you doing here?"

"Abs texted me right after the game ended. She told me everything, so as soon as I got off work, I decided to hightail it over here."

I hadn't noticed it at first glance, but now that he said something, Ty was wearing his Wax and Shine uniform—a pair of black cargo pants and a crimson polo shirt with the car wash's logo embroidered on the left side of his chest where there maybe should've been a pocket instead.

"It's nice of you to worry about me, but you really didn't need to rush over here," I said, snapping on the lights, then squinting because they blinded me.

"I knew you'd be upset," he continued, stepping closer to me.

"I'll still be disappointed tomorrow," I muttered, turning away from him, and heading back to my deserted lounge chair and neglected novel. "There was no need to make time for me tonight."

"But I want to be here, Kay-Kay," Ty said, slowly lowering himself into the chair next to mine. Even though his was a lounge chair too and I was sprawling all over the place in mine, he sat upright, stiffly, almost as if he were afraid of reclining and wrinkling his work shirt. "The game didn't go so well and…"

"I know all about the game," I interrupted, shooting him a silencing stare. "I don't need you to rehash it for me."

"Fine," he said, shifting in his seat, sitting up even further. "Then, if you don't want to talk about softball, what else is on your mind?" He jutted his chin at the book on the end table. "Is that worth reading?"

I laughed, despite my foul mood. "I don't think it's your taste, Ty."

"Oh?"

"It's a romance novel," I said in a silly, high-pitched, papery thin voice that was so unlike my usual alto one that he rolled his eyes in response.

"Grady's inspiring your reading list now too, I see," he muttered and for some reason, that comment just didn't sit well with me.

"Actually, I always read books like this one," I snapped, straightening up so that he and I were on the same level with each other. "I follow this author and read everything she writes. Grady has nothing to do with..."

"Hey," he barked, giving me his own version of the stink eye, "I'm sorry I mentioned Grady's name or attacked your choice of books." He narrowed his eyes. "But I can tell one of those things is a hot-button issue for you right now, so which is it?"

I sighed heavily, then slumped back in my chair. "We both know you don't want to hear me talk about Grady."

"I don't," he admitted. "But I promised I'd listen to you...no matter what you wanted to say, so let's hear it."

"Really?" I eyed him speculatively.

"Really."

I launched into my story at once, telling him all about Grady's invitation to go with him for the week to the cabin on Lake Erie. Ty nodded in the beginning, but by the time I got to the end, he was just staring at me, not reacting in any way at all. "And so," I tried to wrap it up quickly, "the truth is that I think I *do* want to go with Grady and his family, but I know I really can't walk away from my team, either. What if I go away for a week and Coach Davis decides to kick me off the Trailblazers?" I sucked in a deep breath. "Or, what if I go and when I come back, Coach penalizes me and doesn't allow me the chance to pitch anymore? I know my performance on the mound tonight was dreadful, and I'm already on shaky ground, but I don't think I'm cut out for spending the rest of the summer in left field, picking dandelions, and…"

"Kay-Kay," Ty said, leaning forward and placing his hand on my forearm, "you're spinning out of control." His voice was soft, and I got the impression that he was slightly exhausted. Whether that was from putting in a long day at work or trying to keep up with my maniacal raving, I couldn't be sure. "Can't you feel it when you spiral out like that?"

"I try to keep it all bottled up…right here," I said pulling my arm away from him and squeezing my midsection, "but that doesn't help much, either."

"Yeah, I guess it'd probably only make things worse if you tried to put a lid on your feelings."

"Worse?" I groaned. "I'm not sure how things could get much worse." I glanced at Ty, then ducked my head, feeling the weight of my shame. "You should've seen Grady's face tonight. I stomped on his feelings and then just walked away." My hands flew to cover my mouth as the next thought occurred to me, but I was powerless to stop it from popping out of my lips. "What if he thinks I broke up with him? What if…?"

"Stop," Ty said, reaching out to pull my hands away from my mouth. "I told you to slow down, but you sped right back up again. You've gotta quit doing that."

"Okay." I breathed deeply in and out. "I'll try."

We sat in silence for a long moment as I tried to collect myself, but then, before I could say anything else or apologize for going bananas, Ty said quietly, "You know what I think you should do, Kay-Kay?"

"What?" I snorted, not entirely sure I wanted to take his advice. It was no secret how Ty and Grady felt about each other, and I was willing to bet that Ty was going to tell me to just let this thing with Grady go. Call it quits now and move on.

But my best friend managed to astonish me. "You've gotta do what feels right."

"What feels right...?" I repeated slowly, stretching out each word.

He nodded. "If you want to go spend time with Grady, then what's what you ought to do. If heading to the lake with him for a week will make you happy, then you shouldn't miss out on taking that little vacation."

"But..." I faltered, barely able to find the right words. "You just...That's not at all what I thought you were going to say."

Ty laughed dryly. "I think I'm done trying to fight against your relationship with Grady. I know you well enough to understand that you've already made your mind up about him. And, just recently, I realized that Grady's pretty serious about you, too."

"What...how...?" I stumbled over my words, which made Ty grin.

"I'll never come right out and say that I like Grady's brother, Rory, but he's not half-bad."

"Rory? What does he have to do with any of this?"

"He and I work together—remember?" Ty tapped the side of his head. "Even when I don't want to be around him, the guy just pops up out of the blue, and no matter how I react, I can't ever get him to stop talking." He shook his head. "He kind of reminds me of an ornery little puppy, trotting right along behind me, yapping at my heels, telling me about how great Grady is and how I should be happy for you, my best friend, rather than trying to squash something that could be really...special."

"Special?" I echoed.

"Yeah," Ty snorted. "Those were Rory's words—not mine."

"So, you think I should...?"

"I think you should weigh your options carefully, Kay-Kay, but that's kind of the same advice I always give you. Wait and see how things go. Don't jump into anything too quickly. But also, this time around, consider all the possible outcomes. If you go away with Grady and his family that'll sort of cement things for the two of you—really establishing you as a couple. And if that's what you want, I won't try to stop you. But Kay-Kay, is that what you really want?"

I nodded, both to process everything he'd just said, but also because that was the way I was leaning—toward the affirmative. "I think that's exactly what I want, to really and truly be Grady's girlfriend. But Ty...stepping away from softball for a whole week...that's kind of scary. I don't know if I'm ready to face the repercussions that are sure to follow after I leave my team so I can go on a vacation."

Ty stood and stretched his arms high over his head. He yawned broadly. "I'm gonna leave it up to you from here, Kay-Kay. It seems to me that you're going to have to make some sacrifices, one way or six others. And I can't help ya with that. You need to decide on your own what you're willing to give up and how far you're willing to go."

Chapter 24

Friday, June 23rd

Grady

"Why are you slamming your dresser drawer around like that?"

I looked up to see Rory leaning against the frame of my bedroom door. He had one leg crossed laconically over the other, but there was a sharp, inquisitive look on his face, and evidently my behavior had bemused him.

"I'm not slamming anything," I grumbled. "I'm just trying to get changed quickly. I got out of work a little late and if I don't leave now, I'll never make it to Kate's game on time."

"Ah…the terrible, terrible Trailblazers…" Rory said, lifting a hand to his mouth to cover a theatrical yawn. "I can't believe you're giving up another Friday night to go to the park and watch one of their games."

I snorted contemptuously, then pulled a black t-shirt out of my drawer, and yanked it over my head. "And here I was going to ask if you wanted a ride to the field so you could cheer on Syd. Guess I won't bother."

Rory shrugged indifferently. "I was actually thinking of going to the game, but now, I think we ought to have a change of plans."

"What?" I said, rolling my wrist and checking my watch. "Rory, I've only got a few minutes to spare. If you want me to drop you somewhere, you'll have to just come out and tell me where you want to go because I can't miss the opening pitch."

"Why not?" Rory drawled. "It's not like Kate's going to be starting."

At that comment, I slammed my drawer shut for real and glared at him. "Are you trying to be a jerk?"

"Nope," he retorted. "I'm only stating the truth here." He rolled his shoulders. "It's not like Kate's having an all-star summer."

I stalked forward, getting very close to my brother, but he wasn't bothered at all by my proximity or the fact that I was almost a full five inches taller than him. Rory simply held his ground and looked up at me. "Why would you say that?"

"Only because I wanted to point out that she's kind of ruining your summer, too," Rory replied, as if I should've already known as much myself. "You're usually a happy-go-lucky guy, Grady. But right now...you're not exactly having the time of your life, are you?"

I scowled at him. "I hate working at the auto mall."

"Yeah," he snorted. "Summer jobs are the worst."

"And I don't particularly like going to Kate's games all the time, either."

"Bingo," Rory whispered. "There it is. Finally, you admit the truth."

I hung my head. "Am I the worst boyfriend in the world for saying something like that?"

"No." He huffed. "But by saying what you actually think for once, you do seem just a little less than perfect and slightly more human."

"What're you saying? I'm a robot?"

Rory laughed. "We both know that things aren't going well for Kate or the Trailblazers. I genuinely don't think it's her fault that the batters keep taking her for a ride. She seems good enough, but the hitters are talented too, so that's just the way the ball bounces. But the way she treats you after the games? Blowing so hot and cold, never really getting out of game mode...that's gotta be getting old by now."

"I..."

"Don't you just want to forget all about softball for one night?" Rory asked, pushing away from the door, swerving around me, and heading for the closet on the far side of my room. He dug around in the orderly closet, then emerged, carrying my soccer ball. "Come on, little bro. Let's go kick this thing around for a while. Get out some of your own pent-up energy."

"I don't..."

"You deserve to take a break too," he continued pestering. "Let's play some soccer. You can relax a little. And maybe, we can even talk about what's in store for you when you head off to Felding." He made his eyebrows dance up and down. "Things in high school, especially relationships, can get messy, but at college—everything's going to be different."

I was sorely tempted to take my brother up on his proposition. We hadn't kicked the ball around since graduation day and even though it bothered me to admit it, I didn't want to go spend my entire evening sitting on the bleachers at the softball fields. An acceptance was on the tip of my tongue, but I paused before really agreeing to anything.

"Let me just send Kate a text first," I said, palming my phone, pulling it out of my pocket and opening the screen using the facial recognition software. I envisioned how hurt she'd be when she read this message and learned that I wasn't coming to the game, so I tried to keep things short and sweet.

Going out with Rory. Talk to you later.

She didn't reply, probably because she was already stretching and warming up for the game, but I took that as a good sign. If she'd typed back something right away, she might've tried to persuade me to come over to the ball fields, and if she was asking me directly, I wasn't going to tell her no. But since I didn't get ahold of her, that sort of left me free to do my own thing.

"Is it just me or do you look relieved?" Rory joked, nodding at the hallway mirror as we passed by it and headed toward the front door. I didn't need to take a glimpse at my expression to know that I did feel a whole lot better now than I had a few moments ago.

"I *am* relieved," I confessed. "I love Kate, but this softball gig is starting to get exhausting."

"Just think," Rory snickered, "if you and Kate get married and she does end up becoming a softball coach, you've got to look forward to spending the rest of your life sitting on crappy bleachers and eating boiled hot dogs from concession stands."

I cringed. "No way. That'll never happen."

"Which part?" Rory challenged, but instead of answering his taunt, I stole the ball out of his hands and raced him to my truck.

Chapter 25

Kate

One more out. Just one more.

I hadn't felt this good in a long time. My pulse thrummed. My arm was loose and ready. The night air even felt extraordinarily good as it coasted across my face, tousling my ponytail which had come out of the topknot when I struck out the last batter.

Leave it. Don't think about the hair. Don't think about ending the game. Just take this one pitch at a time.

But one pitch was all I needed.

Abs called for a heater, a risky move, considering the girl at bat had already hit two foul balls. But she set up so far outside that if I hit her mark exactly, I'd be throwing an intentional ball, rather than a strike.

I sure hope she knows what she's doing.

Going with the flow, letting the wind carry me a little, I rocked back, then pushed off the rubber, grinding toward home plate as I made the extra effort to snap my follow through hard. The ball rocketed right toward Abs' glove and the batter in the box went for it. Even if she got a piece of it, the ball would fly foul, but she missed it by a million miles. I couldn't help it. I tipped my head back and crowed triumphantly.

Our first baseman tossed her mitt in the air, joining in the celebration and Abs stood right up and pointed her free hand at me. "Yes!" she shouted enthusiastically.

We ran off the field as an elated squad, just glad to finally get a solid win under our belts. The Trailblazers had won a couple of games this summer, but none had been a clear-cut victory like this one. And as for me, I was part of the group once more, stomping, chanting, and full-out experiencing that high a person can only get when they've done something well...really well.

Syd skidded into the dugout right behind me, slapping my backside with the flat of her glove. "Good game, Kate."

"You, too," I commented, grinning right back at her.

"For real," Abs joined us. She tossed her catcher's mask onto the bench, then whipped off her protective mask too to reveal just how much she was sweating. Large droplets of perspiration were rolling down her face and Bianca, our starting catcher, chucked a hand towel at Abs. "Thanks, girl," she said, patting her face. "That was some game."

"You said it." Coach Davis leaned against the fence, watching all of us go through our post-game rituals and put away our equipment. "What do you say you all meet me in right field, and we talk through it real quick?"

I tucked my glove in my bat bag, then trooped dutifully to the outfield with my teammates. It felt good, so good, to finally be on the winning side, and I was so overjoyed that I swung my arms around Syd and Abs' shoulders, pulling them close, and forcing us all to walk like a three-headed monster.

Syd giggled. "Get off me, Kellner."

"Not a chance," I returned, tightening my grip on her arm. "We're winners tonight and that means we've got to stick together."

"So, we break apart when we're losers?" Syd joked, but I was in too blissful a mood to respond to her weak attempt at being sarcastic.

It had been a glorious night, the best I'd had yet as a member of the Trailblazers. We'd just defeated the Oatsdale Otters and while their name didn't sound utterly intimidating, they were a formidable opponent. They'd knocked Lacy around so much during the first inning that Coach Davis had sent Hope out at the start of the second. But she didn't last long either. She did something to her arm that had her calling for relief and running to the dugout so she could immediately ice her rotator cuff. That left me and Becky to fill the pitching spot and for some reason, Coach gave me the nod. I'd taken over in the top of the third inning and because I'd done so well, she'd let me finish off the game. My performance hadn't been too shabby. I'd struck out two batters, didn't walk a single soul, and only allowed a couple of hits. The final score was Weatherfield Trailblazers six and the Oatsdale Otters four. We didn't win by an overwhelming margin, but by golly, we got that W.

Coach Davis talked for a few minutes about the excellent plays our fielders came up with, and she doted on Abs who had thrown out a runner when she tried to steal second. But then, she looked at me and said proudly, "Good job, Kellner. That's the kind of pitching I expected to see from you all along."

It was sort of a back-handed compliment, but I took it anyway. When she dismissed us, I was bouncing on the balls of my feet, feeling like I could go another couple of innings, sort of even longing for the days when I would throw a complete doubleheader for the Farrington Falcons. That was the kind of charge that was coursing through my veins. And that mad rush of endorphins was what made me think of Grady.

"Hey, Coach!" I said, jogging to catch up with her because she was already halfway back to the dugout.

"Yeah?" She scuffed her cleat against the side of the dugout wall, tapping off some of the dirt. "You need a bag of ice like Hope, Kellner?"

"No, thanks." I rejected the offer out of habit. "I was actually wondering if I could talk to you about the upcoming week of the Fourth of July."

"What can I do for ya?"

I paused, trying to think of the right way to formulate my question. I knew what I wanted, but I'd never tried to skip out on softball practices or games before, so I needed a second to get my words sorted. "I was wondering if it would be a problem if I missed the tournament over the Fourth. I've uh...I've got some vacation plans and..."

"No worries," Coach chimed in, cutting off my awkward delivery. "In this league, players have obligations all the time. Work, family, colleges, and school teams that need them. I fully understand that when I have you players here, it's because you're actively missing out on something else. So, if you need to take a week off, we'll be just fine without ya."

"Yeah?"

"I'm not saying we won't miss you, Kellner, but we'll make do until you rejoin us."

"Thanks, Coach." My smile spread so wide that I felt the corners of my mouth twinge.

I can't wait to tell Grady.

Things had been a little rocky between us for the past week or so, mostly because we hadn't really talked anymore about me going with him on his family's vacation. He'd just sort of let the topic drop and even though I knew I ought to say something, to try and smooth over the subject and somehow make things better, I didn't want to get into an argument, either. I wanted the time I spent with Grady to be as carefree as possible. And now that I had Coach's permission, all I needed to do was talk my parents into the plan, then I'd be off for a fun-filled week of water skiing, fly fishing, and tubing with Grady and the Hughes family.

My heart thumped erratically in my chest and by the time I gathered my equipment and raced out of the dugout, I was sure I'd burst with happiness before I could get to him. But

when I reached the fence line where Mom and Dad were waiting, Grady was nowhere to be found.

Where is he?

I looked around quickly, but then, as I was searching for him,
Mom said softly, "He isn't here."

"What?" I turned back to her. "You mean Grady didn't show up
after he got off work?" I hadn't noticed one way or the other,
because I'd been so on point during tonight's game that I didn't
even consider looking toward the sidelines. But now, watching
my mom nod solemnly, I suddenly felt worried. "I wonder what
could've happened to him."

"Where are my favorite brothers?" Syd asked, joining me
and my parents.

"We're just wondering about that ourselves," Mom whispered, nodding at me pensively. "I hope Grady's doing okay."

"I'm sure he's fine," Syd said, flopping her ball bag on the
ground and digging around in the side pocket for her phone.
"Maybe Rory sent a text or something."

I dropped my bag too and started rummaging around, taking
my cues from Syd.

"Got nothing here," she reported, scrolling her slim finger
over her screen, and shrugging casually.

When I pulled my phone out, I saw the red message button
and knew that it was lit up because Grady had tried to contact
me. But when I opened the message, it was bizarre. Maybe I
should've read it aloud, but I was so stunned by the brevity and
the content, that I didn't dare.

Unfortunately, Syd sidled behind me and read over my
shoulder. "*Hanging with Tory. Talk to you later.*" She paused
and snorted. "Who's Tory?"

She'd taken the words right out of my mouth. "I don't know."

Mom inhaled deeply, but then she said quietly, "Why don't
your dad and I leave you girls to it? Do you want to get a ride
home with Syd, Katie, or should we...?"

"Go ahead and go," I said, not looking away from the text to answer her, but appreciating that she was obviously quite intentionally making herself scarce so Syd and I could discuss Grady's text. "I'll probably be home before long."

"If you're gonna be late..." Dad started, but then his words trailed off as Mom tugged on his hand and pulled him away.

Syd gripped my left arm. "Kate. Whatever's going through your mind right now, don't let it get any further. Hit the pause button. Take a deep breath. Maybe even read through some of the last texts Grady sent you before this one."

I did as she instructed because it seemed sensible, but there wasn't much there to calm my racing heart. "Who's Tory?" I whispered and Syd tightened her grip on my arm.

"Is there a lady at the auto mall named Tory?" she asked.

"Nope," I snapped, closing the text message chain, and looking at her.

"What about one of the Hughes' neighbors? Is there maybe an old lady who lives next door that..."

"They live on the Air Force base," I reminded her. "There aren't likely to be many old ladies hanging around there."

"What about...?"

"Syd," I interrupted. "I appreciate what you're trying to do here, but you can stop now. I don't know anyone named Tory and I have no idea why Grady's hanging out with her tonight instead of coming to our game. But..."

"But what?" Syd pressed.

"What really bugs me is how he dropped her name so nonchalantly into the text, like I'm supposed to know who this mysterious girl is and not be bothered at all by his mentioning her."

"Do you think..." Syd began, then stopped, and bit her lip.

"Out with it," I ordered. "You never keep any of your thoughts to yourself, so don't go holding back on me now."

"I'm only guessing here, Kate, and don't bite my head off for making this suggestion, but maybe, before you tie yourself in knots trying to figure out everything about this enigmatic Tory, maybe you ought to just text Grady and ask him straight up."

"Good idea."

Quickly, I thumbed open the message box, then typed the question: *Who's Tory?*

Chapter 26

Grady

"Who's Tory?" I laughed aloud when I saw the message from Kate.

"What's so funny?" Rory asked. We were climbing into my truck, and he was in the process of tossing the soccer ball into the backseat of the cab, so he hadn't seen me check my phone.

"Either my lazy fingers or my phone must've autocorrected your name. Instead of typing Rory, it went with Tory, and now Kate wants to know who you are."

Rory rolled his eyes. "You know, phones are supposed to make our lives easier, not more complicated."

"It's no big deal," I said, while typing a quick reply to Kate, clearing up the discrepancy easily enough. A split second after my message was delivered there was a response from her.

"What's she saying?" he asked, leaning over, and trying to read my phone screen. "Does she have Syd there with her? If she does, tell her I said hi."

"Back off." I brushed him aside and read through her message quickly. "She said she's got good news, and she wants me to come over, if I've got the time."

"See?" Rory teased. "You gave your girl a little space and now she's begging you to come over. Am I a genius or what? Go on. Tell me how smart I am."

"You're a real brainiac," I muttered because I was already typing back to Kate, letting her know I'd be there just as fast as I could. When I dropped the phone into my cup holder in the console, I turned and looked seriously at my big bro. "But sincerely, I wanted to thank you. It was good to get out and kick the ball around and even if I didn't get in the truck to find this message from Kate, I think I'd still be feeling better now than I did a few hours ago."

"I'm glad to see your real smile back on your face," Rory said, punching my shoulder. "Now, let's get moving. We don't want to make Kate wait for you."

"Yeah, we sure don't."

It took less time than normal to drop off my brother and turn the truck around so I could zip back to the Kellners. Or maybe it just felt that way because I was going there beaming brightly, ready to see Kate and hear all about this good news.

I'd no sooner pulled my truck into her driveway when Kate darted out of the house. I had to force myself to park and shut off the engine before climbing out and capturing her in my arms. But when I did step from my truck, Kate was on me, hugging me close and kissing my neck.

"What's all this?" I asked, partially stoked, but also slightly curious.

"Today's been the best," she said right before launching into a full-scale recap of all that had happened during the Trailblazers game. Then, she followed that up by adding, "And... I got permission—on all fronts—to head to the lake with you and your family."

"You...what?"

She nodded excitedly. "I talked to Coach Davis, and she gave me the all-clear. Then, when I got home from the field, I spoke with Mom and Dad. They said so long as your folks were around, they trusted us and didn't mind if we went on vacation together."

"Kate," I whispered, burying my head in her freshly washed hair, inhaling her shampoo and conditioner. "This is the best news I've heard all summer."

I picked her up, swung her around, and she laughed loudly. The sound was so light-hearted and just hearing it coming from her lips made my heart surge with joy. When we stopped spinning, I pressed my lips to hers, but before I could take things much further, there was the sound of someone clearing their throat.

If that's Ty interrupting us again, I swear I'll...

But I didn't even finish that thought internally because I was too pleased by Kate's news to care much about Ty or any of the shenanigans designed to keep us apart.

We've got a whole week together. And Ty won't be following us to the lake.

Sure enough, when I turned, Masterson was standing there.

"I heard about your outing tonight, Kay-Kay," he said taking a step forward, coming way too close to the pair of us. Instinctively, I held Kate closer, and pulled her a step backward right along with me. But Ty didn't seem to notice our incremental movements. "Abs said you were amazing. So, I had to come right over here and congratulate you."

"Thanks," Kate said, grinning from ear-to-ear. "It was a good night. A really good night." She cast a sidelong look at me, and I beamed back at her, but then Ty opened his arms and beckoned her to him so he could give her a hug. She giggled, let go of me, and stepped forward into his embrace.

I know I shouldn't have been perturbed in the slightest and maybe I wouldn't have been if Ty had kept the hug perfunctory and let her go almost immediately. But he didn't. He squeezed her tight, wrapping his arms around her possessively, and they stood there for so long that I was able to pick up on the sound of a mosquito buzzing around my ears. I swatted at it, then glowered at Ty.

Here I'd been thinking that things with Kate were finally heading in the right direction, but Ty can't just leave anything alone. He constantly feels the need to butt in on us. What am I gonna do about this guy?

Chapter 27

Friday, June 30th
Kate

And now...it all comes down to this.

I was on the mound, working my way through inning seven of the third game the Trailblazers had played this week. We usually had two practices and two games, but Coach Davis had found another squad, the Mid-Ohio Monsters, who wanted to pick up an extra game before heading into the big tournament next week. And Coach Davis had been only too happy to sign us up for the battle. The Trailblazers had endured a rocky start to our summer season. Our record was now 6-6 but if we won tonight, like I hoped, we could all prance out of here with an overall winning record.

But I can't get too far ahead of myself yet.

Becky had pitched the first three innings. Hope only threw a little during the fourth, because her arm was still on the mend. And Lacy handled the fifth and sixth. So now, at the bottom of the seventh, I was on the mound, acting as the closer—which was a position in which I never envisioned myself playing. This was nothing at all like being in left field, where I had zero ex-perience. This was my pitching circle. It was me gripping that big, bright yellow ball, wrapping my fingers around the seams, and pressing down hard. But somehow, this new situation was entirely different. If I did everything right, I only had to face three batters and that meant I could throw all out—not hold anything back for later. I could let my arm fly and test just how fast my heater could really move.

Abs had caught a few innings for Hope and Lacy earlier in the game, so Bianca was back behind the plate, which added another new aspect to my situation. But Bianca was good at what she did, and she expected me to be on the ball, too.

"Let's do this," I whispered, before rocking back, taking aim, and firing at the mitt she was holding out right over the center of the plate. It was terrifying, in a thrilling way, to send a fastball directly down the middle, serving it up, just in case the batter, number sixteen, wanted to tee off. But luckily, she swung and missed hugely.

Just that one little bit of encouragement, having my fastball sneak right by a batter, was all I needed. I only had to throw five more pitches. I struck out number sixteen. Then, when the subsequent girls took their spots in the batter's box, they both swung at the first pitches. One popped up to right field and the other hit a lightning quick line drive toward third base, but our third baseman, Brandy, caught it, then looked around as if to say, "That's all you got?"

The Trailblazers cheered. We ran toward the dugout whooping and hollering and congratulatory notes of triumph rang out jubilantly. It was good to be part of a winning team.

"Nice last inning out there, Kellner," Lacy said, pulling the elastic band out of her hair and letting her platinum blond locks fall messily around her face. She ruffled her hand through the ends that fell just beyond her shoulder blades. "I was sure we were going to pull this one out, but it was good to see you make it look so easy."

"Thanks." I stuffed my glove into my bat bag, then, on a whim, I yanked my hair out of its topknot as well. I rarely wore my hair down, even when I was at home, relaxing. I almost always pulled the strands away from my face and eyes, securing the loose ends into a low ponytail when I just wanted to go easy on my tresses. But Lacy looked so comfortable and kind of pretty with her hair framing her face that I was compelled to copy her.

"So, what's your story?" Lacy asked, pulling a small pot of lip gloss out of her bat bag, and slicking some on her lips with the tip of her ring finger. "How'd you get on this team when you're so young? Or are you older than you look?" She turned and sized me up. "I've been guessing all along that you were still in high school, but you showed real skills tonight, so maybe I've got you pegged wrong."

I tossed my bat bag over my shoulder, remembering to flip my hair out of the way first so it didn't get caught underneath the wide shoulder strap. "I joined the team because of Abs and Syd." I cocked my head to the side, indicating where the two of them were, on the other end of the bench, talking animatedly. "We're all going to be seniors this year at Farrington High."

Lacy's eyebrows inched upward a little. "Any of you planning to play ball when you go to college?"

"I am," I chirped, not wanting to sound too overzealous, but also still feeling so elated from our victory that I couldn't keep the enthusiastic notes out of my voice.

"Yeah?" she returned. "You been offered a spot somewhere?"

Not even this sore subject could bring me down, so I plowed right ahead with my response. "Not yet, but I'm trying not to get discouraged."

"Don't be," she said smoothly. "People like to say if you're not snapped up before the end of your junior year, then you're not getting any scholarship money, but that's ridiculous. I wasn't recruited to play for Felding until the coach saw me throw during a fall ball doubleheader during my senior year." She popped a piece of fruit punch flavored chewing gum in her mouth, then offered me some, too. I shook her off. "All I'm saying, Kellner, is that accidents happen. I'd talked to the Felding coach during my junior year, but she'd said outright that she didn't need me. She already had a full pitching staff. Then, her star got hurt playing summer ball and..." She let her words peter out, as if the rest was history and didn't bear repeating.

"So, you're saying..." I prompted.

She nodded toward the exit of the dugout, and I went right along with her, walking side-by-side. "You're good. I think your junk pitches are almost untouchable when you've got them working the right way. So, just don't give up on playing ball in college yet. Things happen. And you could still get the offer you want."

"Thanks, Lacy." I hadn't expected this conversation—not at all. Lacy had been nice enough throughout this first month of our acquaintance, but we were just teammates, not bosom buddies. We got along and cheered for one another, but there hadn't been much more going on there. But now, I felt like she was reaching out, really trying to be my mentor or something like it, and that made me feel pretty awesome because hey, she was Lacy Rider—a living legend in the area softball leagues. "So, what do you think of Felding?" I asked as we rounded the backstop and headed toward the spot where my parents and Grady were standing.

"It's the best." A small, pleased smile crept onto her face. "You thinking of applying there?"

I nodded at Grady, who was grinning languidly at us. He was leaning against the fence and as we approached, he leisurely tossed his head to the side, flicking some of his silky hair out of his eyes. My heart skipped a beat because I was so happy to see him. "My boyfriend is heading to Felding in a couple of weeks. You mind if I introduce you?"

"Not at all." Lacy strode forward confidently, eyeing Grady, and my heart swelled with pride. She was full-on checking out my boyfriend, but I didn't really mind. He was devastatingly handsome and carried himself with such grace and ease that most people gave him at least a second glance just to make sure he was real rather than some kind of perfect statue. "Hey," she said, holding out her hand for him to shake. "I'm Lacy." "Grady," he said, accepting her hand and pumping it kindly. "It's nice to meet you." He nodded toward the field which was now empty. "You threw a couple of good innings tonight. Your rise ball was really working." He let go of her hand and hooked his thumbs together, making his fingers look like a bird's wings. "You had them chasing the ball right out of the strike zone."

Lacy arched an eyebrow at me. "He knows his pitches." She turned her inquisitive eyes back on him. "Did you play ball in high school?"

"I spent a little time behind the plate," he replied, but then he winked at me. "But I learned everything I know about soft-ball from hanging out with Special K."

She snickered. "Special K. Cute."

"Anyway," I said, feeling a blush of embarrassment start to creep up my neckline. "I'm not sure if I told you before, Grady, but Lacy's going to be a junior at Felding. I thought since you were going there too, it'd be nice for the two of you to meet." I shrugged. "I know it's a big campus, but it never hurts to recognize one friendly face."

"When're you heading to school?" Lacy asked, tossing her hair over her shoulder, and fixing her eyes on Grady.

"August twenty-second," he replied. "I took the last couple of orientation days that were available, and I guess I'll just stick around after that and wait for classes to start."

"Good plan," she said approvingly. "It's tough to spend a couple of days there, then have to come home again in the middle of the summer." She sighed, smacking her gum a little as she did so. "I made that mistake when I was a freshman. I took the earliest possible orientation grouping because I needed to be on campus over the Fourth, but then, after those couple of days were over, I had to go home again for a few weeks, and that just didn't feel right. It was like once I was on campus, I didn't want to leave again. Ya know?"

I shook my head, because I simply couldn't relate, and Grady shrugged. "I guess I'll find out what it's like soon enough," he said, giving her his dazzling smile. I wanted to reach up and caress his cheeks to feel those little dimples, but I refrained because I didn't want to mortify either of us.

"It's too bad you're not going to the orientation next week," Lacy continued, shifting her bat bag from one shoulder to the other. "I'm heading up to Felding myself because Coach likes to get all her players together at regular intervals. Some girls don't play ball in the summer because they've got steady jobs, and she says it's important for us to keep in shape."

"You're going to Felding next week?" I knew that she had been directing her comments at Grady, but I couldn't help chiming in.

"Sure." She shrugged. "When Coach calls, we all go running."

"But I'm heading out of town too."

"That's odd," Lacy said slowly. "I was pretty sure you were the only one of us hanging around over the Fourth."

"Wait...what?"

She fiddled with the zipper on her bat bag. "I've got to go to Felding. Hope is going to see a doctor, because she needs to get things with her rotator cuff figured out before she heads back to school this fall. And Becky's got some thing with her sorority sisters." She paused. "Didn't Coach Davis tell you that you were going to be the only pitcher on staff all next week?"

My mouth went dry. It was as if I'd emptied my water bottle before the end of the game and desperately needed a refill, but the water cooler had been kicked too. My tongue felt leaden, and the insides of my mouth tasted of dirt. "What's that now?" I eeked out.

"Eh," Lacy waved her hand flippantly. "Coach must've for-gotten to give you notice, but it's no big deal. Right, Kellner?

I'm sure you can handle it." She slugged me on the arm. "I read all about you in the papers, after our last win. The reporter called you a workhorse. Said you were used to leading your team to one victory after another."

"Whichever sports reporter wrote that was being charitable," I muttered.

Lacy snorted. "Maybe, but it sure sounded nice." She nodded at Grady. "Well, I've gotta get out of here. It was nice to meet you. And if you see me around campus some time, don't be shy about saying hello."

"All right." Grady raised his hand and gave her a goofy wave, which brought a pretty smile to her face. I was still slightly stunned from the news about having to do all the pitching next week, but I didn't miss the way Lacy gave Grady one last long look before turning away from us. "She was nice," he said, once she had sashayed far enough from us that she might not be able to overhear his comment. "Thanks for bringing her over here." When I didn't say anything right away, Grady reached out and took hold of my hand. He gave my fingertips a gentle squeeze. "What's wrong?"

"I don't think I can go to the lake with you," I whispered, looking up into his eyes, and seeing a hint of confusion there.

"Why not?"

Chapter 28

Grady

It was obvious why Kate thought she couldn't go to the lake. I'd heard every word Lacy had said. I knew the others were taking off and leaving Kate to fend for herself next week, but it irritated me that the others got to make plans, while Kate was left to cancel hers.

"Grady," Kate groaned. "You know why."

"Yeah," I said slowly. "I know what Lacy just said, but your coach gave you permission to go. She told you things like this come up all the time and that it wasn't a problem for you to take a week off." I paused and let my words sink in. "At least, that's what you told me she said."

"That *is* what she said." There was a little bit of a whine leaking into Kate's voice and it felt odd to hear that pleading note there. She didn't usually have to beg for anything. She just worked hard and got what was coming to her, mostly. But now, I felt like she'd been crushed between a rock and a hard place, and instead of trying to fight her way out, she was looking to take the easy way. "But..."

"But what?" I pressed. "Why can't one of the other girls back out on their plans? Why do you have to be the one to drop everything?"

"'Cause I'm only going on vacation," she said, running her hands through her hair and tugging on the ends a little in frustration. "You heard Lacy. She's obligated to go back to Felding. And Hope has to take care of her arm and Becky..."

"Everyone's got their own good excuse," I interrupted. "And that's fine. But you asked the coach expressly if you could do this and she said you could. That means one of the other pitchers probably didn't talk over their plans with her. And they're just thinking of taking off. Let them deal with the consequences of not thinking through their actions completely."

Kate clenched her lips together so tightly that I could hear her grinding her back teeth. "I'm not sure that you understand what's going on here, Grady. I..."

"No," I barked. "I don't think you understand, Kate. I asked you to go away with me because I wanted to spend time with you...you, Kate. We never get to be alone—just the two of us— and that was all I wanted." She opened her mouth to say something, but I kept talking. "Yeah, yeah, I know my family'll be there, but even with them around there'll be far less people bothering us than we see when we're here in Farrington." I inhaled deeply. "There's always someone else around and this was going to be our one true chance to have quality time with each other before I left for college in August."

I usually didn't go on and on like that, and I knew, just as soon as those last words came out of my mouth, that I had misworded some part of my statement because Kate's eyes went wide and her lips parted, but she spoke no words.

"I... I mean..." I tried to backtrack quickly, to reverse whatever damage I had just done, but I wasn't sure what I'd said to tick her off and then it occurred to me.

She thinks I'm planning on leaving her.

"I...I'm not..." But I didn't even get a full sentence out before Kate cut me off.

"You *are* going to leave me, Grady," she said the words so tersely, I felt like they were sharp enough to cut glass. "Even if what you said right now was just a slip-up, you've probably been thinking about what's going to happen between us for a long time." She paused and stared at me, evidently waiting for me to intercede. "I know what's coming next is always on *my* mind. But what about you? What do you see happening to us, Grady?"

I shrugged helplessly. "I thought we already had this conversation. I want to stay together."

"But what does a relationship like that look like?" Kate asked, peering up at me with her wide and expectant blue eyes. "Will you come back to Farrington all the time? Am I going to have to drive to Felding? Are we maybe going to come up with some plan to constantly meet somewhere in the middle, just so we can go out to dinner occasionally?" She paused again and that's when I saw the tears welling in the corners of her eyes. "Isn't that a lot to ask...of both of us?"

"You're putting too much thought into this," I said, reaching out to cup her cheek. There was a thin layer of dirt there, but I didn't mind. I wanted to stop those tears from falling at all costs. "You're jumping ahead one, two, three steps too many. And you're trying to plan out a future that's..."

"Yes," she cried, jerking away from me. "Yes, Grady. I'm trying to make plans because that's what I do. I can't just plow into the future blindly, pretending like I'll be cool with whatever outcome drops in my lap. I like to know what to expect, so I can prepare for it."

"But, Kate," I argued, "you can't plan everything."

She stared at me. "I was hoping I didn't have to do it all by myself this time. I thought, if *you* had a plan...if you had thought about how we might make this work, then..."

"I'll think of something," I hurried to reassure her. "I'll..." It was difficult to come up with something on the fly, but I gave it my best shot. "We'll just...We can spend some time...talking over our plans and figuring things out once we're up at the lake. We can..."

She shook her head, then snorted, almost as if she were stifling a laugh. "You know, I can see what you're doing, Grady." "What...what am I doing?" She must've been mighty perceptive to make such a statement because I was floundering. I had absolutely no clue what I was doing.

"The reason you're so gung-ho on this whole heading to the lake idea is because you're already seeing this as our last hurrah. You want to spend one really great week with me, so that when you leave for college, we'll both have this happy memory of our relationship. And then, when you break things off with me, it won't hurt either of us so much."

"I...That's not what I was thinking of doing at all."

My words fell on deaf ears. No matter what I said or how I tried to refute her claims, Kate had already allowed this new idea to take root in her mind and she wasn't done evaluating it. "If you want to end things, Grady, it'd be best if we just did it now. I won't go to the lake with you only to come home and have you break my heart later. I won't..."

"Wait," I said holding up both hands. "Just a minute ago, you weren't going to the lake because you needed to stay here and be the only pitcher for the Trailblazers. But now, you're going to the lake...if I can promise we'll stay together afterwards? I...I'm not following you at all."

She threw her hands up in defeat, which was not the reaction I was hoping for at all. "I feel like you're just pretending to be baffled by all of this, Grady." She stared at me accusingly. "But you're the one who's really pulling all the strings here. It doesn't matter what I say or do, you're the one who wants to break up and..."

"You're putting words into my mouth," I interrupted. "I never said..." But then, a terrible thought occurred to me. "Kate, are you acting like this, starting this fight and saying all these things because *you* want to break up with me?"

Chapter 29

Saturday, July 1st
Kate

I cried all night long.

The conversation with Grady last night had ended tearfully —on both ends. I had never definitively answered his question because tears had slid down his face and I couldn't bring myself to say anything. Instead, I'd just wiped away my own tears, then stalked off. He'd chased after me because we were the only ones left at the ballpark and it was either I accept a ride from him or walk home in the dark, and I'd made the smart choice. But when I hopped into his truck, everything felt different. Neither of us had come right out and said that things were over, but it was certainly implied, and my only response to all that was to feel crushed. Devastated. When he pulled his truck into my driveway, I didn't linger or try to prolong the torturous moment. I just got out of there and ran for the safety of my house.

But now, lying in bed, watching the weak morning light filter through my gauzy, creamy white curtains, I felt an ache in my chest that hadn't been there before.

I turned my hands into talons and clawed at the thin cotton material of my sleep shirt, hoping that I could tear away the pain, but it was resilient and not going anywhere at all. Just then, my alarm buzzed. I'd set it when I'd woken up yesterday morning because then, Grady and I had still been happy together. I'd been planning on getting up early today, throwing my last-minute toiletry items in a bag, then having Mom or Dad drive me over to the base so I could head out on a week-long vacation with my adoring boyfriend and his family members. I'd been looking forward to piling up in the minivan with the Hughes brothers and cuddling close to Grady, feeling the comfort and warmth of our connection. But now...

I could still go. Everything that happened last night...we could talk through it. Just decide to forget what was said. We could make this work...

And maybe, if I had been someone else, someone more like Grady, I would've been able to foster that idea and bring it to fruition. But I was Kate—stuck in my ways—Kellner and I never forgot anything. I'd feared that Grady was arranging this whole trip so we could part on good terms and have one last memory to cherish as a couple. And I couldn't quite shake the feeling that despite what he'd said when I'd asked him if that was his plan, that I'd pegged things correctly. One way or the other, before he went to Felding, we were going to breakup.

So, it pained me to do it, but I reached for my phone, shut off the alarm, then sent Grady a quick text.

I'm not coming. Please apologize to your family for me.

A second later, Grady sent a thumbs up and that right there shattered my heart into a thousand pieces.

I regretted my decision at once.

Maybe if I text back and say I've changed my mind...

But that thumbs up felt so poignant...almost casual and carefree...exactly the sort of reaction I should've expected from Grady, and yet...it hurt to think that the Hughes family would be getting on the road and going without me. But I couldn't very well take back my text now. Grady had sent me a thumbs up after all, which meant he was cool with whatever I wanted to do. As always, he was letting me take control of what happened next.

Irritated, I dropped my phone back on my nightstand, then flung my covers off my legs so violently that they spilled onto the floor. I rolled out of bed, changed into a black t-shirt with the words *Throw Like a Girl* emblazoned near the center in electric yellow writing and a pair of capri-cut leggings, then stuffed my feet into my shoes, and tiptoed down the stairs. I tried to be especially quiet while passing my parents' bedroom. Even though one of them was supposed to take me to the base this morning, it was a force of habit to try and make as little noise as possible. But I wasn't at all surprised when I crept down the staircase to find my mom standing near the kitchen counter. She was dressed in a vibrant purple matching t-shirt and shorts set and her hair looked freshly washed, as if she'd just stepped out of the shower.

"Ready to go, Katie?" She looked at me skeptically over top the rim of her purple spectacles. "Where's your bag?"

"I'm not going on vacation, Mom," I murmured, trying to hold back the tears that were threatening to resurface. "I...I've got to stay around here next week...for the team and..."

"If you're not going to the lake, where are you heading this morning?" She nodded at my running shoes.

"I thought I'd go for a walk," I whispered.

"Not a run?" She stared at me, evidently waiting for an answer.

"I'm too tired," I admitted. The truth was that all the crying last night had zapped my energy. I wouldn't be able to put in any real miles today, but I needed to get out of the house and do something, so walking seemed like my only real option.

"Take your phone with you," Mom said, jutting her chin back toward the stairs. "If you walk too far and get stranded, give me a call and I'll come get you."

"Sure." I galloped back up the stairs, then was out the door a few minutes later. I hadn't taken ten steps away from my house when I heard footsteps behind me. "Mom," I said, before swinging around, "I'm fine, really. I just want to be alone right now and..." But I stopped talking when I saw Ty standing there.

He had on his running gear, a well-loved pair of white, red, and black sneakers, and a Farrington Falcons Cross Country tee. His red hair was a mess, twisting in every which direction, as if he'd just rolled out of bed, jammed his feet in his shoes, then sprinted outside so he could catch up with me. I waited for him to say something, maybe just something as simple as good morning, but he didn't utter a word. Instead, he fell into step right beside me, and we walked on. Ty didn't whisper a peep about going for a walk instead of a run and he didn't ask about the tears that I had to hastily brush away with the back of my hand.

We'd gone almost a full mile in nearly perfect silence when he said out of the blue, "I got you an early birthday present, Kay-Kay."

His words were so surprising that a laugh bubbled right out of my lips. "We both know my birthday isn't until January. So...you're about six...er...seven months too early."

"Doesn't matter," he replied. "I bought this gift for you. And I want you to have it." He snorted grumpily. "I almost thought I was going to have to give it to someone else, when you said you were going to the lake with Grady, but now..." His words fell away, and I was grateful for that because I didn't want to talk about Grady...especially not with Ty.

I turned to look at him squarely. "What kind of birthday present did you buy me that has to be used this week only? And why would you buy something for me, then even consider giving my gift away to someone else?" I elbowed him playfully in the ribs. "That doesn't seem very nice."

"Well, we don't have to worry anymore about what I *would've* done. The point's moot, 'cause you're hanging around and I can give it to you now."

I chuckled. "You know I don't like suspense and I'm not real big on surprises, either."

"Yeah..." he said slowly, drawing out the moment even longer.

"Aren't you going to tell me what you bought?"

"I'm getting to it," he murmured, smiling slowly, showing all his teeth, looking a little like a cartoon crocodile. "I was sort of hoping to keep it a surprise a little while longer but..."

"Ty," I demanded, "just tell me."

He laughed. "Next Saturday, July eighth, you, Miss Kate Kellner will have the best seat in the house to watch the Cleveland Guardians take on the Cincinnati Reds."

"What? No!" I punched his arm. "You got us tickets to a Guardians game?"

"You betcha, Kay-Kay. And we aren't sitting up in the nose-bleeds or out in the bleachers with the riffraff. I used all the tips I've made from the car wash this summer to get us prime seats, right behind home plate and...Kay-Kay...what's wrong?"

A sob escaped me. "Nothing," I moaned. "Everything."

"You...you don't want to go to the game with me?"

"No," I answered, feeling a terrible shudder wrack my whole body as the words bubbled over my lips. "I want to go, but I'm sad about Grady, too." I cried mournfully. "I know you don't like talking about him, and you probably really don't want me to mention him right now, but I'm just so...so sad that I won't get to see him all week." I brushed wretchedly at my tears, swiping them away only so a fresh batch could fall into place. "Ty... how can I be so happy about going to a ballgame with you, but also so upset about missing Grady? Is it really possible to feel so many contradictory things, so intensely, all at once?"

Ty shrugged. His expression had become closed off once more, almost like he was afraid of the weeping girl walking along beside him. "You're going to feel the way you feel, and because you're you, it's not possible to do anything halfway. If you're going to be blue, you'll be practically indigo. But...all we can hope is that the sadness will dissipate, and you'll eventually be able to move on."

"Move on," I squeaked. "But I..."

"Not today, Kay-Kay," he said hastily, nudging his shoulder against mine. "But soon...maybe?"

I looked up into his green eyes and saw that he was being sincere. He didn't know what to say or how to comfort me, but he was hoping that I'd figure it out and once again be myself, the girl who didn't break down crying and sniffling just because one thing didn't go the way I wanted.

"Thank you," I whispered.

"For getting the tickets?" he asked.

"Yeah," I breathed. "I'd really like to go to the game. But...I'm also glad that you still believe in me. You...you can see that I'm going to make it through this and..."

He scoffed. "You're Kate Kellner. You can make it through anything."

I knew I'd endured greater hardships than breaking up with my first real boyfriend, Grady Hughes, but right now, the pain was unbearable. All I wanted to do was keep walking and I was glad to have a friend like Ty by my side to keep me company.

Chapter 30

Saturday, July 8th

Ty

The game couldn't have gone better. Just as I'd planned, our seats were six rows behind home plate. We weren't just close to the players and all the action. We were right on top of it. Whether one of the batters hit a foul ball or a pitcher struck out the side, we were synced up with the professional athletes, living and breathing the same rarified air they were, feeling the thrill of victory when the Guardians won with a score of 5-3 after Franklin Gomez hit a home run in the bottom of the seventh, sealing the win for the home team.

When I pulled into Kay-Kay's driveway, after making the long drive back from the ballfield, it was late, but she was still bouncing in her seat, recapping every exciting moment of the game, squeezing that big red foam finger we'd been gifted as part of a promotional giveaway. "We're number one! We're number one!" she chanted as I shut off the engine.

"Tonight, the Guardians looked pretty good," I agreed. "But I think they're still a few games back from the Yankees."

She guffawed loudly. "Seems like we're always trailing the Yankees."

I shrugged. "They've got the money and the talent..."

"But we've got all the heart," Kate crowed, tipping her head back and letting her ponytail settle against the headrest.

"That's right," I murmured. "We keep the faith, even when it seems like we're down and out."

Kay-Kay took off the big foam finger and pressed it into her lap, then she swiveled in her seat to look squarely at me. "I've really got to thank you again, Ty. I needed this like…like you don't even know and tonight…this game…it was the best."

"Yeah?"

She beamed at me. "Best night of my life…for sure. I mean, have you ever sat that close to home plate before?"

I snickered. It was nice, not only to see my pal so enthused, but also to hear her say this was the best night of her life. She'd done some pretty phenomenal things over the years, but knowing that she liked being here with me…and she placed this experience above all others? Well, that was an even better compliment than what I'd been hoping for when I bought the tickets. "The only way we could've gotten closer was if we'd served as the batboys."

"Ahh…" she groaned. "We'll have to remember that and get jobs as batboys next summer."

"Deal," I agreed, not so much because I wanted to spend my summer running bats back and forth from a dugout to a major leaguer's hands, but because I wanted to continue making Kay-Kay smile.

We looked at each other for a long moment, and then she plunged back into a retelling of the way Franklin Gomez had hit that final home run. I watched her talk and gesticulate, acting out all the parts of both the hitter, Gomez, and the opposing pitcher who'd been stunned and dismayed when the ball went sailing into the right field bleachers. But Kay-Kay…She was on fire, getting into the story, reciting what happened for me, as if I hadn't been sitting right there next to her.

She's so beautiful…

I'd had this thought so many times over the last six months, but watching my best friend, seeing that look of pure joy on her face, it reminded me that for the first time in a very long time, she wasn't just my exquisite neighbor, attached to some other guy. She was my Kay-Kay, the girl who was sitting in my SUV, and, if I wanted to, I could be the one to kiss her goodnight.

That realization was slightly unnerving, not because I didn't want to kiss Kate, but because I knew that this week, outside of tonight, had been difficult for her. She'd been awfully fragile and even though she'd pulled it together during the Trailblazer games, eeking out a couple of wins in the tournament, she'd spent an inordinate amount of time thinking about *him*.

I had to stop myself from sneering when I thought of Grady Hughes. He'd gone and broken Kay-Kay's heart, then didn't even have the decency to reach out and checkup on her all week. I knew some guys, when they ended their relationships, just forgot all about their former girlfriends. But after spending the first half of the summer listening to Grady's big brother, Rory, extol his good qualities and swear that Grady was madly in love with Kate, I was sure that he'd at least text her or call and ask how she was dealing. But, at least as far as she'd told me, she hadn't heard from Grady even once all week long.

He's a real jerk.

I pictured that stupid smirk he always wore on his face, like he had a secret, and if you were lucky enough, he'd share it with you. And just thinking about him made my blood boil.

Nobody gets to hurt Kay-Kay the way he did.

I was nearly simmering with rage, but then, all my anger just seeped away when Kate laughed.

"What?" I asked, floating back to the here and now.

"You've got the strangest look on your face," she tittered. "What're you thinking?" I started to open my mouth and she interrupted. "Uh-uh...I caught you looking all wild-eyed. Don't try to come up with a quick lie. I want to know what was really on your mind."

She leaned closer to me, and it was then that I realized now was my shot. If I was ever going to kiss Kate Kellner, I had to do it now, while she was still bubbling with exuberance, and I was feeling primed and ready.

"Ty," Kay-Kay said softly, wriggling even nearer to me in her seat, "you may not understand this, but this night was exactly what I needed. Being at the ballpark...getting to share all that with you...it really was the best."

I noticed the way she didn't qualify things by calling me her best pal or saying it was good to get together with me, her best friend. Kate was just simply happy to be with me. Inspired by her words and feeling slightly intoxicated by the way she was gazing at me, I moved forward, fully intending to kiss her.

She lifted both of her hands, and I was sure she was going to wrap them around my neck and pull me close, but then a flood of lights illuminated the interior of my SUV and Kay-Kay inhaled sharply.

Chapter 31

Grady

What is Masterson up to now?

I paused at the stop sign near the intersection of Parkland Street and Sixth, but because the Kellner family's house was right on the corner, I could see Ty's green SUV parked in Kate's driveway.

For crying out loud, the guy lives right next door. Couldn't he have parked in his own driveway and left some space for the rest of us?

It had killed me that I didn't get to see Kate all week, and I hadn't been able to talk to her either. The cell phone reception at the lake house had been spotty, so my phone had sat on a nightstand, in the bedroom I shared with Graham all week long, just charging. But as soon as we'd gotten home and I'd helped unload everything, I'd hopped in my truck and driven over here quickly.

I really need to talk to Kate, but it looks like I'm going to have to contend with Ty hanging around once again.

A blip of annoyance simmered in my stomach, but I squashed it quickly.

I can't go into this conversation starting from a bad place. I'm here for Kate, not Ty, and I'll just have to grin and bear his presence.

I flicked the turn signal and as I started to pull into the driveway, a thought occurred to me.

What is Ty doing parked here? If they'd gone out for a run, they'd both be on foot. And if they'd just gone to a movie or out for pizza, he'd could've easily parked in his own driveway and let her walk across the lawn back to her own house. Ty would only park in front of Kate's house if he was dropping her off after going on a date and...

That's when my headlights flashed over the backside of his SUV and I saw very little, other than the silhouettes of two people who were dangerously close together.

What the...

I jammed my index finger into the dash, killing the engine, but then I was out of the truck in a flash.

Hit him. Knock out his two front teeth. He's crossed the line this time.

I took three big steps forward, moving toward the driver's side of Ty's SUV. My hands were already balled into fists, and I was itching to slug the guy, knocking him from here to next week, but then I stopped short.

I'm not going to hit Ty.

While I might rough house with my brothers or enjoy being on the mat, facing off against a fellow wrestler, I wasn't a fighter. I'd never really popped anyone in the nose before or socked them in the gut because I was unable to control my temper. So, I just stood there for a long second, allowing my fury to simmer.

Maybe I won't punch Ty, but...doesn't he deserve it? Kate's my girlfriend and he's trying to kiss her. So yeah, I think he's already earned everything coming his way.

I marched forward, seething, then just as I'd put my hand on the driver's side door, Kate yelled my name, "Grady! No!"

She was out of the passenger's side and standing behind me in a split second. Her hand wrapped around my bicep, and she tugged hard, pulling me away from the driver's door. "Let go, Kate," I hissed.

"No!" she shouted. "You can't...You can't do...whatever it is you're thinking about doing." She sounded almost breathless, and I recognized that tone. It was the one she fell into naturally after we broke apart from kissing each other.

I growled. "You can't stop me."

"Yes," she pleaded, tightening her grip on my arm. "Yes, I can. You...you're a sensible guy. You know we weren't doing anything."

Her words struck me as being honest, even though her voice was still fairly faint and airy, and my gaze flicked toward her. It looked like her whole body was tensed and ready for action. Her eyes were stretched wide, and her upper lip was drawn into such a tight line that it had practically disappeared. I hadn't realized just how hard she was working to keep me away from Ty, but seeing the strain on her face brought some clarity to the situation. I let go of the door handle, then stepped away from the SUV.

"We...we weren't doing *anything*," Kate reiterated, stressing the last word, putting special emphasis on it.

"Yes," I whispered gruffly, "you were. If I hadn't pulled up just when I did, you would've kissed him and that would've meant..."

"No!" she interrupted. "That wasn't what was happening at all."

"Really?" I said snidely.

"Really," she insisted. "Ty took me to a baseball game to-night, and he was just dropping me off. I was thanking him by giving him a big hug and...that was it." She finished rather lamely, then relaxed the hold she had on my arm. She didn't let go of me completely, maybe because she could read the dubious look on my face and had to make certain I wouldn't follow through with my original plan and sock Ty a good one.

"So...a hug...that's what I saw you doing?"

"That's it. That's all," she said, sliding her hand down the length of my arm so that she could interlock her fingers with mine. "I've had a terrible week and Ty has been my rock. He took me to the game and just being there...having fun...it was so nice. I almost forgot for just one second how miserable I was since you...since we..." She swallowed hard. "The least I could do was hug my best friend and thank him for showing me a good time."

I barked a dry laugh. "I'll bet he was only too eager to *show you a good time.*" I made a point of saying those last few words with a hefty helping of sarcasm ladled all over the top.

"Ugh," Kate groaned. "Get over it, Grady. If I wanted to kiss Ty, don't you think I would've done it earlier in the week? I didn't have to wait until now. I could've done whatever I wanted all week long while you were away and..."

"Is that why you broke things off with me?" I interrupted. "Did you end our relationship so you could be with him?"

"No," she grumbled. "No, no, no." She met my gaze then and when our eyes locked, I could see how distraught she was. There were deep frown lines around the corners of her mouth and a serious indentation furrowing between her eyebrows. "I wasn't the one who ended things between us, Grady. I know I got worked up last week and what I did...bailing on you and your family like that last minute...that was despicable. But never, not for one minute, did I stop wanting to be your girlfriend."

"Never?" I ventured.

"I love you," she whispered. "You can't think I'd just say something like that, then forget all about it a few days later."

"I..." My rebuttal sat heavy on my tongue because that's when Ty opened the door to his SUV, pushing Kate and I away a few paces, and he stepped out of his car, once again, placing himself firmly in between us.

Chapter 32

Ty

"Yeah," I said, slowly closing the door behind myself, then turning to face them. "Listen to her, Grady. From Kate's perspective, everything she just told you was the God's honest truth."

"*From Kate's perspective?*" he hissed. His words were laced with vitriol, but I wasn't intimidated by him, so I shrugged and decided to take my time and explain.

"Yep," I replied. "From where Kate was sitting, she probably did think she was just going in for a hug. But for me? I was totally going to kiss her."

"Ty! What?" Kate questioned, giving me a bewildered stare.

My eyes drifted to hers and I could see that I'd not only managed to shock her, but also bring a sense of dismay to the already emotionally heavy atmosphere. "Sorry, if that surprises you," I murmured, "but I wanted to kiss you and I thought that's what you wanted too, so..." I held up my empty hands. "Can you really blame me?"

Kate groaned. "Ty...why did you...?"

"Yes," Grady interrupted, stepping closer to me, using his height to his full advantage, and looming there. "I do blame you for behaving like a creep. Kate's *my* girlfriend. You knew that and yet you were going to..."

His words must've failed him because I watched as Grady balled his hand into a fist. I know I should've been startled and maybe even frightened a little because judging by the livid expression on his face, he wasn't just posturing. He wanted to hit me. But I just couldn't see Grady taking the first swing. He'd always come off as having a *laissez-faire*, live and let live attitude, and only when he'd been intentionally trying to get under my skin this summer had I ever seen him break that mold. But now, the guy standing in Kate's driveway glowering at me wasn't the Grady I recognized. He wasn't smirking or winking or languidly draping his arm around Kate's shoulders. And he certainly wasn't the self-sacrificing goody-two shoes that his brother, Rory, told me so much about, either. He wanted to hit me, and so I was going to stand right here and let him do it.

I leaned back against the driver's side door of my SUV and crossed my arms over my chest, practically daring him to make his move. But before he could act, Kate grabbed his hand. It was an awkward movement, because of his fist, but she wrapped her long fingers around his, just the same way she did when she was roughing up a game ball during the first few innings, trying to make it easier to grip by getting rid of some of the slipperiness on the surface.

"Grady," she whispered, "Ty doesn't know what he's talking about. He...he must've had too much popcorn at the game. He wasn't going to kiss me..."

"Yes, I was," I interjected.

"Ty," she barked. "Will you shut up already?" I shrugged but didn't interject any further. So, she continued, "I guess... I guess it doesn't matter what Ty was thinking of doing, because I know how I would've reacted. He's my best friend, but you, Grady, I love you. And I want to be with you. If we all could've gone to the game together tonight, that would've been so much fun and..."

Grady grimaced and I was pretty sure that I'd just made a nearly identical face, because my internal reaction to Kate's words had been just as chagrined.

She didn't really want to be there with me. She wanted him. All this time...if he could've been the one by her side, she would've gladly made that trade.

The reality was painful, but also stark. I simply couldn't deny what I was hearing. Kate had continued talking, elaborating, maybe even overdoing it a little, in her efforts to calm Grady and placate him. But I didn't need the long-winded speech or the handholding. I'd finally heard her, and the message sank deep. She was speaking loudly, making her feelings crystal clear. How could I not get the picture?

"Kay-Kay," I said, holding up my hand and interrupting her right in the middle of a sentence, "give it a rest." I turned my gaze on Grady and his eyes narrowed. She had managed to relax his hand and he was no longer staring pointedly at me, but I got the impression he was continuing to size me up, trying to guess what I might say next. "Listen to her," I said, nodding at Kay-Kay. "Really listen to what's she telling you. She's spent this whole week pining for you and I can't count the number of times she told me that she wished she could've done everything differently." I sighed deeply. "This week, I witnessed a first. Since we were nine years old, all Kate's ever really wanted to do was play softball or practice or go running to build her endurance. But this week? She wanted to be with you. She was willing to pick you over being on that ball field and well...that's gotta mean something."

Grady's eyes flicked toward Kay-Kay, then they shifted back to mine. "If you knew all that...how she felt and what she wanted...why were you going to still try and kiss her tonight?"

We'd come this far being honest, so I didn't feel the need to lie now. "I'd have tried, because the opportunity was there, but I'm not sure Kay-Kay would've let me get too far." I waved my hand dismissively at the pair of them. "She's so wrapped up in you and hearing her go on and on tonight, trying to soothe you, that just makes me think that if I had planted a kiss on her, it would've been the absolute wrong thing to do. I might've ruined our friendship, so I'm almost glad you saved me from making such a colossal mistake." I stopped and smiled smugly. "Almost."

Kate groaned, evidently not too pleased with my attempt at smoothing things over, but Grady's expression softened, and his face broke into a slow, easy grin.

"You really are the worst, Ty Masterson," he said as the corners of his lips curved up into something resembling his normal smile.

"Right back at ya," I retorted. Then, I left my SUV where it was because Grady's truck was parked behind it and tossed a wave at them over my shoulder as I took off, striding purposefully toward my own house. I was done stepping between Kay-Kay and Grady and even though I was mildly curious about how things would pan out between the two of them, I figured I'd just ask her all about it in the morning.

Chapter 33

"So, where does this leave us?" I wanted to know. Ty had already disappeared across the lawn, and I was still holding loosely onto Grady's hand, massaging it, willing him to calm down, but I needed him to clarify our situation and let me know what he was thinking.

"Us?" he whispered.

"I want you to trust me, Grady. I know that a few weeks ago, near the start of the summer, you'd worried about what might happen between me and Ty if we were left to our own devices but...I swear, I wasn't going to..."

"I know," he said softly. "I heard what you said before."

"Then...why...why do you still look so conflicted?"

He pulled his hand away from me, then leaned heavily against Ty's SUV. "I'm just thinking," he murmured. "Trying to make sense of everything."

"I've spent a lot of time this week trying to do just that," I said, leaning my hip against the driver's door, making it so we were still close to each other, but not too close. "And you know what I've come up with?" He shook his head. "I was wrong."

"You...?" The word was barely audible as it tripped off his lips. "You were wrong?"

I nodded. "I don't like saying that out loud, or even thinking it, for that matter, but it's glaringly obvious. I've done almost everything wrong this summer." I sighed wearily. "I told you I was taking a break, but then, I went and joined the Trailblazers at the last minute and we both know that hasn't been quite what I was hoping it would be."

"Yeah," he scoffed. "Just a couple of games...a few practices here and there...no big deal."

"Don't remind me," I moaned. "I had this idea of how things ought to play out, but nothing—nothing went according to plan. The only good thing, the one constant thing I had in my life was you." I frowned while staring at the ground, and concentrating hard on the words I was saying. "That was just so...strange because normally softball provides all the consistency that I need. But between Abs getting hurt last year, losing all those games, then sitting on the bench during this summer softball season, I realized that I didn't just need softball. What I really needed was you, Grady." I paused and looked up, wanting to meet his eyes. He was gazing at me, unwaveringly. "That's why I'm really hoping you won't make this breakup a permanent thing."

"From where I'm standing, Kate, we never really ended things," he whispered, scooting closer to me, sliding his body so that it was just a few inches away from mine. "We just called a timeout while I was at the lake, but now that I'm here, maybe we should get back in the game."

I laughed. "Is that really what you want to do? Give this whole thing another try?"

He reached forward and touched my arm gently, grazing his fingers lightly over my skin, causing goosebumps to appear. "I made up my mind about you months ago. At the reservoir...the first time we kissed. I knew right then and there that I wasn't getting into a relationship with you just so we could hang out this summer. When I said I wanted you to be my girlfriend, I really meant it. Softball...college...Ty..." He paused and rolled his eyes, which made me giggle. "None of that is going to come between us."

At that point, I wanted nothing separating us, so I flung my arms around him and pulled him into a bear hug. He laughed, but I didn't allow my grip to slacken. "This is going to be hard," I whispered in his ear.

"Tremendously," he said teasingly. "If I can't breathe, how will we ever be able to talk to one another again?"

I relaxed my hold on him a little, but I didn't let go entirely. "I'm serious," I breathed.

"You're always serious," he returned, and I could almost hear the laughter ringing in his voice.

"Grady," I said insistently, "please. I...I need to acknowledge...I need both of us to recognize that staying together isn't going to be easy. We'll be in different places, and we won't be able to see each other all the time and..."

"We'll be fine," he said, lifting his hands, rubbing them over my back muscles, giving me a gentle massage. "The time we do get to spend together, we'll just have to make memorable."

"Okay," I breathed, laying my head against his chest, and burrowing into him. "Fine. Then, we shouldn't waste any more time. We should start making memories just as soon as we can." He laughed, but I continued, "What do you want to do tomorrow?"

He backed away a little then and I looked up to see a question in his eyes. "You don't need to go to practice, and the Trailblazers don't have a game?"

"There's nothing on the schedule." I disentangled my hands from around his neck so that I could slide one finger underneath his jaw and feel the light layer of stubble that was growing there. The hair was fine and soft, and I liked rubbing my finger over top of it. "And I know I'd usually spend the morning working out, but I'd rather be with you and let you decide what we're going to do."

"I get to pick what we do?" he asked. And I nodded. "Anything I want?" he pressed, which made me laugh.

"Anything you want," I whispered.

"Good," he said, leaning forward and rubbing his nose against mine. "'Cause I've got a couple of ideas." But he didn't tell me any of them. Instead, Grady just lowered his head even further and placed his lips softly against mine, giving me the longest, sweetest goodnight kiss imaginable.

Chapter 34

Sunday, July 9th

Grady

"Over here, Kate!" I shouted, waving my hand, and beckoning for her to join me. Since she'd let me pick what we were doing this morning, I'd decided to throw my butterfly nets in the back of the truck and drive us out to the reservoir. We'd spent the first few minutes traipsing through the tall grass, trying to find a few specimens, but it wasn't until we got closer to the rim of the water that I saw a spot where the dragonflies were swarming. "Come on!" I called before running toward the winged creatures with my net held high, ready to scoop them up quickly.

"Wait," Kate hollered after me. "I...I can't keep up with you."

"Yes, you can," I assured her, not slowing down one bit. "You're the one who goes running all the time. This should be child's play for you."

She sprinted even faster then and by the time I was swinging my net through the air, she was right at my side, copying my movements, trying to ensnare a dragonfly that had lacy, iridescent purple wings. "Ha!" she shouted triumphantly. "I got one."

I captured a green winged one just then and we both grinned at each other. "Let's go put them in the jar."

She tipped her head to the side, like she was analyzing what I'd just said, then reached her free hand out to stop me. "I thought you didn't like the idea of keeping insects in a jar. You told me they live only for a short amount of time and that..."

"Do you always remember everything I say word-for-word?" I teased.

"Pretty much."

"Well, then I guess I should remember to give you all the details, so that you'll always have the facts straight." I twirled the net in my hands, making sure the soft gossamer part was doubled over itself and the dragonfly wouldn't escape while we were talking. "I don't think people should just capture insects and hold them in jars, but these dragonflies are for my collection."

"Oh," she said softly, then gave a dramatic shiver. "I should've known you'd be wanting to stick these little suckers to your bug board."

"Yeah," I snickered. "My bug board. My folks can't decide if they want me to take it to college with me or if I should leave it at home. Rory says if I take it to school, I'll run the risk of having my room nickname me *bug boy* and..."

Kate laughed. "Bug boy? Really?"

I shrugged. "I'm sure there are worse nicknames. And besides, I do really like bugs."

She rolled her eyes. "Yeah, you'd have to like them a whole lot to pick chasing a bunch of butterflies through a field on a day like today instead of..."

"Instead of...what?" I asked.

"Nothing," she shrugged, and a small, secretive smile played on her lips. "It's just that last night, when I told you that you could pick whatever we were going to do this morning, I sort of thought you might be thinking of doing something else..."

I nodded toward my truck, indicating we ought to take the dragonflies back to the jar. As we walked along together, I questioned, "Was there something else *you* wanted to do today? Are you disappointed that..."

"No," she said quickly. "I kind of like mixing it up like this." Her smile broadened. "It's sort of fun, isn't it? One day, you get to decide what we're doing. The next day, I'm in charge. Maybe we could make this into our thing."

"Cooperating?" I said jokingly. "Taking turns?"

When we got to my truck, Kate handed over her butterfly net then picked up the empty glass jar. She held it steady while I dropped the two dragonflies in, then safely secured the lid. In a soft voice, she said slowly, "I know we can't help your summer schedule at the auto mall, and I've still got quite a few ballgames to play throughout the next month, but I'm thinking, when we're together, we ought to stick to this routine. One day, you decide what we do. The next day, it'll be my turn."

"All right," I agreed, handing her back the net, then leaning against the corner of the truck bed. "What's your big idea for tomorrow?"

"Well, I've got a game in the evening, but I was thinking of a few things we could do both before and afterward."

"What?"

She reached for me with her free hand and grabbed ahold of my t-shirt, towing me toward her. "I'm picturing you...me...lying together in a lounge chair next to my pool..."

"Looking at the fireflies?" I teased.

"Yeah," she said, staring up at me heatedly. "We could do that, too."

When Kate kissed me, I felt the same way I did when I was squatting in my catcher's crouch, catching the pitches she liked to hurl in my direction. I was exhilarated, fully alive, and a little scared too. Going forward, things weren't bound to be easy for us, but no one could make me feel the way she did. I wanted to catch dragonflies with her and watch her play softball and lay around by her pool, just talking about everything that was running through her mind. But more than all that, I wanted to stand perfectly still with Kate and just enjoy making this memory, one which I hoped would be able to sustain the both of us through the challenges that were sure to lie ahead.

Epilogue

Friday, August 11th
Kate

"All right, girls," I called, walking through the tunnel that had been created by the row of middle school aged pitchers and the catchers who were there to support them. "Let's see what you've got." I got to the end of the line, spun on my heel, then strode slowly in the opposite direction, gazing at each girl in turn, really wanting them to listen to my advice. "Just remember that this is your first official clinic. I've taught you a couple of the basics, but you're just learning to throw. So, if a pitch goes wild, there's nothing to worry about. You just keep throwing and don't worry about making your catchers do some work." I paused and winked at my pals who were interspersed throughout the group, ready to perform catching duties for the pitchers. "They're used to it."

I nodded at Abs, who was in the thick of the group, near the center. Early on, we'd paired her up with the oldest middle schooler. She was tall, even for her age, and she'd towered over the others. Her name was Eliza, and she was going to be in eighth grade when school started on Monday. I was glad to see that she'd turned out because it never hurt to help the next generation of Farrington Falcons point their feet in the right direction and start taking strides toward future victories. "You heard her," Abs said, yanking her cushiony soft mask over her face, but going without her proper catching gear. "Let's get to work."

The other catchers gave a soft cheer in response, and I glanced down the line, so proud of all my friends who had shown up to assist. Aside from Abs, Syd was there too. She was working with a girl named Taylor who was small and spoke in a high-pitched voice. Smitty was wearing her full set of catcher's gear, and she was catching for a player named Sally who had bright orangish-red hair but wore a navy-blue Cleveland Guardians cap over top of it. I liked Sally immediately.

There were a couple of catchers who were representing the middle school age group, and they were lined up next to Jennica and Isabel, a few other Farrington Falcons who'd gamely reported for duty this morning. But then, there at the end of the row was Grady. There was a handful of dads standing around, listening to the instructions I'd given their girls, but Grady was the only baseball player in sight. He seemed to be in his element though, crouching over top the round paper plate we were using to make it seem like every pitcher had a home plate.

He's going to be leaving in a few days.

I had tried not to think about that fact very much, but now, surrounded by all these softball players, knowing that I was starting school on Monday and practices for fall ball were kicking up on Tuesday, I realized that I couldn't avoid the truth any longer. Grady was here for me now, but soon enough, he'd be off, discovering what he wanted to do with his own future.

Which brought me back to the task at hand. Graham had wisely suggested that I do some coaching, maybe something akin to teaching, so I could decide if this was really what I wanted to do with my life, and so far, things had been swell. The pitchers had been receptive to my instruction while I was taking them through the warmups, showing them how to grip the ball and snap their wrists on the follow through. But this was only the first session. It'd take time for these girls to really accumulate knowledge, which meant, if I truly wanted to see them learn and grow, I was going to have to dedicate myself to running future pitching clinics.

And I'm just not sure I'll have the time for that going forward.

"Ow!" One of the girls yelped and the sound caught my attention. I'd been looking at Grady, but he wasn't making any noise, and his pitcher was right in the middle of throwing him another pitch. My eyes darted down the line and that's when I saw Eliza, Abs' partner, bending down. I ran to her side.

"What happened?" I asked, dropping to my knees so I could be right next to her. "What hurts?"

"It's my ankle," Eliza answered through gritted teeth. "It turned in a funny way when I brought my foot down and..."

"She was reaching," Abs supplied helpfully, appearing at my side, still holding her glove in the air with the ball cradled safely inside. "I thought to warn her about overdoing it, but she's only just learning, and I knew she needed to try out striding off the rubber, figuring out what felt right for her, so..."

"It's cool," I said. "No one did anything wrong." I nodded at Eliza. "Do you mind if I look more closely?"

She sniffed. "Go ahead."

She'd been wearing a pair of shorts and tall white softball socks that had red stirrups stitched on them. I considered rolling down the socks, so

I could see her ankle more clearly, but the extra movement wasn't necessary. I could see that there was a tiny bulge near the joint, indicating that she'd twisted it, and the area was already starting to swell.

"We're gonna need some ice," I said, looking up, squinting into the sun. "And where are your parents, Eliza? I'm gonna need to talk to them."

"Here's the ice," Grady said, handing me a plastic bag that was already dripping wet. It was hot outside and we'd only packed a couple of bags of ice in a small soft sided cooler, just in case of emergencies like this one. But he'd anticipated my directions and showed up right on time to hand me exactly what I requested.

"What happened?" A man's voice asked and when I looked to Grady's left, I realized I was now speaking to Eliza's dad. He was tall, like her, and his lips were drawn into a concerned frown.

"She'll be fine," I said, handing her the bag of ice, and waiting for her to position it on the already-swelling ankle. "I think she just tripped over a rock or something." I plucked a small pebble from the infield, then flung it aside, over my shoulder. "She was doing a fine job, really trying to fire that fastball. But when she strode out a little too far, she probably connected with a rock and because her balance was off-center, she twisted her ankle."

Her father sighed deeply. "Do you think I need to take her to a doctor?"

"She ought to be all right." I tucked one of my hands around her waist and placed the other on her elbow. Abs moved forward and copied the motion and together we helped Eliza stand. She was no longer bending and pressing the ice bag to her ankle, but I figured it was better we got her off the ground than let her sit there much longer.

"Does this...do injuries like this happen often?" Eliza's dad questioned, which made Abs snicker.

She tapped her face covering. "Softball's not exactly a dangerous sport, mister. But it isn't for the faint of heart, either."

"Should I..." Eliza whispered, "what should I do now, Coach Kate?"

"Take a few days off," I recommended. "We've got school on Monday, so spend the weekend icing that ankle. When you're not walking around, get an ice pack on it and prop it up using a couple of pillows."

"So, she can still walk on it?" her dad asked, and I nodded seriously instead of snickering the way Abs was doing.

"It may hurt if she tries to put too much weight on it right away," I said. "And I wouldn't recommend she go out running over the weekend, but by Monday, she'll be raring to go to school."

"Maybe," Eliza quipped.

"Right?" I laughed. "It *is* school, so maybe you won't be hurrying out the door on Monday morning, but if that's the case, it won't be your injury that's keeping you in bed."

"Thanks, Coach Kate," Eliza said, and her dad echoed the sentiment.

"You're welcome," I replied, giving them both my most sincere smile. Then, I turned my eyes on Abs once more. "Will you help Eliza to her car, please? I've got to stay here and keep working with the…"

"Yeah, yeah." Abs waved me off with her glove. "I got you, Lady K."

With that minor fiasco handled, I turned my full attention back to the other players. Some were still going strong, but others, the younger ones, looked timid now.

They don't want to trip and get hurt, too.

I could understand those sorts of qualms, so after watching the girls throw ten more pitches each, I called it for the day. "Hands in," I instructed, and all the players, boys, girls, pitchers, and catchers alike did as I requested. "Farrington Falcons on three," I coached. "One, two, three!"

"Farrington Falcons!" They all chorused, and then, my teammates like Syd, Jennica, and Smitty started *caw-cawing* loudly and flapping their gloves like they were sets of wings.

Some of the parents hung around a moment longer to thank me for arranging this clinic. One mom, Sally's, asked, "When do you think you'll be having another one of these, Coach Kellner?"

"I'm not sure," I replied honestly. "We'll have to see how the fall ball schedule works out and I've got some other commitments pressing on my time." I cast a sidelong glance at Grady, who was smiling at me.

"Well, let us know," Sally's mom continued. "I think the girls had fun today and it'd be nice if we could keep this going."

"Sure thing," I said, giving her a chipper smile in return. Once the moms, dads, and young athletes had all walked away from the diamond and headed to the parking lot, Grady joined me. "Help me pick up the paper plates?"

He laid his gloved hand over his heart and pretended to swoon. "I never thought you'd ask." We collected the plates, then gathered the plastic strips we'd been using for pitching rubbers, and it was then that Grady finally said what I knew he must've been thinking for the last several minutes. "You did a good job out there today, Special K. Not just with the pitching clinic, but while handling Eliza's injury, too."

"It was nothing," I said, waving away his praise as I deposited the stack of paper plates into a nearby trash can. "Just a twisted ankle. Maybe not even that."

"It wasn't nothing to Eliza or her dad. Didn't you see the stressed-out look on his face?"

"He's her dad," I replied, turning to look up into Grady's eyes. "He's allowed to be worried."

"But you weren't," he retorted. "You knew exactly what to do. And you handled taking care of her injury like you were already a doctor."

"Huh," I snorted. "I'm guessing you're not going to let this go."

He shrugged. "I know you came out here today, trying to figure out if teaching and coaching were the right fit for you, but maybe, your future's already knocking on your door, and you've got to just open wide and embrace it."

"There's only one future I want to embrace right now," I said, leaning toward him and smashing the pitching rubbers he'd been carrying between us.

He laughed, but I could tell he wanted to kiss me, and I certainly wasn't going to stop him. But then, Abs interrupted us. "Yo! Lady K. Grady. Look who I found lurking around out in the parking lot."

"Coach Cobb," I said, happy to see our varsity coach striding toward us. I hadn't laid eyes on him all summer and it was good to see him again. I'd known ahead of time that he wouldn't be making any surprise appearances at any of our Trailblazer's games because he'd told us that he was spending his break in Florida, working at a restaurant that was owned by his sister. But he was so tanned that he looked to me like he might've been laying on the beach rather than doing any real work. I didn't say that though because Coach Cobb was devoted to teaching and coaching throughout the school year, and he, like everybody else, was entitled to take a vacation every now and again. "Thanks for swinging by today."

"I was trying to get here earlier, because I wanted to see you and the middle school kids in action, but Abs informed me that I didn't make it in time."

I stepped away from Grady and waved my hand at the now-empty ball diamond. "You'll have to be here for the next clinic. I think the middle school girls will like getting to know their future coach."

He smiled. "Sounds like a plan."

It was then that he shifted to the side slightly and I noticed the lady standing behind him. She was tall, maybe a full inch or two more than me. She had a curvaceous figure, which was accentuated by the very short pair of cut-off jean shorts she was wearing. Her hair was shiny, black, and slung into a low ponytail. I couldn't see her eyes, because they were covered by a pair of overly large, thick black sunglasses, the kind athletes wore during a ballgame when they were playing the outfield. She looked effortlessly cool, even though the sun was scorching this morning, baking the infield dirt, and making not just me, but everybody else who'd been participating in the pitching clinic sweat profusely.

That can't be Coach Cobb's girlfriend. She's young, much too young.

But it was hard to tell. They didn't look anything alike, so I surmised this wasn't his sister either, taking a break from her restaurant in Florida to visit Ohio for a few days.

But if this person isn't Coach's girlfriend or sister, who is she?

"Hey," Grady said, stepping forward and nodding at the newcomer. "I'm Grady. I don't think I caught your name."

"That's because I didn't throw it," the girl said, taking off her glasses and gracefully sliding them up her head, using them to pull several long, wispy tendrils of hair away from her face.

Grady scoffed. "Yeah, I guess you didn't." He nodded at Coach Cobb. "Is this a friend of yours?"

That's when Abs stepped forward. She held her hand out to stop Coach Cobb from speaking. "You mean you don't know who this is?"

Grady and I both shook our heads. Our combined befuddlement seemed to amuse the girl and she smiled, cat-like, wide and displaying a set of glistening, white teeth.

"I'm Rosita Cruz Alvarez," she said crisply. "Friends call me Rosie. Team-mates call me R.C."

"R.C. and I met last year playing in the girls' basketball all-star game over at First Trinity," Abs explained. "You remember that. Don't you, Lady K?"

"Sure." I nodded. "I remember going to watch you play in the game, but I don't recall you ever mentioning an R.C."

"Shoot," Abs groaned. "I didn't think I'd needed to. She scored like half our points."

R.C. laughed haughtily. "You're exaggerating."

"No, I'm not," Abs retorted, still being a tad playful, but also firmly sticking to her story. "You weren't just another all-star on that team. You were the MVP."

"Really?" Grady asked, showing his interest. "Where'd you go to school?"

"I used to go to Perry City," R.C. explained, "but now…"

When her voice trailed off, a funny feeling came over me suddenly. It was the way I felt sometimes when Grady started talking about insects. I could've sworn I had a thousand tiny little ant legs crawling all over me, making my skin tingle and prickle. "But now, *what*?" I prompted.

"This is why I brought Alvarez out here today," Coach Cobb said, looking from me to Abs. "Perry City had to close its doors because it just wasn't getting the funding it needed to stay open. They had asbestos in the ceiling and the water heater was shot."

"Our school was rickety," R.C. added.

"Yeah," Coach agreed. "So, the city decided to close the high school and now the students are being shipped elsewhere. We're not quite consolidating schools here, because Farrington High isn't big enough to accommodate all the city kids who'll need somewhere to go, but some of them are coming our way so..."

"Dang," Abs interrupted. "That means R.C.'s going to be playing ball with us this winter?" She held up her hand and offered Rosita a high-five.

"And in the spring, too," Rosita said, grinning at Abs as if they were already best friends.

"For real?" Abs was obviously thrilled. "I didn't even know you played softball."

"I love it," Rosita returned, still smiling broadly. "Been the starting pitcher for Perry City since I was a sophomore."

Abs laughed. "Then, I guess you'll be giving our girl Lady K here a run for her money, won't ya?"

"Oh?" Rosita said, looking at me and blinking innocently. "Are you a pitcher, too?"

I scoffed. "I just held a pitching clinic for a bunch of middle school girls. So yeah...I dabble."

Grady laughed, then after shifting the pitching rubbers he'd been holding so they were tucked underneath one arm, he draped his other across my shoulder. I felt marginally better the second he touched me, but not even his proximity could mellow me entirely.

"Oh, man," Abs hooted. "This is going to be great. I can't wait to see what you can do on Tuesday, R.C."

"Oh," she said, softening her voice and smiling sweetly at Coach Cobb. "I won't be coming to practice on Tuesday. I actually won't be playing fall ball at all this year."

Abs pooched out her lower lip and pouted prettily. "Why not?"

"I run cross country," R.C. answered, putting her hands on her waist then popping one hip to the side like she was striking a pose.

"Great," I said, trying hard to stay polite. "My friend Ty's the team captain for the boys. I'll have to introduce you sometime and..."

"Ty Masterson?" she interrupted. "I already know all about him. He's one of the fastest runners in the state. I heard he could do the four hundred meters in forty-six seconds flat. Is that true?"

"I...uh..." I wasn't sure exactly what Ty's personal best was. He was speedy. I knew that much. But he didn't usually brag about his times, and he never showboated when we were running together, so it was hard to say.

"Well," Coach Cobb said, jumping in just in time so I didn't have to try to come up with some vague answer, "It's time for Alvarez and me to get going. I promised Coach Armstrong I'd bring her by the school so we could introduce her to the cross-country team too."

"It was nice to meet you," Rosita said, slipping her glasses into place, then jutting her chin in Grady's direction.

I wriggled closer to his side while he replied genially, "Yeah. You take care, Rosita."

As she and Coach walked away, I stood there watching her, trying to figure out what had just happened, but I didn't have long to sit with my thoughts because Abs started yammering. "I can't believe how lucky we are," she said, staring after Rosita. "Do you know that she currently holds the state record for points scored in a single season?"

Grady snorted. "I'd have thought with her being that tall that she played center or maybe as a forward. But she's got a good jump shot, too?"

Abs let out a low whistle. "The best."

I flicked my eyes toward my friend, who was still gazing after Rosita's disappearing form. "And she's a three-sport athlete," I murmured. "Have you seen her play anything other than basketball?"

"I've never seen her run," Abs started, but then stopped herself. "But I guess that's not true because she jogged up and down the court like a pro." She turned her gaze toward me then and I could see a spark of curiosity flit through her dark eyes. "Are you really trying to ask what kind of pitcher she is, Lady K?"

"Maybe," I mumbled.

"Come on," Abs cajoled. "You can't be worried about a little competition. We just spent all summer playing with a bunch of pitchers who were your idols. You shared your position with Hope, Becky, *and* Lacy. And the four of you got along just fine."

"That was different," I retorted. "Those girls on the Trailblazers were living legends. They were people I knew could hurl the ball and get the job done. But this girl..." I waved my free hand at the parking lot. "I'd never even heard her name before."

"Rosita Cruz Alvarez," Abs said, spelling it out slowly, taking her time and rolling her r's in all the correct places.

I gave her an annoyed look. "I don't care who she is. This is *my* senior year. And I'm not just going to step aside and let her start throwing half the games because..."

"Woah, there," Grady said, laying on the thickest southern accent I'd heard him use in a long time. "Let's just hold our horses." I twisted my head slowly to look at him. He dropped his arm off my shoulder, making it easier for us to stare at each other. "Everything's going to be just fine, Kate. You're the starting pitcher for the Farrington Falcons. There's no disputing that. It's a fact...Etched in stone, even." I could see that he was trying to lighten the mood, but I was still reluctant to crack a smile, so he proceeded. "And it doesn't matter how many people move into the district or come to Farrington and try to take your spot. You've got this all locked up."

I nodded at my boyfriend who looked downright adorable, doing his very best to cheer me up while still cradling an armload of plastic pitching mounds. "Come on," I said, jerking my head over my shoulder. "Let's have one last pool party before school starts on Monday."

"Sounds good to me," Abs said, reaching forward and taking the plastic strips right out of Grady's arms. "I'll just put these in with the rest of my equipment and we can sort out where they go on Monday."

"All right," I agreed.

As she walked off, Abs turned and called, "See you at your house in a few minutes, Lady K?"

"Sure," I replied. "And be sure to text Syd. Invite her to come over too."

"Done," Abs chirped.

When she'd left Grady and me alone, and we were no longer burdened by the pitching rubbers, he reached out and took hold of my hand. "Are you sure you want to have a pool party right now?"

"Why not?" I asked, gazing up into his cloudy eyes that looked more blue than gray today.

"Because I can tell that this thing with Rosita has already gotten under your skin," he returned softly, lifting his hand, and using his fingertips to caress the side of my face.

I leaned into the softness of his palm, then said quietly, "I'm not going to let Rosita's presence get to me. And I won't be intimidated by a little competition. I'm going to be the starting pitcher for the Farrington Falcons this spring. And that's all there is to it."

"You're right, Special K," he said, winking at me. "There's no doubt in my mind that you'll do whatever it takes." He laughed quietly. "So, I guess I sort of feel sorry for Rosita."

"Why?" I grumbled.

"Because she has no idea what she's up against."

I kissed Grady then, not just because he was being supportive and making me feel better, but because he understood me completely. I wasn't going to let some other girl coast into my town and steal my starting spot, and Grady knew that. I was thankful that I had him in my corner, and I hoped that with him sticking by my side, I'd be able to fend off the competition, no matter what form it might appear in later.

THE END

Be sure to read the exciting conclusion in the Kate Kellner Trilogy: Kate Kellner Throws a Perfect Game.

Book Three

Monday, August 21st

Kate

Zzzzuuuu...whap!

It was so hot outside that I could practically hear the ball sizzling as it left my hand and careened toward home plate. Grady caught the pitch, held the pose for a second, so I could see how close I got to hitting the true mark, then fired that highlighter yellow ball right back in my direction, so I'd have the chance to go through the motions all over again.

Zzzzuuuu...whap!

This time I grunted a little with the effort of pushing off the rubber and striding toward home plate.

Grady caught the ball, held his glove in place, then readjusted his position so that he was sitting on his knees, rather than in the catcher's squat. He tipped his head to the side, using the heather gray sleeve of his t-shirt to wipe the sweat from his brow and push the silky strands of his sandy brownish blonde hair out of his eyes, then called, "This is brutal, Special K. I'm practically boiling over here."

"A good athlete trains in all conditions," I shouted back, snapping my glove at him, intimating that I wanted him to toss me the ball so we could get back to work.

He snorted, then gifted me with a wry smile. "That may be true, but there'll never be cause for you to throw two hundred pitches straight during the middle part of the day, when the heat is almost baking the dirt around you. You'll strike out the side, then go into the dugout for at least a little while so you can cool..."

"Is this your way of saying you need a break?" I interjected, teasing him a tad.

"Yep," he said, climbing to his feet. "That's exactly what I was trying to say."

I nodded toward the dugout where we'd left our bat bags and a couple of water bottles, but Grady missed my acquiescence. He was already heading for the shade of the dugout and since he was carrying the ball along with him, it wasn't like I could keep throwing without the proper equipment.

I watched as he took a long glug from his water bottle, swishing the cool liquid around in his cheeks, then squirting some of it over his head.

"Sorry," I mumbled, grabbing my own bottle, and taking a slow sip. "Just because I was ready to go all day, didn't mean you were. I should've figured that you'd want..."

"We're good...now," he said right before chugging another gulp of water. He emptied the entire bottle, then placed it back on the bench, where it wobbled a little now that it had been drained. Using the tail ends of his shirt, Grady wiped the sweat from his cheeks, and I stared at him, appreciating yet again just how gorgeous my boyfriend was.

He was tall, maybe six-two or six-three and slim, but he also sported well-defined muscles. Sometimes, guys who were as tall as Grady were rail thin or gawky, but he had broad shoulders and taut arm muscles, probably because he played so many sports in high school and was constantly training. His hair was a little on the long side and the strands were generally soft and silky. They almost always hung in his eyes, but that was never a problem, at least not for me, because I adored watching him brush the forelocks aside. His grayish blue eyes were squeezed shut, but as if he knew I was staring at him, his lashes fluttered open, and he fixed me with an amused stare. His lazy smile, the one where dimples showed on both his cheeks, slid into place, and I breathed a sigh of contentment. "What's up, Special K?"

"Just admiring the view," I answered, not feeling the least bit shy about making this confession. A few months ago, when we'd first met, I couldn't make eye contact with Grady without blushing profusely. But now that we'd been dating all summer and gone through our fair share of struggles as a couple, I was completely relaxed in his presence and didn't hesitate to speak my mind, especially when he was looking right back at me, smiling in a way that still made my heart pound erratically.

"Take your time," he joked, tipping his head from one side to the other, making his sweat-soaked hair flop back and forth. "We could both use a minute to cool down."

I cringed. "Sorry."

"Why do you keep apologizing?" His heavy eyebrows lowered, and he looked at me quizzically.

"It just occurred to me that maybe you don't want to spend all day at the ballfield and..."

"Hogwash," he drawled, adding a liberal and extremely exaggerated dose of his southern accent to his response, "there ain't nowhere else on God's green earth I'd rather be right now."

I shook my head at his nonsense. "That can't be true. We both know it's your last..."

"Uh...uh..." He clucked his tongue while lifting one hand and holding it up, apparently wanting to stop me before I could say anything else. "I thought we both agreed not to talk about that today."

I groaned. "I don't remember agreeing to anything." Today, I wore a black tank top with the words *Throwing the High Heat* stenciled across the front and I lifted the hemline so I could fan myself a little and stir the stagnant air that was hanging between us.

"I want to be here, Kate," Grady said, stepping closer, prompting me to give up on my fanning operation. "With you," he whispered. "And you want to be on the softball diamond, so..."

"But we can go somewhere else," I said softly, looking up into his eyes. "I should've let you pick today because..."

"It was your turn," he reminded me gently.

"Yeah, but this is your last..."

"Don't," he cautioned, slowly lifting his hand, and using the tips of his fingers to brush some of the sweat-soaked tendrils of my blonde hair away from my forehead. "You might not remember agreeing to anything specific today, but we did promise each other last week that we wouldn't bother saying goodbye. We wouldn't..."

"But you're leaving," I blurted and as I said the words, Grady winced. I knew that the thought of all those packed boxes and suitcases which were just waiting to be loaded into his truck and taken to Felding University tomorrow morning brought me all kinds of feelings of despair and loss, but until now, Grady had been masking his own emotions. Whenever I wanted to talk about his imminent departure or discuss whether he was excited about making this big move, he steered the conversation in a different direction entirely. But right now, it was just the two of us, standing face-to-face. And I could see that Grady was just as chagrined about going to college as I was about being the one who was about to be left behind in Farrington. "Why can't we talk about this?" I asked quietly.

His eyes darkened a little, becoming grayer and slightly more intense. "I don't want to think about leaving you."

"We were able to talk about you going to Felding all summer long. What's different about today?"

He sighed and dropped his hand away from my face. "Everything's different. When we talked about Felding before, we were just mentioning something that was going to happen...way off... in the future. But now..."

"The future's here," I finished his statement, and he nodded his head curtly. I wanted to say something spectacular and provide some sort of comfort for the two of us, but nothing came to mind, so I just reached out and placed my hand on his chest, settling my long fingers right over his heart. "Maybe we shouldn't be here. On your last day in town, we should've done something that would've been memorable...something that would've..."

"Hey," he interrupted softly, "this *is* memorable—at least it will be for me." He laid his hand over my own, connecting us completely. "My whole high school career, I've been on a ball field, soccer pitch, or rolling around on a wrestling mat. But in a few days, I won't have any of that." He swung his head, whipping some of his hair out of his eyes, then he nodded at his ball mitt. "I'm not even planning to take this with me."

"No," I moaned. "You've gotta take your baseball gear."

He snorted before chuckling. "Who's gonna throw with me, Kate?"

"I don't know," I returned, thinking quickly. "Maybe your roommate. Or maybe..."

He shrugged in that nonchalant way of his and his lips turned up at the corners. "Maybe I'll try to walk onto the baseball team or..."

"You could play intramurals, right?" I asked, staring at him hopefully.

"I guess I could," he said, letting go of my hand, and taking a step back. "I'd thought about playing some intramural soccer or maybe even finding a lacrosse club to join. So..."

"You play lacrosse?" I questioned, blinking at him rapidly, trying to recall a time when he'd ever mentioned being interested in that sport before.

"Nope," he replied, picking up his glove and tucking his hand inside the soft, well-worn leather. "But if I'm going to college, I'd like to think that I'll have the freedom to try something new."

"You will," I encouraged, reaching forward, and taking the softball out of his mitt. "When you get to Felding, you'll be able to do pretty much anything you want."

"Yeah," he grunted. "Do anything, except see you every day."

My heart gave a violent twinge. His words were achingly sweet, and it hurt to think that he wasn't joking around anymore. This time tomorrow, he'd already be on campus and there would be miles, so many miles, separating us from one another.

"We'll see each other," I promised. "And we'll talk all the time. We'll find a way to make this work."

"Sure," he said, smiling at me warmly. "We'll do whatever it takes." He took off his glove, patted it along his thigh, then tucked it underneath his arm.

"Really," I said, grabbing hold of his elbow and forcing him to look at me. "I'm Kate, Special K, Kellner...remember? If there's something I really want, you know I'll fight tooth and nail to get it."

His grin broadened. "I'm counting on that." Our eyes locked and we stared at each other for nearly a full minute before he added, "How's the arm feel? You ready to get back out there now?"

I stepped a few paces back from him and rolled my shoulder slowly, then made a windmill motion with my arm, moving at just half speed. "Ehh..." I said, feeling a slight stiffness. "We may have waited too long."

"We could take a few minutes and warm back up again," he suggested, looking at me with concern in his eyes.

"Naw," I replied. "I don't think it'll be worth it."

"But don't you have your first fall ball game right around the corner?"

My eyes flicked up and down his form. His posture was relaxed, and he still had his ball glove tucked under his arm, like he was ready to go, should I say the word, but something seemed off. "What's going on?" I asked, figuring it was best just to be direct. "A few minutes ago, you were ready to take a break, but now, you can't wait to hustle back out into that blazing heat."

"I...I'm not sure," he said slowly, faltering over his words as they tripped out of his mouth. "I don't know if I'm ready to go yet." He paused and exhaled a hot, dry breath. "As soon as we're done here, I've got to go home. I still need to pack everything up in the truck and my dad's van because we're leaving first thing tomorrow morning and..."

"So, this is it?" I prayed silently and selfishly that I was mishearing his words. This couldn't be the last time I'd see Grady Hughes before he left for school. There had to be more time for the two of us to spend together.

"I guess." He shrugged and averted his gaze so that he was looking out at the pitcher's mound. "But Kate...I'm glad we got to do this." His eyes coasted slowly back toward mine. "When I think of you, I'd like to remember you just like this..."

"With sweat dripping down my face and sunburn making my nose peel?" I quipped both wanting and needing to lighten the mood before I started crying.

"No," he whispered, closing the distance between us, and wrapping his free hand around my waist. "You're the girl who never gives up. Plenty of other people could be and maybe should be out here right now, putting in the extra hours, practicing, getting ready for the Farrington Falcons first fall ball game, but you're the only one who's actually doing it. I've always admired your dedication and determination, and I think, above all other things, that might be what I love about you the most."

Helplessly, I flung my arms around his shoulders, pulling him into what should've been a hug, but wound up being more like a strangle hold. His glove was pressed between our bodies, and it dug into my ribs, but I didn't care. "I wish you didn't have to go," I whispered, saying the one thing that was utterly and completely true, but also totally irrational.

Of course, he has to go. You've known since the day you met him that this moment was inevitable. He was always leaving for Felding in the fall and no matter what happened, that was never going to change.

"I love you, Grady," I said, pressing my nose into his chest, inhaling one last time the strong scents of perspiration, dirt, and fresh cut grass—the aromas that reminded me of my favorite things, including the guy I held in my arms.

We stayed locked together, our warm bodies radiating heat, for a very long time. But then, quite suddenly, Grady broke our embrace. "I've got something for you," he said, walking toward the bench, and unzipping his bat bag. He produced a shoe box and held it out to me.

"What's this?" I asked, looking at him, rather than the gift.

He chuckled. "Exactly what you think it is."

"Huh?"

"Here," he shoved the box at me. "Just open it. You'll see."

I flipped the lid of the shoe box open and sure enough, right there, nestled between wispy bits of white tissue paper, was a pair of softball cleats, nearly identical to the pair I was currently wearing. "You bought me...new cleats?"

He laughed brightly. "I know you like to wear yours until they're practically falling off your feet, but I noticed the other day how the hole in the toe of your right cleat was gaping."

I glanced down at my feet. He was right, of course. Because I was always digging the right toe of my shoes into the rubber and pushing off with all my might, I tended to wear down the leather quickly. The hole in the toe of my black cleat was so big, at present, that my cherry red softball socks were visible.

"This is really nice, Grady," I said, looking into the box once more, thumbing over the tongue of the shoe and seeing that he'd even picked out the right size, "but, I'm not sure I can accept this gift. My mom and dad probably already bought me a new pair for fall ball and..."

"They didn't," he said, hastily speaking over top of me. "I ran this idea by them before I made the purchase."

"But these had to have cost a lot of money," I said, allowing the flap of the lid to close on its own. "I know you worked all summer long, but you're going to need that money at Felding to pay for pizza and be..."

"I need you to have those cleats," he insisted, placing both his hands on the box, and gently pushing it toward me once more. "These last few months, I've rarely missed seeing you play and you and me...we've had so many good times together, just tossing the ball back and forth." I looked up to see tears swimming in his eyes and that made the ache in my chest intensify. "I know that I won't always be around this year to watch when you take the field, but I'd like to think if you're wearing the cleats that I gave you...then...then you'd have a little piece of me with you...always."

"Grady..." Tears slid down my cheeks and a ball of sadness fit itself neatly into my throat, making it so I couldn't say another word. I rushed at Grady, barreling right into him, ramming the box of cleats into his chest, but also pressing it against mine.

He backed away slightly, then snickered. "It's a good thing I didn't get you a cake, 'cause if I had, that thing would be all over the two of us right now."

I blinked at him, letting all those hot tears course down my cheeks and dribble off the tip of my chin. "If you bought me a cake, it wouldn't mean so much."

He took the shoe box out of my hand, put it on the bench, then hugged me to him tight. "I wanted to give you something practical...but also a little sentimental." He nuzzled into my neck and whispered in my ear, "I hope you don't mind."

"I love the gift," I said softly then stood on my tiptoes and kissed him lightly, "almost as much as I love you."

About the Author
Mindy Killgrove

Mindy Killgrove is the author of the Kate Kellner Trilogy, the Missy Lawrence Trilogy, the Kanedy Productions Trilogy, and is the creator of the Riley Roundtree Social Story Learning Adventure Series for children. Most notably, Killgrove is a professional ghostwriter. She has penned one play, forty-one short stories, and thirty-six novels all while working as a freelance author.

She has a bachelor's degree from Heidelberg University and a master's degree from Bowling Green State University. She lives in Orlando, Florida with her adoring husband and three rambunctious, but beautiful children. When she's not writing or reading, she's exploring local theme parks, lounging on the beach, or aiming to bake the very best chocolate chip cookies in the world.

Explore more at www.mindykillgrove.com

The
Mindy Killgrove
Collection
Don't miss one of Mindy Killgrove's stories.
THE MISSY LAWRENCE TRILOGY
Meet Me at the Pond
Meet Me at Fountain Park
Meet Me at Blessed Creek
THE KATE KELLNER TRILOGY
Kate Kellner Throws a Wicked Changeup
Kate Kellner Throws a Filthy Drop Curve
Kate Kellner Throws a Perfect Game
KANEDY PRODUCTIONS PRESENTS TRILOGY
Royally Engaged
Majestically Married
The Princely Prize
EDUCATIONAL MATERIALS
If Teachers Could Talk...
CHILDREN'S BOOKS
The Riley Roundtree Social Story Learning Adventure Series